DATE DUE

D0467502

THE FAR CALL

Center Point
Large Print

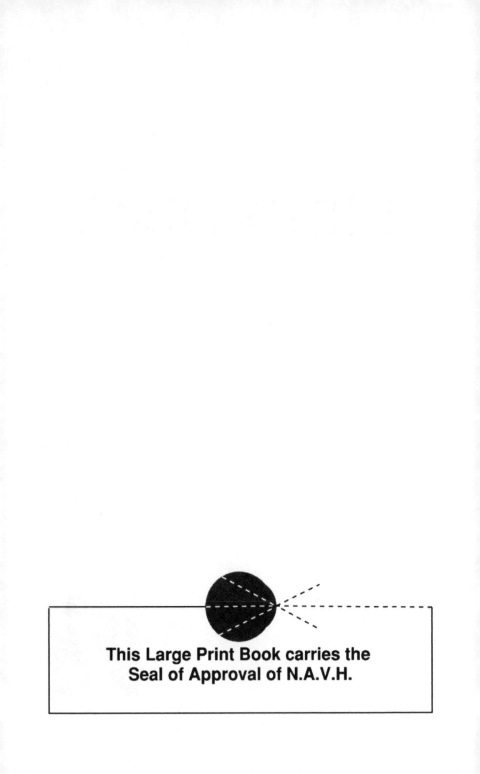

**This Large Print Book carries the
Seal of Approval of N.A.V.H.**

THE FAR CALL

Jackson Gregory

3NECBS0096851Y

CENTER POINT LARGE PRINT
THORNDIKE, MAINE

This Center Point Large Print edition
is published in the year 2015 by arrangement with
Golden West Literary Agency.

Copyright © 1940 by Jackson Gregory.
Copyright © 1940 in the British Commonwealth
by Jackson Gregory. Copyright © renewed 1968
by the Estate of Jackson Gregory.

All rights reserved.

First US edition: Dodd, Mead & Company.
First UK edition: Hodder & Staughton.

The text of this Large Print edition is unabridged.
In other aspects, this book may vary
from the original edition.
Printed in the United States of America
on permanent paper.
Set in 16-point Times New Roman type.

ISBN: 978-1-62899-704-0 (hardcover)
ISBN: 978-1-62899-709-5 (paperback)

Library of Congress Cataloging-in-Publication Data

Gregory, Jackson, 1882–1943.
The far call / Jackson Gregory. — Center Point Large Print edition.
pages cm
Summary: "After Jesse Bodine and Kate Haveril witness a murder and
see the murderer brought to justice, Jesse and Kate's brother Ransome
head west to answer the call to adventure. The trials and surprises they
encounter demand all they can give as they move toward full manhood
and an unknown future"—Provided by publisher.
ISBN 978-1-62899-704-0 (hardcover : alk. paper)
ISBN 978-1-62899-709-5 (pbk. : alk. paper)
1. Large type books. I. Title.
PS3513.R562F37 2015
813'.52—dc23

2015020677

To Glyneth

For Chinchilla

From J. G.

CHAPTER I

A FAR CALL SOUNDING

Maytime came laughing over the hills into Pleasant Valley, with wild roses in her hair. Maytime has a way of dancing and of wearing wild roses—and of playing fitful airs upon heartstrings, an ancient way always as new and fresh as young Maytime herself.

With the whisperings of a sundown breeze there came throb and thrill into wild young hearts, and a new, strange wildness. There came a pleasant riffle up along quick blood streams, a heady tumultuousness which would not be stilled.

Pleasant Valley was as lovely a place as its name. But to the westward rose the high purple mountains which, in young eyes, could become a wall and a barrier shutting out the real, true world of high purpose and rich adventuring, the golden world of the still farther west. And now came arrant young Maytime putting a fine new quality into swelling daybreak and pulsing dusk. Men, and women, too, breathed deeper; steps, old and young, were quickened. Hearts swelled like young May buds; blood streams became as uncontrollable as the quicksilver creeks leaping down from the mountaintops.

The skies were as blue and serene as eyes of angels; then of a sudden, over the mountains, thunderclouds boiled up, and a chill wind shrilled out of nowhere, and the storm did its tyrannical best for a time to black out the smiling valley; jagged streaks of angry lightning ripped open the water-swollen clouds, and the rain came down like Noah's flood.

Then the storm passed, and loveliness came glancing back into the valley and was lovelier than ever.

The pink-tipped petals of a boy-and-girl love were unfolding that day while the sun shone; and when the clouds were at their blackest, murder was done. The beginning of a long, wavering trail opened up; a far call was sounding.

CHAPTER II

THE WILD ROSE OF PLEASANT VALLEY

"It seems a sort of wonderful thing," said young Jesse Bodine. He didn't look at the girl sitting on the grass so close beside him; there were times when he had to keep his eyes off her. Times as now when they were following the idle wanderings of his lean brown fingers up and down the long barrel of his muzzle-loading rifle. "Sort of wonderful that your folks and my folks—not knowing one another at all, never even having heard tell of one another, your folks coming all the way from Kentucky and my folks coming all the way from Tennessee, and with maybe millions and millions of folks living in the world—happened to be the ones to come to the same spot out here and pick out their places right smack-kerdab together."

It was one of the longest speeches he had ever made, but the girl didn't stir, and her slightly parted lips, readied for speech, were still until after the expulsion of the long deep breath he drew when he had finished. Even then she waited an instant for his eyes to come up to hers; when they didn't, she said softly, sounding awed and all but breathless:

"I know! I've thought that, too, Jesse. It—it's like a miracle! And I've thought something else: People, millions and millions of them, have been coming into the world, being born you know, for centuries and centuries; and just think, we might have been born at the wrong time! Maybe with a hundred years between us! Oh, Jesse! It's fate, that's what it is!"

Even then he didn't look straight at her; he wanted to but couldn't. Just the same he knew exactly how she looked, how wide open her eyes were, soft and warm and lovely, and how in a moment the long fringe of lashes would come down and make shadows on her delicately flushed cheeks, and how there were shadows, too, of the brown curls against her cheeks, and how in her bared throat there was a tiny pulse beating, and how altogether she was so sweet and darling a thing that she put a pain in a man's heart.

He came very close then to putting out his strong, lean hand to her two little hands clasped in the lap of her blue-and-pink gingham dress; the words came up into his throat: "Oh, Kate! You are like a wild rose!" But he couldn't bring himself to saying a thing like that. Of the two she, though she was but sixteen and he nearly twenty, was the bolder; but her boldness was that of the little wild things of the forest country, readiest for scampering flight at moments when some high curiosity in their bright eyes restrained them briefly from scurrying into their thicket homes. Neither of them had ever said, "I love you," and they had never kissed; but their hearts were beginning to talk during their long silences. They knew, though it all seemed too wondrous possibly to be true. But everything in this Maytime was wonderful.

The Bodines from Tennessee had been first of the two families to come as far west as Pleasant Valley; they had found the valley marked off already into lusty young farms and dotted with green log cabins, and so had kept on to the farther rim of the valley, finding a place to suit them among the foothills. Then, the next season, the Haverils had arrived, the girl's people, a thin, worn caravan straggling out toward the setting sun, seeking land and water, a place where wild game abounded and where the seasons were bountiful. Old Abner Haveril, the father and patriarch, had visited with old Tom Bodine, had been received with quiet welcome, had watched with still-eyed interest as Tom's long arm pointed out certain desirable free lands, and had settled with his family and few goods and chattels on the farther side of Buckeye Creek. A scant two miles—what hereabouts was regarded as a stone's throw—separated the new Bodine cabin from the newer Haveril.

The two families saw little of each other, saw little of anyone, having plenty to do right at home.

11

Yet Jesse Bodine saw and took notice of the little Haveril girl. He was seventeen or eighteen then, not thinking particularly of girls, having an older sister and a younger one and very little in common with either, and Kate Haveril was about fourteen or fifteen. Yet after a while he got into the habit of looking after her whenever at rare intervals he saw her, his eyes trailing the flicker of a gay ribbon or the pastel of a faded calico when she went running down the crooked path through the trees, hurrying not to be late to the school at a crossroads down in the valley. He fished the pools of Buckeye Creek, and she came there sometimes to gather blackberries; and she would always put flowers in her hair and sometimes would sing. He would hide, silent and stoic like an Indian, watching her.

Now it was their secret that they met at this grassy spot ringed about by its brushy wall, shaded in late spring and hot summer by a grove. Neither had ever said, "Don't tell"; that had not been necessary. Gradually they came to realize that most of the time there was no need of words between them. And now Kate Haveril was a big girl sixteen years old and Jesse Bodine was almost twenty, a tall, manly fellow who looked, little Kate thought, somehow like an eagle; and when by chance his hand brushed hers or a wisp of her hair blew across his face, a delicious thrill, troubling and ecstatic, ran through them, and her swift color mounted and he would not look at her.

And it was not that either of them was usually a retiring sort of individual; the Haveril household knew that it had a head-strong entity to deal with in one of its youngest, and men even beyond the Bodine boundaries already spoke of young Jesse as a man to reckon with. Wild hearts beat alike in the two of them, tamed only when a sort of magic fell over them shutting them away in a secret place.

Jesse Bodine ached to say: "You are like a wild rose! You are the prettiest and sweetest thing in the world, and some day I am going to marry you and take you 'way off somewhere, and we'll have a place all our own as big as all outdoors, and I'll build us the biggest, finest cabin you ever saw, with bearskins on all the floors, and I'll send a string of pack mules off to the nearest city and it will come back all loaded down with dresses for you and ribbons and things and factory-made furniture and books and pictures and a little organ for you to play and sing at." Instead of all that, he remarked on the weather, saying, "I don't think there ever was such a fine day, do you?"

Their speech, when words took the place of their more eloquent silences, was all about common-place things. She spoke of berries in berry time, and of school and the things she had read and learned, and of little everyday happenings at home, whether of someone ailing or a new baby calf or the owl with the broken wing which her youngest brother had made a pet; he, of manly things, work in the fields and woods, hunting and trapping. Today he was giving her part of his kill to take home with her, a heavy, fat gobbler. She would explain to her mother, all in a rush, "I saw the big Bodine boy; he had been hunting and sent this."

"I ran plumb out of powder," said Jesse. "I've got to go to town tomorrow. There's a sort of valley hunched up sort of on the lap of the mountain where there is more game than you can shake a stick at. I wished I'd had one more shot left."

"Tell me again what it's like when you get clean to the top," said Kate, and their eyes were lifted to the high, blue barrier. "On the other side, Jesse. I want to see it too, sometime."

He took a deep breath.

"If a man just keeps on going, long enough and far enough, over those mountains and some more mountains and across plains and valleys, you get to California. Where all the gold is."

If his eyes brightened as they always did when his quick fancies led his hopes, so and not less did hers.

"Oh, Jesse! I wish—"

"Look, Kitty!" There again he called her Kitty; it was only recently he had done that, just exactly four times in all now; she wondered if he noticed or if the new name just slipped out without his knowing. He even touched her hand lightly with his; she wasn't sure that he noticed that, either, his hand was lifted so quickly to point. "There's a storm coming; I can feel it, can you? Can't you smell it? And look at those clouds, how black they are, and how they're rolling up over the peaks. The rain's going to come down like water sloshed out of a rain barrel, and you'll get soaked through if we don't hurry."

But they didn't hurry; in so wonderful a world there was wonder in a gathering storm with the blue skies going black, with a queer light making the grass greener than ever, with a queer hush in the air so that the murmur and bicker of the creek sounded louder and clearer, with a sudden blast of wind through the pines.

"It's beautiful!" said Kate Haveril, scarcely above a whisper. They stood up and looked at each other now. "It scares me, it always does when there is thunder and lightning, but it's beautiful."

He nodded.

"It'll catch you long before you can get home. We better take to shelter and wait till it's over; it won't last long."

She smiled; he stood staring at her while she smiled, at the way her gay eyes made silent laughter, at the whiteness of her teeth, at the full ripeness, berry-red, of her parted lips.

They knew better than to look for shelter under the trees; the lightning when it came would run in liquid fire down some of those tall fellows from lofty top to bottom. Young Bodine snatched up his game and led the way, striding long-leggedly, while Kitty Haveril broke into a little trot close behind.

When the storm broke over their heads, thundering through the mountain gorges, crashing through the shivering pines, with the torrents of rain lashing the earth with its million whips, the boy and girl stood in a place of adequate shelter. Here the creek banks were high, the watercourse gouged deep through the years, and in a crook of the stream there was a tiny strip of sand-and-pebble beach over which the bank, carved grottowise at the base, extended like a roof; above their heads they could see the naked roots of trees, and a fringe of berry-bearing vines hung down like curtains. They didn't even get their feet wet coming here. They looked across the darkening curve of water and to the opposite bank. And when the first clap of thunder made them twitch, and the heavy drops of rain came threshing down, they looked at each other and smiled and were as happy as they had ever been in all their lives.

Jesse Bodine thought, "I wish it would never stop!" and Kitty said, "Oh, I wish—" and stopped, and they both laughed. Then they looked again at all they could see of the world outside their snug haven, and saw the bank with its buckeyes and alders and willows tossing about, and a little clearing along the edge; and, in an electric moment which came almost immediately and which stood out from all the rest of life as vividly as dark treetops flashing out of the pall of shadow when a blinding flash of lightning tore through the sky, they saw one man kill another.

The two men stood out quite clearly revealed less than a dozen yards away. What few words they spoke came with sufficient clearness, through the first crashing sounds of the storm, to be understood. One of them was a small, yellow-bearded man whom his companion called Joe, shouting after him: "Hi, Joe! Wait a shake."

"The crossin' is right here somewheres," said Joe, stopping and turning when near the brink.

The other was a large man, tall and heavy and of great girth; he, too, was bearded, wearing an enormous black beard that forked under the chin and was twisted into two horns. He hurried and overtook Joe and clapped a big hand on Joe's slight shoulder.

Some familiar chime rang in Jesse Bodine's memory. That little fellow Joe, with the yellow beard! Young Bodine could have sworn he had seen the man somewhere, perhaps a long way from here and a long time ago. Given time he could puzzle the thing out. But no time was granted him.

Joe said impatiently: "What you want, Miller?

Can't you see there's a lalapalooza of a storm coming? I tell you right here somewhere is the reg'lar crossin', and then a wagon road."

Both men carried long rifles and there were sheath knives at their belts. The big man, Miller, wore two pistols at his belt. As Joe paused, Miller came up to him and stood towering above him, looking in all directions as though seeking something. Then he struck with never another word, but with a little grunt of effort, and drove a horn-hafted knife into the little man's chest close up to the throat. Joe was hurled backward and came close to going over the edge of the bank and down into Buckeye Creek.

Miller snatched at him and dragged him back and struck again, sinking the broad knife blade deep into a scrawny body that jerked into rigidity and then went horribly limp. Miller squatted and wiped his blade clean on the wet grass.

Kate Haveril instinctively started to scream; she couldn't; her throat was locked tight. Then she clapped both hands to her mouth and cowered back, crouching down, trying to make her small self smaller. Also instinctively Jesse Bodine jerked his rifle up to his shoulder; then, remembering, he lowered it slowly and stepped back closer to Kate. Even then, before there was time for a single clear thought, he arrived at a determination to which he was to cling all his life; he would always save a last shot in his gun for the unexpected emergency. If he had only one more charge of powder! A man owed it to himself always to have in reserve one last charge of powder and ball.

Miller again glanced all around him, then set to work tugging and jerking at something tied securely, hard-knotted to Joe's belt. It was a little buckskin bag. Miller got it free, got its mouth untied, poured a part of its contents into his palm. Then hurriedly he poured it back into the bag, tied the bag to his own belt and stood up.

He seemed such a long time doing anything after that! Such a long time moving. He just stood there, and Kate's heart was beating so that it seemed it must burst through the wall of her fear-tightened breast. He just stood there while Jesse Bodine, his face drawn, his lean jaws locked hard, stood equally as still, one hand gripping his rifle, the other on his own knife. At last clear thought came to him; he was telling himself that if he or Kate in any way betrayed their presence they were as good as dead. Big black Miller, who had killed like that for the contents of a little buckskin bag, would never turn a hair at further killing to cover up his other murder.

Jesse turned slowly and looked down at Kate; her hands were still tight pressed against her mouth, and her eyes, flashing up at him, were wide and round with an agony of horror. He frowned at her and shook his head warningly.

When he turned again toward the killer the man had at last moved, and now was in all haste to be gone. He ran across the little clearing, plunged into the underbrush and disappeared, and Jesse couldn't even tell what direction he took. For a moment all had been still; now again the thunder rolled its reverberating drumbeats and jagged thunderbolts tore the sky wide open.

CHAPTER III

THE HANGING ON BUCKEYE CREEK

All color had drained out of Kate's face; Jesse Bodine had never seen anyone look so white and ill and stricken. Somehow, all involuntarily, she had come to her feet; he had to help her stand. And he, too, looked pale and gaunt and wild-eyed, shaken to the foundations of his being. Neither of them could get the thing they had just seen out of their minds; it was as though burned for all time into their eyeballs. That horrible knife—it was almost as though it had been plunged into their own bodies. They could see it yet; they could feel it tearing into their flesh. But at last they got themselves in hand.

"He is gone?" whispered the shivering girl.

Young Bodine nodded. He cleared his throat quietly and said huskily, "If only I hadn't used up my last shot!"

"Yes! You would have killed him! I wanted you to. For one minute I wanted you to kill him; I wanted to kill him myself! Now—now I'm glad, Jesse, that you haven't killed a man, too!"

"We've got to hurry—"

"Maybe he'll come back for something! If he saw us, he'd know we saw him, and he would—"

21

She broke off with a shudder; she wiped her staring eyes with her hands, trying to wipe the memory of that knife away.

"No. He's gone for good. We've got to hurry and tell folks what happened. I've got to hurry home and get some more powder; there's always a little. God, what a fool I was! And you run to your home too, Kitty; tell your father and brothers. He can't get far before we run him down."

She clung to him.

"I can't go alone! Don't leave me, Jesse! I'll go with you."

"All right. Now come ahead."

First they stood a moment looking out, listening, hearing and seeing nothing but the storm. She said in a small voice: "That other man—are we sure he is dead, Jesse? Maybe we ought to go to him first?" But Jesse shook his head. The man must be dead or, if not, there was nothing they could do for him until they brought help. So, hand in hand and cautiously, they left their retreat, going a little way downstream alongside the darkening water, then clambering up a bank and coming right away into a dim, winding path through the trees and thickets. When they could, they began to run.

Soon they left Buckeye Creek behind them and passed out from under the wind-tossed trees and came into the upper edge of the Bodine clearing. Already they were drenched to the skin, but they had no thought of that; the steady downpour beat into their faces and made a fluttering curtain through which they could see but short distances; the Bodine cabin, still almost a mile away, was cloaked in invisibility. It was all that Kate could do to keep up with the running Jesse Bodine, but just then she would have run until she dropped, with never a thought of calling out to him to wait. They raced across the pasture land and crawled, panting so that each could hear the other, through a stake-and-rider fence. When at last they hurtled into the cabin, it was as though the storm had blown them along with such leaves and stray branches as it had caught up on its way through the woods. And at first they could not speak the news which instantly their eyes were prefacing.

The Bodine household were gathered in the kitchen, a long, ample, rude room, high-raftered and homey. A dark, bearded, thick-shouldered man, sitting on a bench tinkering with a pair of hames on the table before him, looked up and stared at them. He said nothing, just waited. That was Tom Bodine, Jesse's father, and such was Tom Bodine's way, a man slow to take action but quick enough to act when once started.

A tall woman, middle-aged, still fine looking and with something proud in her bearing, Jesse's mother, was at the stove. She, too, looked at them and was silent, waiting the way her husband did, but with a livelier quickening of her jet-black eyes.

Then there were the younger ones, Jesse's brothers and sisters—Jimmy, the oldest, twenty-four and with a small curly brown beard; Luella, twenty-two, who looked like her mother, a dark beauty; Bert, a boy of twelve with a dash of red in his tousled hair and a glint of brown in his round eyes; and Baby Molly, a plump, impulsive little thing of eleven. And these younger ones, from Big Brother Jim to little Baby Molly, broke into a volley of question and exclamation.

Jesse Bodine shut the door behind him and a moment stood looking down at the blackening pool of water draining off him and Kate, getting his breath. Kate still looked frightened as she glanced all about her; she had never been in the Bodine home before, had never seen the Bodines themselves at such close range. And she saw how they looked at her.

Then Jesse took a deep breath and started talking, and, save for the lash of wind-whipped rain on the shake roof and the frequent booms of thunder and the boy's quiet speech, there was not a sound. While he was speaking, his mother came closer and sat down on one of the benches and lifted her face toward his, listening quietly, watching his eyes. Then, even before he finished his curt recital, she got up again and went to Kate Haveril; she took the girl's hand in hers and led her to the bench and the two sat down together, Mrs. Bodine still holding Kate's hand snug in hers.

Tom Bodine stood up and went for his coat and hat and rifle; he was thinking and didn't say a word. The others were quick to emulate him; the small amount of powder on hand was divided swiftly.

"We'll get him," said old Tom at last. "He won't go far in all this rain before he hits for shelter. Bert, you duck over to the Haveril place; tell 'em there. Any of the men folks that's home can overtake us."

"I'm coming with you!" cried young Bert excitedly.

His father, a hard man in family discipline, was just. He regarded his youngest son a moment thoughtfully then said:

"Yes, you come along, Bert; 'pears like you're a man grown and I didn't notice. One of the girls can go tell the Haverils."

Kate said: "I'll go. I'm Kate Haveril, you know."

"Yes, we know, Kate," said Jesse's mother in her quiet, pleasing voice. "It's best you go, you knowing as much about it as Jesse does. Luella, you go along with Kate; she'll be feeling sort of jumpy, all alone."

"I'll go, too!" cried little Molly, and, as the men folks started with their guns, the three girls ran out into the rain, headed for the Haveril place.

Hoping to pick up the fugitive murderer's trail, the Bodines went straight to the spot where the murder had taken place, where flight had begun.

With the rain beating down upon them they stood, a small, stilled group, looking down into the dead white face of the man with the yellow beard. There was no blood to be seen; the rain had washed it all away.

Closest of all stooped old Tom Bodine. For as long as a man could have counted ten, he stood stooped over, intent and rigid. Slowly he straightened up and looked at his son Jesse.

"So you heard the other feller call him Joe, did you?" He spoke quietly and gravely, his words well spaced. "And you sort of seemed to rec'lect having seen him some place? Well, it's Joe all right. You saw him back down in Tennessee, Jesse. Funny you even remembered, it was so long ago—"

"My God!" said Jimmy, the twenty-four-year-old Bodine. "It's Uncle Joe!" And then the mists blurring a time past faded away for Jesse, and he remembered.

"Yes, it's Joe," said their father. "It's Joe, all right. He was my youngest brother. It's been more'n ten years since we saw him that time. He said he was on his way to Californy; he said he'd come back sometime with his pockets full of gold for us. He said—It don't matter now what he said. He must have found out where we went; he was coming to see us and was almost home when this had to happen." He bent over again, this time to straighten the dead man's body properly, the stiffening arms at its sides, and placed Joe's battered old black hat over the upturned face. "Show us which way the man went, Jesse," he said then. "And you better lead for a spell, tracking; you're better'n the rest of us at that."

Jesse stepped swiftly to the spot where the big man with the forked beard had broken through the bushes; he found traces aplenty in broken branches trampled underfoot and even in the deeper imprints of heavy boots that the rain had not washed away. Once having picked up the trail, he had no difficulty following it to where it brought them into an opening through the pines. After that there were difficulties in plenty—dead leaves and matted brown pine needles and the pounding rain itself might have been in league with the murderer, concealing his tracks.

But the grim determination of the questing men and their knowledge of the woods and their shrewd, hard eyes constituted a relentless force which consented to be patient but was not to be thwarted. They spread out in a long line, and scarcely a broken twig as large as a pack needle escaped them. Some minutes passed before Jesse waved to them. He showed them a clear track in a bit of black, sticky soil; it was rain-filled and its edges broken, yet the track was there and pointed their direction for them. The big man, Miller, had headed as nearly as he could in a straight line that would lead some three or four miles farther on

27

into Wagon Road Gap, one of the steep passes through the mountains.

"Guess we know now which way he's going," said Tom Bodine. "Headed west, through the Gap and towards Californy. Best, just the same, we should keep our eye skinned for more tracks a while longer, less he turns off. Step along, Son."

So Jesse again led them—swiftly again, then more slowly, questing about, this way and that, jerking his head up to stare ahead, for all the world like a hunting dog. And after a while they heard shouts behind them, and then the Haveril men, three of them, old Abner, the father, and his two grown sons, Ransome and Richard, came hurrying to join them, each one of them with his rifle over his arm. There was but a minute or two taken off for talk; it was young Bert Bodine who blurted out the news that the man murdered was their Uncle Joe. Then the seven men moved forward again toward the lifting mountain.

Of a sudden the storm passed away, the rain ceased, and the sun, as bright and glorious as though it had been washed in the cloudbursts and scoured by the blasts of lightning, shone from a rare blue sky; and rain drops on branch and leaf were sparkling jewels, and a new, ineffable green was upon the open grassy slopes and valleys, and a happy bird, no longer hushed and fearful, began to sing until presently other birds near and far released their spontaneous, bubbling notes, and the world was fair and fresh and clean and joyous again. And yet the man with the yellow beard lay dead just back there, and the man with the black forked beard twisted into rough horns was somewhere ahead.

After a while old Abner Haveril said to old Tom Bodine, "Your boy tracks like a Injun." And Tom nodded and was proud of his keen, stalwart son. It's a fine, heartening thing to hear praise spoken of your son by a just man like Abner Haveril.

"My girl Kate tells me," said Abner, "that the killer couldn't have any sort of notion that her and your boy Jesse was anywhere near. If that's so, well, he can't have any notion anybody's after him. That being so, we're apt to run him down real soon, being as he's no doubt holed up somewheres for shelter."

"That's so," said Tom Bodine. "I'd thought of that."

Young Bert had the way of always sticking close to the older folk; he liked to listen to what they said. Now he spoke up.

"What do you think he killed him for, Papa? What do you think Uncle Joe had in that buckskin pouch? Gold, Papa, do you s'pose so? And that's why he got kilt?"

"Maybe, Bert; I don't know," said Tom Bodine patiently. "Now you keep shut up."

"What are you going to do with him when you ketch him, shoot him like a dog?"

"Bert!"

"Oh, all right," said Bert.

It was but a few minutes later when they came upon their quarry with an unexpected suddenness which startled them and left him thunderstruck. As they had deemed likely, he had sought shelter during the worst of the brief storm; where a shoulder of a hill broke down into a bit of rocky cliff, he had crept into a deep cleft with an overhang of rock and turf like a section of ragged shed roof. Had he lain quiet, there was the bare chance that he might have escaped, for among the rubble strewing the slope he had left no track. As it was, the men were passing silently when he crawled out into their view.

He had no chance then and knew it, with those several unwavering rifle barrels a bristling arc before him, and did not even lift hand or foot in his own behalf. They closed in on him and disarmed him without a word; he remained as silent until after the thing was done.

He kept looking at one face after another until he must have stamped every face indelibly upon the tablet of his memory; he saw the same expression everywhere; even that on young Bert's face seemed a reflection of the look on old Tom's.

"Come along," said Tom Bodine.

The black bearded man didn't speak even then; he stumbled along in their midst, back toward the spot where so short a time ago he had killed Joe

Bodine. It was likely that he knew from the first sight of them, though he could not understand how it came about that retribution came so swiftly; he could not possibly fail to understand when at last they came to their destination. Tom Bodine removed the hat from Joe's face; the clear sunlight glanced into Joe's eyes.

"You killed him," said Tom.

"No," said Miller. He moistened his lips; he brushed the tangle of beard away from his lips that were full and red and sensuous. "I never killed him. I never saw him."

"My son saw you kill him," said Tom Bodine. "Jesse saw you kill him and rob him just now."

"Which is your son? Which one?"

Tom pointed. Jesse's lean, hard face was scarcely a yard from Miller's.

Miller shook his head.

"No. I didn't kill anybody. If this man, your son, says so he's a liar. I'll tell you how it is." He twisted the forks of his coarse beard with both hands together. "Your son must have killed him, so he says I done it."

"This is the right man all right, ain't it, Jesse?" his father asked.

Jesse nodded. Also he stepped closer and untied the buckskin bag at Miller's belt; he opened it and poured its contents into the dented crown of his hat and showed them what it was. Gold, as young Bert had thought it ought to be; gold that Uncle Joe had brought them from California.

"We'd ought to brought a rope," said old Abner and sounded fretful. "Here we come off in a rush and nobody brought a rope." He unpocketed, a hard, dry slab of chewing tobacco and a broken-bladed clasp knife and started whittling a chew. "Ransome Haveril, you go down to the house and bring a rope."

There was a cold fury in Jesse Bodine's eyes, a fury that was a stranger there until today.

"We don't need any rope; we don't need to wait," he said very quietly yet very distinctly. And when Abner Haveril demanded tartly, "What in tarnation does the boy mean? To turn the skunk loose?" Jesse said, "No."

"Go get that rope and hurry, Ransome," said old Abner. Ransome hurried away on his errand, and Abner got his tobacco shavings into his mouth, pocketed plug and knife and said to Jesse, speaking placidly again: "I dunno, Jesse Bodine, but somehow a execution don't seem reg'lar 'thout the rope. We got ammunition and guns aplenty and could shoot this feller, or we could stick him like a pig with his own knife, and I don't know's it would make any hell-fired diff'rence. Only a rope seems more sort of reg'lar."

There was a log handy and he sat down on it; so did Tom Bodine and young Bert, though young Bert's feet kept shifting and a slow greenish pallor was creeping into his face and a look of distress into his eyes. For a long while he stared in fascination at the man about to die; then he jerked his eyes away and didn't look that way again.

Miller said, "Got any whisky, anybody?" Nobody had. He said, "God-a'mighty, I never wanted a drink so bad!" Then he asked for a smoke. Jimmy Bodine gave him tobacco and papers; Miller's fingers were slightly unsteady but he managed.

"It's reg'lar," said old Abner, "to ask a man if he's got any last wishes, if there's any word he wants sent to anybody."

Miller hurled the cigarette down and stamped on it.

"I tell you I didn't kill him!" he shouted. "Nobody saw me; this boy's a liar! You got to let me go!"

"My girl saw you," said old Abner.

Miller was sullen and silent until he saw Ransome Haveril returning, saw the coil of rope in his hand. Then he made his hopeless, desperate, maniacal bid for escape, flailing with his thick arms, clawing and kicking. They had to pile on him, three or four of them, and drag him down. He fought to the last second, fought with his last breath as the noose tightened. They hung him to kick his life out a few yards from the still, aloof thing that had once been the gay, wild, generous, likable Joe Bodine.

CHAPTER IV

A GLEAM IN THE RISING SUN

Jesse Bodine and Kate Haveril did not meet again on the banks of the Buckeye. No matter though the sun shone and warm little wandering breezes rippled the grass and May buds opened, their old familiar haunts had lost something that would never come back, just as something new and sinister and ugly had come to stain the world hereabouts horribly and indelibly. Nor, for several days, did they meet anywhere.

That same evening Jesse Bodine went down into the valley to the little crossroads settlement they called The Town, for ammunition. The next daybreak found him "gone hunting" far up into the mountains. He was silent when he left; when, after two nights of sleeping out in the open wherever night found him, he returned, he was silent.

In the Bodine household itself nothing seemed changed, nothing beyond that subtle change in Jesse Bodine himself. Uncle Joe had been brought down to the wood lot out at the loveliest sunny rim of the pasture and decently interred, his grave properly marked and mounded, with a low, neat, tight picket fence around it. His murderer had been promptly returned to the earth at the spot where he had so swiftly expiated his crime, and there was nothing left of the two of them save memories and Joe Bodine's little buckskin pouch with its California gold.

The pouch lay for days untouched on the ax-hewn oak mantel over the fireplace, for the most part even unmentioned, hardly regarded, maybe touched only now and then by the flick of a sidewise glance. But at last, on the third or fourth day, Tom Bodine took it down in the presence of the assembled family.

"Joe wanted us to have it, some of it anyhow, I reckon," he said.

"How much is it, Pop, in money?" asked young Bert.

"I don't know," said Tom Bodine, hefting it in a measuring sort of way in his horny palm. "I'll get it weighed down at Lunt's hardware store; Charlie Lunt will know. It's a heap of money, though. Don't know; maybe six-seven hundred dollars."

"Maybe a thousand, even?" said Baby Molly, and grew rounder-eyed than ever. That was Molly for you: she could say a thing, freeing her fancies for wild flight, then grow awed over her own words.

"I wish I could remember Uncle Joe, what he was like, when he was to visit us that time in Tennessee," said Molly.

"You were only a baby then, maybe couple years old. You wouldn't remember."

Later her mother told her all about Uncle Joe, how he was the gayest, jolliest of all the Bodines, the youngest too, and always going off to faraway places, bringing back amazing tales for many a retelling. He played a fiddle, too, the only one of the Bodines to do that, as far as Tom's wife could remember.

"Do you s'pose the man that killed him follered him all the way from Californy, Ma? How'd he know about Uncle Joe's gold?"

"We'll never know, Pet. Joe was always careless, oh, about everything; about his companions, I'm afraid. He might have talked; you can't tell. He wouldn't have hurt a fly himself, not for anything; he wouldn't be the likely kind to suspect any man of wanting to kill him."

"I wish Uncle Joe hadn't died. I wonder what Californy is like, Ma? I wish he could have told us."

"Other folks have been there. Some of 'em come back, some don't. Someday maybe you'll get to hear someone talk about it that knows."

Jesse was back from the mountains but somehow still seemed as far away from them as if he had not returned. He sat on a bench at the table and cleaned his rifle; he melted lead in the fire shovel and molded bullets; he went outside about his daily chores; he grew vocal sufficiently to express his creature wants, as when he passed his plate at supper; and that was about all from Jesse Bodine those days.

He met up with Ransome Haveril in the foothills where Jesse had gone with the two bays and the sled for firewood; it was the first time he had seen any of the Haveril family since the affair at Buckeye Creek. Ransome Haveril, on a like errand, left his team standing and came over, ax on shoulder. Ransome was the oldest of the young Haverils, four or five years Jesse's senior, though scarcely more mature, tall and dark like Jesse, handsome in the eyes of the Pleasant Valley girls, a Big Brother next to Godhead in the eyes of his favorite sister Kate. He and Jesse had always got along, much to Kate's delight.

Ransome's dog, a shepherd with round yellow spots over its soft brown eyes, followed him and flopped down close to his feet when he stopped. So the two young men spoke briefly of dogs. Ransome told how a skunk had raided the chicken pen last night; cut the throats of seven hens.

They idled over to a log and sat down and took out their knives.

"I'm going west," said Jesse.

"Wonder what she's like out that way?" mused Ransome.

"I've been thinking about it quite a spell. Now I've made up my mind. The folks don't need me around; they wouldn't have needed me anyhow, and now with all that gold Uncle Joe brought they're fixed up fine."

"When are you going, Jesse?"

"I don't know. Any time now. I haven't told anybody about it, Ransome."

Ransome nodded. A man would naturally keep his mouth shut until the last minute; no use starting a wind at home, a lot of talk stirred up by the old folks.

"My folks don't need me around particular either," he said after a while. The two didn't look at each other; both had their eyes lifted toward the bulwark of the mountains. Both were looking through the mountains, over them, far beyond. "Might go along with you, Jesse, if you want me to."

"We'll need plenty ammunition; good, stout shoes, too."

"A man can tote along enough jerked venison and parch corn to last him the hellofa ways. There'll be plenty game."

"I've got ten dollars of my own," said Jesse. "I've been saving it."

"I spent mine the last dance I was to," Ransome admitted. "But I've got extra ammunition."

"Tomorrow morning? I'll meet you right here at sunup."

"Suits me."

They stood up and closed their clasp knives.

Jesse had something else to say but took his time, hesitant though determined to get it said.

"I've got to see your sister Kate before I go," he said after a while. "You see, I've got a going-away present I want to give to her. You ask her will she come outside tonight after supper, will you, Ransome?"

"All right. G' by, Jesse."

"Tomorrow morning. Sunup."

That evening Jesse told his mother first. Somehow, he couldn't make out why, he found it hard to do. She was in the kitchen alone; he followed her around, got into her way, brought her unneeded wood for the wood box, told her how good the dry-apple pie smelled.

She washed and dried her hands and sat down.

"Well, Jesse. What is it? It's not a girl you've got in your head already, is it?"

"I'm going away, Mother. Going west. Tomorrow early."

She didn't say anything for a long time. He stood head down, vaguely sad and troubled. He knew that he had hurt her. She kept looking at him, her hands placid in her lap, her mouth placid. Into her eyes came, he thought, the strangest look in the world; he couldn't make anything of it. Maybe she was just thinking, trying to get it straight in her head, trying to realize what he had said, for it must be a surprise to her; maybe she was looking back over old memories; maybe she was looking, in her own way, westward, too; westward with him.

"Told your father yet, Jesse?"

He shook his head.

"I've known a weary long time it was coming, Jesse, just waiting to hear you say it. Well, better go tell him. He's out by the smokehouse." Then suddenly she threw her arms around him and hugged him tight. He saw her dab at her cheeks as she went back to whatever it was she had been doing. He hurried out to speak with his father.

"I'm going, Father," said Jesse, hurrying to get it said. "West. In the morning."

"So you're going west, are you?" Tom Bodine, like his wife, sat down; there was an upended keg handy and he settled on it and pulled off his hat and ran his toil-hardened hand through the thick thatch of his black and grizzled hair. "Well, Son, I don't know as I blame you. Folks keep on a-moving fu'ther and fu'ther west all the time. My father got as far as he did; I got this far; you'll be aching to move on ahead. Well, your mother's been telling me so a year; she said it was coming unless by chance you stayed on account Katie Haveril."

The sun had gone down; shadows were thin over the brooding world; one lonely star shone in the low pale sky. In the eerie, uncertain light of the dusk, Jesse Bodine stood like one bemused. His mother knew a year ago, before he himself knew? And his mother knew of Kate, too. He said:

"You know how it is—And you won't be needing me—"

"No. I never needed any man, Son, not hard enough to want him to stay when he had some other place pulling him. So you're going in the morning?"

"Maybe Ransome Haveril will go along with me."

"That's good. He's a good boy. Told your mother yet?"

"Yes. Just now."

"That's good. She say anything?"

Jesse shook his head. His father, the session done, stood up and for an instant laid his hand on his son's shoulder.

"Take care of yourself, Jesse," was all he had to add.

It was just before supper that the news came out into the open for all the family, and instantly the big cabin became a place of turmoil from puncheon floor to smoky rafter; even the candles seemed to sputter in brand-new fashion and the smoked hams and sides of venison to turn and sway with an electrified will all their own. Jesse's brothers exclaimed this thing and that, and had many wise remarks to make; his sisters gasped and stared at him as at a new creature in their midst, and caught him by the arms and shook him, and all the while, after the first astonishment, were half between laughter and tears. Tears did pop out from Baby Molly's eyes at the very first word, and her mouth quivered and she couldn't speak. But after the shock of the thing, hers was the wildest and noisiest excitement of all.

What Jesse was doing was exactly what she would do if only she were a boy! California! The wonders of its mountains and plains and valleys, its forests and rivers and waterfalls, its gold, gold, gold! Gold everywhere! And glorious new things to see and to do!

"Haven't forgotten Uncle Joe, have you?" put in brother Jim.

That hushed them, and little mercuric Molly came close to crying again, and grew fearful and hugged Jesse's arm tighter than ever. But her sister Luella's smile returned quickly, a mite of malice in it as she said sweetly:

"Jim would like to go too, but we know why he can't. Sarah won't let him."

"Lou!" her mother chided. It was a recent discovery in the family that Jimmy had been sparking Sarah Fairbanks all spring, and Sarah, though not a day older than Luella, was a widow. A young widow, a pretty, vivacious one; one who had married a man much older than herself and who now, childless, had heired her husband's property. Well-to-do, they had called him. There were those who would say that Jim Bodine would be making a fine match; there were others, and

Jim's mother was one of them, who were apt to say, "Well, maybe I'm old-fashioned," but did not think it a very nice thing for any woman to have two husbands in the same lifetime. When Sarah's name was mentioned Mrs. Bodine usually found some excuse to leave the room.

In the lull young Bert, who hadn't found a chance to get a word in edgewise, offered wistfully:

"I wish I could go, too! Couldn't I, Jesse? Say, Jesse—"

"Dry up, Bertie," said his mother, as nearly sharp with him as she knew how to be. "And go bring me a bucket of water. It's most supper time."

Altogether Jesse's brothers and sisters made a great to-do over his impending departure, and somehow they began to put a new flavor into it, making of it a high, chiming adventure with a dash of danger and a red cloak of romance, whereas until now he had just looked at it as a thing to do, a natural and almost inevitable step, simply the thing he was going to do. Before they were done he had caught a fervor which, beginning with Baby Molly had extended to the others until its atmosphere created a little warm, golden mist about them, and his eyes, which had been so sober-serious these latter days, sparkled like Molly's. Questioned, sitting on a bench with Molly on one side and Lou on the other holding his hands, he began even to grow boastful. He began to dream aloud, to live in heroics, to bestride Youth's charger and let it prance. His mother sighed and went into the kitchen and, behind the kitchen door, lifted the hem of her apron to her eyes.

Jesse didn't eat. He told his mother that he wasn't hungry yet and slipped outside while the others were gathering at the table; he knew that Kate would have had her supper and would be waiting for him by the time he could hasten over to the Haveril home.

And waiting she was, all excitement. All that her brother had told her was: "Jesse's coming over. He wants to see you right after supper. He—he is bringing you a present." And when she and Jesse met on the path a couple of hundred yards from the house, he could see in the starlight the shining eagerness in her eyes.

"Ransome told you?"

"Yes! What is it, Jesse?"

"What did he tell you?"

"Just that you were coming, that you wanted to see me."

"Nothing else?"

There were trees about them, still and dark in the starlight, but they stood in an open spot; her eyes were held up to his and he could even see the tremor of her lips in a secret smile.

She nodded, and her curly hair shook as though the wind were in it.

"He said you were bringing me something! What is it, Jesse?"

He brought it out of his pocket, a pretty gold locket on a fine gold chain. He had seen it one day in town, among the few gay trinkets at Charlie Lunt's store, and had hoarded for it a long while, thinking with an anticipatory shiver how lovely it would be around her white throat. He gave it to her in silence and stood rigid while, wondering, she took it into her hands. Suddenly her hands shut tight about it and she clasped it to her breast.

"Oh, Jesse! I love it! I am going to keep it forever and ever!" She lifted it and brushed it against her lips and cuddled it against her cheek. It was the first gift and spoke with poignant eloquence to a heart all atuned to its musical whisperings; of a sudden her heart beat so hard that almost it pained her.

"It's a going-away present, Kitty. Didn't Ransome tell you? I am going away."

Her hands came down slowly and she stiffened so that she was rigid, too; he heard her deep intake of breath.

"Going away? What do you mean? Not far, Jesse? Not for long?"

"West. All the way to California." He knew then that he was going to hurt her, too, somewhat in the way he had hurt his mother. He felt crude and clumsy; he wished he had spoken to her first of all, that he hadn't come out in this blunt fashion.

46

He felt all mixed up inside, oddly embarrassed. He had to go; he knew he had to go. Right now he wanted to stay, to be with her. It was with an effort that he went on. He tried to speak with a cheery heartiness which he did not feel now but which he had felt an hour ago when talking with his admiring and mildly envious sisters.

He spoke rapidly, and it was the first time she had ever heard him speak with a rush of words; he told her of what he meant to see and do and experience; he grew with her, as with them, boastful.

California was waiting for him, that was it, fair, golden California! Oh, there'd be dangers and adventures and hardships; he laughed at them. There were fame and fortune waiting out there for the man who was man enough to wrest them into his own grip. A man couldn't tell how long he might be gone, how many years. But some day he was coming back; he would come back laden with gold. Then he would come to her, and—and—

Oh, he hurt her then! Going away like this, was he, just blurting out the fact at the last minute, going maybe for years! Filling his hands with gold, then coming back—and counting on Kate Haveril endlessly waiting!

She thought that her heart was broken; she thought at sixteen that hearts did truly break. She wanted to cry, she wanted to scream. She began laughing at him. She showed him altogether a flaming, fiery, scornful, mocking Kate Haveril that he had never dreamed existed.

"You big, overgrown baby!" she taunted him, lashing raw flesh. "Oh, how smart you are and what fine noble deeds you are going to do—in that faraway *California!*" She said California as spitefully as if it had been another girl's name. "You'll fill your hands with gold, won't you? Will you come back riding in a golden carriage drawn by six white horses? And will you let me run along at your wheels or run ahead and throw flowers for your white horses to prance on? But maybe by then I'll be an old lady with white hair—and maybe it will be my daughter who will throw flowers for you!"

He had turned pale and his eyes were flaming, but she could not see that. Weakly he said: "Kitty, don't you see? Don't you understand?" She heard herself laughing again. Then she whipped about and ran, and as she ran she flung the tiny locket on its fine golden chain over her shoulder. He stared down at it but didn't touch it. He stared after her, stunned, incredulous, and saw her vanish in a pool of dark at the cabin corner.

He stood a long while, watching the lamplit window, yellow in the thickening night, waiting, hoping that she would come back. Then he heard voices in the cabin, heard her gay laughter.

He turned slowly then and walked away.

It was late when he returned home that night and all had gone to bed except his mother and Baby Molly. He had a few mouthfuls of food in the kitchen, pretending to eat rather than really eating. Molly yawned and went off to bed; she was going to be awake and tell him good-by in the morning no matter how early he left.

But only his mother was standing out there by the woodpile in the daybreak, though he suspected that his father was awake. His mother tucked her arm through his and they walked slowly a few steps together.

"It's all right that you are going, Jesse," she said quietly and steadily. "I understand. Maybe you won't ever come back, and maybe you will. Maybe if you do come back I'll be alive and maybe I'll be dead. It's a far way, Jesse. God takes care of things. You just be a good boy, Jesse. Be a good boy and you'll be a good man. Now kiss me and go."

She hugged him in a fiercely strong embrace, then almost pushed him away. She hurried back to her kitchen, going around the cabin, and did not once look back. He strode off toward the hills and a meeting with Ransome Haveril and the mountains beyond, and neither did he look back.

But both he and Ransome, from a high place, before they came to the Gap, making an excuse of resting a moment after a rapid climb, turned their faces toward the valley lands they were discarding for an inviting unknown. They could see still columns of smoke standing straight up into the clear new day from the two cabins; the sun was just up and the smoke columns were almost black down close to the chimneys, bluish gray at the top.

Ransome affected to laugh but seemed vaguely disturbed and ill at ease.

"Get away without any row, Jess?" he asked offhandedly.

Jesse nodded. "They said it was all right. Funny, they already had a notion I'd be going. What about your folks, Ran?"

"My father just said, 'Go 'head if you're a mind to and get it over.' Mother, well she cried a little but said she wouldn't keep me. I don't know what come over Kate though. I never saw her act up like that. She sure give me hell and what for, Jesse." He tried his laugh again. "Funny, she put all the blame on you, and you'd have thought we were a couple of scum of the earth. I always thought she liked you, too."

Jesse was looking now at the spot near the Haveril cabin where last night Kate had come to meet him. Something gleamed faintly in the sun, just where she had flung the little locket on its gold chain. A fleck of mica in a rock, no doubt. He shouldered his rifle and started on.

CHAPTER V

THE ECSTASY AND THE GLORY

It was to be a full two years before they saw the distant high blue ranges of California under a high blue sky, with snow on the mountaintops looking like fragments fallen from the soft-bosomed cottony clouds, clouds standing so still that one wondered what kept them in their places, so motionless that the black shadows which they dropped on the sunbright slopes seemed fixed immovably. And during that time many experiences came to them, and some of them, in one way and another, became a part of them; some were tangible facts that hard hands could grapple with, and some were evasive and insubstantial thoughts and dreams and scraps of knowledge that touched their hearts or maybe sank into their souls. Sometimes a year merely makes a man a year older; these were different years, doing far more than that.

That first day of their westward wandering they were quiet and thoughtful; something hushed them as children are hushed entering a dark room or a deserted house. The mountain solitudes pressed upon them as never before, and for a time their shoulders were slack and heavy. Not so soon had they shaken off all that they were so deter-minedly leaving behind; their thoughts turned inward instead of leaping ahead in anticipation; they were carrying their homes, mother, father, brothers and sisters, familiar daily routines, on their backs as a plodding turtle carries his shell. They didn't talk much that day; they didn't take the interest they had expected to take in the land about them; and the next day was like the first, as was even the third in lesser degree. Distance, both in miles and in time, needed to be put between them and their homes before they could shake off something that trammeled them, before the free stride came.

But then, sudden and emphatic like the flash from powder ignited, came the ecstasy and the glory! They awoke as the sun came flaming up, beside their dead campfire on the rocky rim of a plateau high above the sleeping world, and that world was instantly their world. Overnight the shackles had been struck off. They were free in a rich and intoxicating freedom. It was still Maytime, and buds on hardy mountain shrubs were still bursting. The skies were clear, no clearer than their eyes, than their inner vision. Already they were ankle-deep in the Great Adventure! They could shout to the mountaintops and no human ear save their own could hear. They could say, "This is mine," and "I want that," and there was no will but their will. They were young lusty gods on Olympus. Better, they were young men. They were just stepping proudly and masterfully into their birthright. They were setting their eager lips to the golden cup from which to take deep, electrifying draughts of the sheer joy of Youth running wild. All that lay behind them was suddenly as far away, as dim as a dream dreamed long ago. What belonged to them was the vibrant Now with vast, undulating expanses extending below their foot-level; what belonged to them was all that lay in the future; a sunset with the sun going down into a field of vivid and colorful radiance was not so bright and beautiful and beckoning as was the life over which their ardent young sun was only risen. Risen and still rising, to fuller, incomparable glory.

That sense of mastery born in them so overwhelmingly, so mysteriously, went on with them; it did not fade with the passing days but grew. The sap was rising in them as in young trees.

From the first it had been Jesse Bodine's expedition. To the end, and no matter what end, it must be Jesse Bodine's. Younger than Ransome Haveril, he was stronger; stronger in everything. Physically he grew swiftly to be far stronger; intellectually he was stronger. His hands could grasp and hold; his mind could grasp and hold. His lean, hard jaw, his dark, burning eyes, his high forehead with the mane of black hair tossed back from it—these were the signs of the inner man that already existed, that was being retouched here and there as last details may be lined upon a bronze statue. Already the hardness of bronze was in him. And deep within was a hot, bright fire. That fire was a fierce ecstasy.

Youth running wild! The youth of the lone pioneer. To do as you please, to think as you please, to go as you please. Take what you want; grasp it in your iron fingers and it is yours. Keep it, throw it away. Do what you please with it. Go on, go on to what is next. There's always something better ahead. Stand on a high place and look with low-lidded, insolent eyes at the world spread before you. Well, whose world is it anyway? You can stamp on it. You can take up handfuls of soil, of stone, and fling them over the cliff's edge. Far down yonder is a little laughing, dimpling, green valley, soft in the sunshine in its kirtle of flowers. Whose? A strong hand makes it yours; yours the Conquest and the fruits thereof. Wide fields with only a herd of deer grazing; do you want the fields and the herd too? Take them, young man. They are yours. Swing an ax against the wall of a centuries-old forest, and the forest in surrender yields you whatever roof you demand. Every created creature and thing pays you tribute and brings you full-handedly food and drink and raiment. How many furred things ask you to honor them by wearing their coats before the chill of winter! "Splendid!" says

Youth, and then laughs and says: "But I want something still more splendid. Something farther on."

They lay on their bellies on the bank of a green, winding river, with the sun warm on their backs. They had eaten to the full of fish and of fowl, too, and of parched corn, and had drunk deep of the cold water.

Ransome said murmurously into the crook of his arm on which his face was bedded, "It feels good to be alive, don't it, Jess?" He turned his head lazily; he sounded half asleep. "I like it here fine. A man could have himself everything he wanted. I never saw so much game; fish, too. Someday maybe there'll be a town not too far away; a store, you know, and folks; there'd be some girls and there'd be dances once in a while. There'll be girls living here, too. I bet there will someday, Jess. Huh?"

Jesse rolled over and sat up, but he didn't answer. Ransome dozed off and snored faintly. Jesse nibbled at a blade of grass and looked off above the treetops to still farther, bluer mountains.

Ransome came out of his doze, scrubbed his forehead with his knuckles and said:

"Talking about girls, there was one I was getting to like pretty much, back in Pleasant Valley. You know Sarah Fairbanks that your brother Jimmy's been shining up too, well it's a friend of Sarah's; I saw her at a dance the first time." He laughed chucklingly. "I don't know, Jess. Might have married her if I hadn't come along with you. This is better though, ain't it?"

Jesse got up and stretched, and went for his rifle leaning against a tree. Shouldering into his light pack he said:

"I've got a hankering to see what it's like the other side that next ridge, Ran."

They knew, as they had known when they started from Pleasant Valley, that most folks traveling westward followed an established route which lay nearly a hundred miles to the south; that they had but to turn southward to strike into that emigrant trail provided they craved companionship of their own kind. They'd find families, groups of families with wagons and some livestock, all California-bound. And there'd be an infrequent trading post or a farm or some sort of settlement. Following sign, asking what lay ahead, planning. The clank of a caravan, the grinding of wheels, dust rising under plodding hoofs. Night camps, campfires, men congregated talking, a fiddle or guitar some-where, voices singing, old folks remembering and advising, young folks eluding and finding one another on the outer rim of fire-flickered circles, an old man dying and a boy and girl falling in love. A wayside funeral, maybe; maybe a stop by a river for a wedding and a dance.

It might be fun, all that.

We might as well have stayed at Pleasant Valley.

The two, always friendly, grew with passing days and weeks and months to be stanch friends. They were sufficiently like, sufficiently unlike, to complement each other; at times they argued, seeing the same thing in different lights from different angles; at times they knew quick flashes of irritation, anger even; but, despite these things, and partly because of them, their friendship grew steadily and became a fine, loyal bond between them.

Time and experiences, quiet happiness and hardship tooled tirelessly at their characters; as a great rock in the desert is worn and carved and shaped by the fine chisels of sand in the hands of the winds, so were these two, at least in part, shaped by the wilderness through which they roamed and in which they lived; as a sandstone cliff and a granite outcropping, blown upon by the same gritty winds, may be worn in varying degrees, at unequal speeds, into dissimilar shapes, so these two in their pilgrimage. Jesse Bodine had begun to grow hard back there as a boy on the rim of Pleasant Valley. That day when he had seen the fork-bearded man drive a broad-bladed knife into Joe Bodine, the day he had helped hunt the murderer down, had watched with pitiless, inscrutable eyes as the man died horribly, he had hardened perceptibly. His adoration for the lovely Kate Haveril had constituted a tender influence that drew him strongly toward a gentler way of thought and deed; but all he could remember of her of late, and that a slowly dissolving picture, was the Kate Haveril whose passionate denunciation and bright, brittle mockery had been salt and acid upon all tenderness within him and had made him hard again, and, more than that, bitter.

And now the slow, steady hardening process went on, with many factors to contribute.

With Ransome Haveril there was a difference. Jesse more and more led the way, and Ransome grew content to follow. Ransome loved the life they led, largely because it put no restrictions upon them, because here and now all former responsibilities were sloughed off. He found life easier, simpler; his reaction was to grow soft where Jesse turned hard. He was like any man who finds a support to lean upon, and leans upon it more and more with each succeeding step.

One late afternoon they were so startled that they stood and stared at each other slack-jawed as though they could not believe what they heard without assurance. And it was one of the commonest sounds in the world. It was the barking of dogs.

They were going down the slope of a long

mountain flank toward water and rest; below them was a ravine so steep and thick with timber that it would harbor a green dusk at midday. Down in the bed of the ravine was a swift stream; they had heard its splash and gurgle before the dogs barked. They hurried on again; the dogs burst into a perfect frenzy of barking. Then, where there was a bit of a clearing on a strip of level land bordering the stream, they saw the small cabin made of sapling poles chinked with mud, and the flurry of dogs, and the man.

He saw them at the same time and ran a few steps and stooped for something; as he straightened up they saw that he was holding a rifle. He stood irresolute an instant, then started running again as though to dart into the fringe of forest behind his cabin. They shouted, and he stopped again; he stood there seeming of two minds at once, seeming frightened, bewildered. The dogs ceased barking and, as Jesse and Ransome came close, began to growl and draw back. But they did not go any nearer their master. That was a strange thing. It would seem that they were suspicious of the strangers, which was as it should be; but also they were afraid of their master. There were three of the dogs, all shepherds with a bar sinister.

Jesse and Ransome looked at the stranger not as they would look at a man but as at some marvel of the animal kingdom. Jesse, for one, remembered a book he had read at the country schoolhouse in Tennessee; here was a very evil, dirty looking Robinson Crusoe. The man was clothed in the tatters of skins from head to foot, from shapeless fur cap with a bushy tail hanging down against a shoulder to shapeless moccasins. Nose and eyes was all the face he had, for the rest was a mat of black whiskers, and a fringe of hair from beneath his squirrelskin cap came down to his brows. His eyes were just two small, round, black living beads, and were restless and furtive and cruel and alive with fears. He was like a thing that had been a man of sorts once, that had dwelt too long among the animals he preyed upon, that had turned all animal himself. When he spoke it seemed a strange thing that such an animal could speak.

It was not that he was in any haste to speak. He stood and stared at them and blinked his beads of eyes; at last a soft, low growl came into his throat. That seemed quite fitting. But when Jesse said a quiet, "Howdy, stranger," the growling sound died away, or altered, rather, into human speech.

"Howdy," he said. Then one of the dogs started growling again, and he shouted angrily: "Shut up! Shut up, you damn' bitch or I'll kick your guts out."

The dogs subsided and slunk away. The man snapped his eyes back to his visitors; he had nothing to volunteer in addition to his surly

"Howdy." They looked about upon the slovenly camp with idle curiosity.

"We heard your dogs barking. That's how come we dropped in," said Ransome after a silence, and got a grunt for an answer. "Many folks around here?" he asked.

"There ain't nobody. Just me." The man clawed at his chin, lost in the tangled thicket of his beard; his hand was greasy and black and hadn't been washed in years. "This is my trappin' country— all up an' down this crick, over yonder. All over, up here. Nobody but me."

All the while he kept blinking and clawing at his chin; his other hand was like a foul talon about his rifle. He had a sheath knife at his belt, and a hatchet.

Jesse Bodine, disgusted with him, having no flicker of interest in him, turned and stalked off downstream. Ransome hesitated a moment, then followed him. Suddenly Jesse stopped and turned a cold, thoughtful stare back at camp and cabin and man.

"There's something damned funny here," he said in a low tone. Then he lifted his voice and called out, "Where'd the other man go?"

His Robinson Crusoe stopped clawing his chin and again seemed bewildered, at a loss, irresolute.

"What other man?" he demanded.

"The man that was here with you. Your pardner. Where'd he go?"

There came no answer. Ransome looked questioningly at his friend.

"What are you driving at, Jess? I didn't see anybody else."

"There's another rifle leaning against the cabin," said Jesse. His eyes, narrowed down to details, swept the whole camp again. "And I saw another powder flask; it's hanging on the extra rifle. And those dogs don't belong to this man."

Ransome showed a lively interest. "I'll be damned," he said. Then he shrugged. "What do we care? This old goat's crazy anyhow. Come ahead."

Jesse turned and walked slowly back toward the cabin.

"What happened to your pardner?"

"He's dead, if you want to know. Died last night. I was just fixing to bury him when you come along. Now git to hell out of here an' leave me alone. Git, I tell you! This is my place an' I ain't askin' comp'ny."

"What did he die of? What killed him?"

"He et something; he got a bad bellyache and it kilt him. Some rotten meat, it was."

Jesse pushed the cabin door open and looked in. There, flat on its broad back, lay stretched a man's body. He, too, was grimy and bearded, not beautiful to look upon in death; no, nor would he be in life, either. Dead from poisoned meat? Or a knife thrust? There was nothing to show, no wound, no blood.

"It's murder, that's what it is," said Jesse, not taking the trouble to lower his voice this time. "This place stinks of it."

The evil, blinking eyes never left his face. The man had lifted his rifle a little bit; he would fight like a rat in a corner.

"There's a bundle of furs in there; I saw them," said Jesse. "You killed him for the furs."

"You're a liar! You're a nosy damn liar. I tell you a bellyache kilt him. He et a lot of that rotten meat."

"Come ahead, Jess. Let's get out of this," said Ransome.

Jesse hesitated. For a moment his finger had itched on the trigger. He had meant to kill this man who he was dead sure had killed his own partner. But in the end he shrugged and went along with Ransome.

Here again had a blast of wind blown against granite, scouring the rock with the tiny grains of sand that were like chisels. Those chisels cut away first what was softest, leaving in marked relief what was hardest.

CHAPTER VI

INTO THE SUNSET

They came one summer day to a little round lake; at one end where a creek fed it were pines mirroring themselves in the water. They stripped and bathed for the fun of it, and Ransome swam out a hundred yards from shore and dived and threshed about and swam back. He stood up, laughing, mopping his hair back from his wet face, the water dripping from his naked white body. Jesse, wading close to shore, frowned.

He didn't like to see his friend doing so easily what he could not do at all. As a boy down at a swimming hole in Kentucky, Ransome, along with the rest of the boys, learned to swim when six or eight years old; Jesse, in his Tennessee hills had never heard of a swimming hole.

"Show me how you do it, Ran," he said. "We're going to stay right here until I can swim like that."

Ransome was delighted. Lessons began immediately. They tarried day after day after day. They made a semipermanent camp with a rock and clay stove, a lean-to of boughs and willow branches. They hunted and fished, but mostly they loafed and daydreamed, each in his fashion, and swam.

And Ransome said, "Your grandpappy must have been a duck," before they took up the westering trail again.

Frost was in the air nights and mornings, and even in the noondays there was a blood-tingling crispness, before they came to that little wild valley lost in the heart of a vast wilderness of rock and pine where a certain Bob White tainted the air with his presence and his manner of living. At least "Bob White" was what he chose to call himself when any titular label was required. He claimed to be a Texan, boasted of the glories of Texas, was always about to go back home, had been boasting that way for thirty years, would never go back. He and his woman lived in a cabin at the edge of a meadow with a creek silver-threading through it; he and she and "them damn Injuns" and the Injuns' colony of dogs.

At first they thought the woman was Indian, too, such a black-tan was burned deep into her skin, so glittering-black her eyes, so straight her thick hair. Bob White himself, a man of fifty now, was not to be mistaken; his hair, rippling to his shoulders, was still tawny brown, his eyes blue. Fine blue eyes they might have been those thirty years ago, red-rimmed and bleary and heavy-lidded now.

Bob White, sagging against his door in the sunset, saw them from a distance and shouted and waved welcome as though here came old friends. His woman, of an age with him, a hag of a thing, withered and ugly and bitter-eyed, came to the door and leaned there and mumbled. A quarter of a mile away a group of a score of Indians, bucks and squaws and their litters, watched without interfering.

Bob White was drunk. On the doorstep close to him were his gun, his knife with its point sunk into the puncheon, a jug of reddish liquor. He said "Howdy" a dozen times and went lurching for his liquor, oozing fulsome hospitality.

They drank with him out of a tin cup that had been stepped on, then more or less straightened. Ransome downed his drink, made a face, gulped some water and was no worse off. It was the first time that Jesse Bodine had even tasted such stuff as this; raw and violent, it might have been a devil's brew of fire and red pepper. He had eaten nothing since noon; the draught he put under his belt flew to his head. He choked, drank his water hurriedly and sat down in the late sun, his back to the cabin wall.

He heard Bob White's voice, thin and far and vaguely disturbing, like a mosquito's, proffering further hospitality, urging, insisting; Bob White himself drank and slopped his precious liquor and cursed and laughed and tossed a cupful skyward and said he didn't care a damn. He'd just been 'way down to Temlock's Cross Roads, a good forty mile, and he'd brought his pack horse loaded from mane to rump, and you could go and bet a man your last bottom dollar that he'd brought plenty to drink.

They stayed with Bob White and his woman that night, and all four of them got drunk. Jesse Bodine had been taken by surprise; after that first slugging cup he found he couldn't think things out clearly, that everything about him, along with life in general, was a blur; he laughed unsteadily and felt foolish for laughing, not knowing what it was about; he heard himself talking. He listened to himself talking and frowned over it and laughed at it and said: "Hell, what a talker I am. Didn't know that, did you, Ransome?"

He went to sleep, lying out in the open. They awoke him with their head-splitting clamor inside, all yelling at once, yammering like hound dogs; singing was the worst. And Bob White and his woman talked; they fought over the things they said and Bob White knocked her down and she ran for a hatchet. God, how those two hated each other! After a while they were all jabbering together, jabbering and singing and quarreling until the cabin suddenly quieted and Jesse knew they were all sprawling asleep.

You wouldn't think two people would live together like that, alone out here—you couldn't understand such a thing unless you had heard some of the things that Jesse Bodine had caught in the wild jumble of their incoherencies. He didn't know the details, but details weren't necessary. This man and woman long ago had been young, as young as he and Ransome Haveril; maybe the man had been fine looking, the woman pretty. As young as Kate Haveril? As pretty as sixteen-year-old Kitty? Didn't seem possible!

Yes, once they had been young. Back down in Texas. Then what? A crime, a man killed. What man? It didn't matter. They had had to run for it, these two who had been young. They had been in love; anyhow they had thought they were in love. They couldn't go back; they never could, never would. They hid and they grew older fast and their crime hung about their necks like a dead albatross. And now, God, how they hated each other!

Funny sorts of people in the world, funny people everywhere—even in wild places like this.

All the next day, too, Jesse and Ransome stayed with Bob White and his woman. Bob White was lurching around when Jesse's splitting headache brought him back to his dizzied senses. Ransome looked white and sick; he took one drink to straighten him up. Jesse crept away into a thicket and vomited.

The woman, her hair hanging all about her face, muttering to herself, made soggy flapjacks and a bitter pot of coffee. Jesse drank three cups of strong black hot coffee and sat down again by the wall. He listened to the talk. Bob White had an arm about Ransome's shoulders and was offering another drink. They drank together. Bob White planned for the future: The two newcomers were welcome, were always welcome and always would be welcome. They were going to stay right here all their lives, the way Bob White did— the best place in the world. Bob White had his woman; they could have their women, too. Just walk a few steps over to the Injun camp. Hell, whoop and have the Injuns come over here. Some young squaws; hell, take your choice. Buy 'em for anything you got in your pocket; got a red undershirt? That would be fine! You could get the shirt back, too, before it got real cold. Or just take the wenches, and if any young buck got cocky and raised a rumpus about it, shoot the dog. This was a white man's country, wasn't it?

And Jesse Bodine understood at last that the man was terribly lonely.

Winter was on the way. They struck southward at last, heading for the traveled way along which the westward wagons rolled. And so, on a cold, black autumnal day, they came to Temlock's Cross Roads.

Cress Temlock kept a trading station of sorts; he was known as a well-to-do man whose slogan was: "This is a great country! Yes-siree, she sure is a great country!" His store was an eye-arresting structure, long and narrow, that had been put up in sections as time and expansion demanded, so that it looked like several log cabins jammed together end to end. Sturdy and broad and bald, he had for helpmate the tall, angular but richly warmhearted Mrs. Temlock, some few years his senior, of whom he was inordinately proud and whom he treated always, in private or in public, with the sort of deference a good son paid his mother. He traded in everything; on his shelves or stacked away or hanging from crossbeams were nearly always to be found flour and sugar, salt and tobacco of both kinds, boots and shoes and guns, picks and shovels, calico by the bolt; he had scales for weighing raw ore; on his wall was a price list of furs, from Boston; ammunition, tools and steel traps were his stock in trade. He dispensed raw liquor at four bits a shot, the same hell-fire which, in bulk, to those like Bob White, he sold or swapped far cheaper.

"Yes-siree! It's a great country! Why, we already got a stage running through three times a week! What more do you want? Look at them bosses out into the corral back of the barn; them's stage hosses, and when they shove their naiks into their collars they're off for Bantam Springs like the wind. Pshaw, we'll be having us a town right here where I'm standing in no time; no time a-tall! A town? Pshaw, a city! Temlock City, you just watch.—All right, Mrs. T.; I'm a-coming. What's that? Oh, just a couple young fellers dropped in. They passed by Bob White's and are on their way to California. Come in, boys."

A voice shouted, "Here comes the stage!" and men gathered to watch, their gradual appearance smacking of slow magic. Where they came from neither Jesse nor Ransome knew. "Must of popped right out of the brush," said Ransome. There were a couple of swarthy, black-mustachioed Mexicans among them, an Indian in a worn red and black blanket, an old, gray, stooped man, a gangly youth in high boots and a broad hat too big for him, and a Texas longhorn, so called more from his enormous yellow mustache than from the land of his problematic nativity, the woods being full of Texans.

The old gray man screwed up his mouth and put puckers into his sunken cheek in order to get one eye properly squinted at the sun. He spat tobacco juice and observed with obvious relish:

"Hank's late ag'in. He cain't bring the stage in like George Bill used to do. Shucks!"

"You step inside an' take a look at Cress's clock," spoke up the Texas longhorn, "an' I bet boots with you that Hank's on time, right on the dot, too."

"Clock!" jeered the old man. "God made the sun an' some damn tinkerin' fool Yankee made the clock, an' Hank's always late, anyhow."

The stage came rolling in with Hank's long whip

cracking for the final spurt, the horses in a lather, fine, fast horses as western stage horses had to be.

There was a flurry in the station's hard-packed yard, with Hank climbing down from his high seat, the three passengers alighting and pressing in at an open door, horses being led away, fresh horses brought. To Jesse Bodine and Ransome Haveril looking on, everything was very gay and lively.

Of the travelers one was a man of slightly more than middle age, with a set and stony look to his eyes. He was Chris Anders who had made his stake in gold in the West, who had started back home with his fortune in an old carpetbag, who had been robbed only a couple of hundred miles east of Temlock's who was on his way back west, to make his pile again. Another was a seedy, nondescript man whom nobody particularly noticed. The third, however, demanded attention and got an amazing amount of it. His appearance, his dress, his carriage, all were distinctive.

The old gray man exclaimed when the trio had passed inside:

"Claude Purcell, by thunder!"

"Minister?" asked Ransome Haveril.

"Minister, hell! Cain't you hear good? I said that was the gambler, Claude Purcell!"

The stage pulled out with its full complement of passengers and one in addition; the longhorn

Texan climbed aboard, bound for Bantam Springs. The old gray man announced with relish, "Got here late, left late. That's Hank for you," and went his wide-legged way to a scrubby little mustang tied at the corral, crawled up into his saddle and rode away. Cress Temlock, again in his doorway, regarded Jesse and Ransome.

"Thought as maybe you boys was taking the stage," he said. His eyes asked, "Well, now you're here anything you want?"

"Ammunition," said Jesse.

All this while he had spent little and sparingly of his original fortune of ten dollars, and that little almost exclusively for powder and lead. Even so, when he had finished bartering with Temlock, and his eyes and Ransome's ranged the well-stocked shelves, the two realized that a bit more of the coin of the realm might come in handy.

They loitered all afternoon at the trading post, spent two dollars for a banquetlike supper of coffee and hot biscuits and gravy and potatoes and beans and a sort of pudding with brown sauce poured thick over it and—this alone brought no thrill—generous helpings of a savory venison stew. After that they sat with the others in a small smoke-filled room watching a listless game of poker. The players were Temlock, the gray man who had slid in again unostentatiously, one of today's Mexicans whom they called Chico Fuerte and a raw-boned youth who evidently was Temlock's hired hand. The men bet quarters mostly; a dollar bet for a showdown was an average high. They played just to pass the time; it was October and the feel of the break of the season was in the air, and they were waiting for winter. One falls into the way of doing something or other when he's just waiting.

Jesse Bodine had never played a game of poker in his life and had but a sketchy idea of what it was all about. He watched and was interested; this was a change for him and Ransome, as good as going to a show. Ransome had played a few times, understood more. He and Jesse, sitting slightly withdrawn, spoke now and then under their breaths; Jesse asked questions of the values of certain hands, of the broader rules. And when Temlock, sensing his interest, said, "Want to set in?" Jesse pulled up his chair to the table.

"I've got only about four dollars left," he said.

He put his money on the table and was dealt a hand. Beginner's luck stood at his elbow; he drew four aces and was lucky enough to catch Temlock and the old man both with hands good enough to draw them along for a look-see. So Jesse pulled in his gleanings and counted ten dollars.

Beginner's luck pressed even closer and breathed down his neck. He won the second time, hands running. There were bright, dancing lights in his eyes; his breath came faster, freer; he felt the tingle of the game, the flush of gambler's fever. Here was a man's game; here was zest. And beginner's luck seemed to have picked him for her darling, and it was as though she meant to be true to him always. But every man knows that luck alone is a poor part of draw poker. In a few minutes of play Jesse Bodine sat back, a blank and empty feeling replacing the short-lived zest, his four dollars looking aloof and far away under the old gray man's tapping fingers.

They moved along westward again, making what speed they could against the slamming of winter's white gates in their faces. For a time storms held off, though their threat was a frequent reminder; they crossed parched, waterless valleys and traveled flinty mountain ways. Jesse Bodine was long ago the dominant factor in their world; he didn't say, "Let's do so-and-so"; he would say, "Here's what we'll do next." He passed his twentieth birthday in a region of high, lonely mountains. Exultant on a pinnacle, he shot the stern glance of an eagle into the far, wavering distances. There was the poise of a young conqueror about him.

When winter's great guns started thundering, the two were within a day's travel of a new camp which they knew nothing about until, through icy wind gusts sharp-edged with sleet, they came within sight of it. It was a rough-and-ready encampment forced into existence through the grim realities of death and birth and some other paralleling factors. Three families after sober council had elected to wait for springtime in a parklike, mountain-sheltered valley. They were the Olsens, the Robertsons and the Crabtrees. A baby had been born to the young and delicate wife of an elder Crabtree boy; that was one thing. Then a very old man, one of the Olsens, the grandfather of the youngest of that clan, had come painfully to the end of his trail in this remote place; his foot had slipped on the iron frosted tire of a wagon wheel as he was climbing down, and he had fallen. He was slow in dying; his feeble old wife followed him to make a twin hummock with him in the shade of a cottonwood. And three horses belonging to the Robertsons had eaten something in their pasturage that killed them— loco weed, Clay Robertson thought, but no one knew.

Here were water and timber, and, if they hastened garnering, fish and game and wood. They estimated that they were long on provisions if they had run short on luck. Among them they had company, and all were helping hands. They built three log cabins; they were digging in for the winter when Jesse Bodine and Ransome Haveril saw smoke and sparks from their rock chimneys in the dreary early dusk and shouted, "Hello, there!" and so took the first step toward becoming for a time a closely knit part of the small, isolated community.

Welcomed to tarry, they immediately fitted in like a hand in its gauntlet. So they fell to with a will, building their own small cabin, one room, fireplace, two bunks. Later would come table, benches—winter tasks. And there followed a space of time for them which was to be recognized later on as one of the fullest, most complete and profitable of their lives.

It was Ransome's thought, filled with love of company and athrill at this season with the youthful vigor of bursting sap, to construct a community building, a long, low, sturdy cabin with an enormous fireplace in each end—a place for getting together on the hardest days and darkest and coldest nights to come. Never was a task more heartily entered upon, every member of the small group filled with suggestions, their hands filled with endeavor.

At first, as this first storm blew itself out, a man would take one of the wagons with a four-horse team and drive out to Lusk's Meadows, a trading post that was a tiny settlement in the germ some eighty or ninety miles away, taking with him a list of articles the camp would most need—potatoes, flour, tobacco, Mustang Liniment, Wizard Oil, salt and grain were high on that list.

Meantime white chips flew under flying axes, and on a crisp, clear, frosty day the thudding and ringing of the ax blades carried far and made merry and deeply soul-satisfying music. Men went out with their rifles; a rifle-shot carried far and clear. The men swinging their axes would stop a minute, say, "That's Will," or "That's Frank," and would wonder whether the new addition to the winter larder was going to be bear meat or deer, or maybe elk.

It grew into quite a little settlement, for now the smokehouse was added. In the clear cold starry nights or on a rare bright day with the sun shining on a clean fall of snow, it was as pretty as a picture.

Here Ransome Haveril found a pretty, blue-eyed and pink-cheeked girl; Ransome was girl hungry. She was Nellie Crabtree, seventeen years old, sister of April Crabtree, and sister-in-law of Ann. Ann was the mother of the new baby. April was the Crabtrees' youngest, not quite in her 'teens.

Logs were dragged in, two horses, a doubletree and a log chain pulling them into camp, and some were used for housebuilding, some were corded for the fireplaces' maws. The women cut the meat; the children operated the smokehouse. Through all this, Ransome and Nellie were forever conscious of each other. And, after the first day or two, Nellie's father was fully aware of both. There was something very eloquent, a thing no one could possibly take exception to yet which no one could fail to feel, in the manner he set his double-barreled shotgun down at the corner of his cabin.

And winter came and found them laboring hard for the luxury of mere existence, but somehow living far more richly than they took time or had time to think about; the smell of wood smoke was brave and heartening in the cold, and sparks up chimneys were as lovely as stars. In the long, general cabin they played cards with old, thumbed decks, and checkers on boards newly made; they talked, swapping experiences and advice; they sang, all together, the old songs which were the songs of all such people; there were a guitar and a fiddle among them; they even danced, though less and less frequently. For it took young people to dance, and the old people had eyes which never blinked, which somehow discouraged this sort of thing; their glances were as eloquent as a shotgun against a cabin wall.

Here no doubt before the winter was over every single one of them found something which sank as deep into the core of him as a pebble in a pool. Later they would go on, break up, each tread his own trail, and so they'd not come to know how much they had meant to one another, nor in how many ways.

Here Jesse Bodine found something—a new tender influence that for a time permeated his whole being as the fragrance of a flower may seep through a fabric. It came to him through a child, little April. She, like her sister Nellie, was blue-eyed; hers were the great big blue eyes of a little maid of ten or twelve. She was as pretty as a fragile doll, and you felt you must treat her with delicate touch. Somehow, he couldn't tell why, she made Jesse Bodine think of his own little sister, Baby Molly.

April was dear and sweet and sensitive; her lip quivered easily and her eyes swam; she was a fairylike little thing, and when she laughed—she laughed as readily as she wept and far more often—it was tinkly, irresistible music.

And all she wanted to do after the very first was sit and look at handsome Jesse Bodine, to follow him around, to bring him things and—how she thrilled that first time!—to walk along at his side, her hand in his!

To little April, Jesse Bodine during the whole of that time was that Jesse Bodine which no one else had ever known, the young conqueror ecstatic and exultant on the rocky pinnacles of the mountains. To her he was a young god; she thrilled to him as inevitably as a harp thrills in the wind.

To Jesse Bodine, though he never thought of such a thing, she was perhaps the single softening influence a rigorous life had brought him since Kate Haveril flung his little locket and fine gold chain down in the dust.

CHAPTER VII

SOMEONE ELSE TAKES THE TRAIL

And Kate Haveril traveled her own burning desert stretches, and likewise penetrated deep dark ravines of her own mountains; was lost, got her bearings on a dim star, had the star blink out and fail her, and was lost again, traveled on. Traveled through the days at first, and a day can be a desert; through the weeks, the months, the years. When Jesse Bodine failed her, he tore something vital out of her and left where her heart had been an emptiness which not even an agony of anguish could fill.

She did not cry; what had happened to her lay too deep for tears. No one in her busy home noticed that anything untoward had occurred. Saving of course that all missed their well-loved Ransome. But Ransome was a young man full of spirit, and had gone along with that Bodine boy, and that was a thing natural enough, no more remarkable than the fading of springtime, the coming of winter. It was the inevitable, the expected, and so left no sore, no subsequent scar.

"I expect you miss your big brother," Kate's mother remarked, and came no nearer than that to the tragic truth.

Kate had stopped going to the school down in the valley, because she was sixteen, which was to say a mature woman, and besides there was her secret thought that she would be married soon. "Mrs. Jesse Bodine!" After Jesse's desertion of her it grew intolerable just staying at home and thinking all the time of how they used to meet at the creek, and would never meet there again. She gathered up her books bright and early of a Monday morning and informed her mother that she was going to finish school.

The teacher, Mr. Yancy, was an elderly, ascetic looking man, tall and stooped and watery-eyed; who wore a long black coat, shiny and threadbare along the hems; who in his time had been clerk, preacher, peddler; whose flair was along lines of culture; who could play a mournful violin; whose educational qualifications, if thin and threadbare like his raiment, had, also like his coat, taken on a shine from long years of usage. He wasn't strong; his asthma was very bad at times and forced him to take his regular dosage of corn whisky. Folks sent their children to him for book learning and felt generous and charitable in sending him also at odd times either small sums of money or things to eat. He was an old bachelor and lived at the village over behind the store.

Kate Haveril at sixteen was the oldest and prettiest girl in his elastic scholar group, of which at times there were four or five humped over their whittled desks, rarely a dozen, sometimes even more. In ages they ran from five or six up to Kate's age.

She sat on a hard bench in the little log schoolhouse, a book before her, a pencil in her hand, and dreamed daydreams. She read and read and read until her father, skeptical about all this, warned her of her eyes, eyes which certainly looked to be quite all right. She took spurts of interest in her school work, and a few of these flying attacks took her to the outer confines of Mr. Yancy's knowledge.

One day when his asthma was bad and his supply of medicine exhausted, he was about to declare a holiday; his watery eyes took stock of his little flock, just six little boys and girls all about five or six years old—and Miss Kate Haveril. He beckoned Kate up to his desk with the long pointer he used all day as a cane, rod and scepter, practical aid and insignia of his high estate, and said to her with dry facetiousness:

"How'd you like to be schoolteacher today?" And he called her Miss Haveril, and the children giggled and whispered to one another: "He called her Miss Haveril. And she's going to be the teacher!"

So Kate taught the school that day, and was mighty serious about it. There came a glow from the small thing she was doing; it became a large thing, working with the tools of words and thoughts, molding, if only in a little, these few handfuls of human clay. And it was the first glow she had experienced since Jesse Bodine broke her heart. She had come to believe that glows were all gone out of the world.

Mr. Yancy came back in time to dismiss school; he found the children busy and behaving themselves; he discovered Kate looking capable of the task he had thrown at her. His asthma was better; he had had a pleasant few hours outing; he had stumbled upon an inspiration, and the result thereof was one which might bear repetition.

It did. No one paid any particular attention to what was done at the school, and Kate found herself more and more frequently at the teacher's desk, staying there for longer times. She began to feel a warmer feeling for Mr. Yancy; she was grateful to him. He had opened a door for her, and it led into a bright place while there was so much darkness elsewhere.

And he opened another door for her; rather, this time, Kate herself did the opening, using him for a key. She loved music; she had a soft, rich, murmurous voice and was always singing around home. That was, she used to sing; she hadn't sung so much of late; she began unconsciously again. And then she thought of Mr. Yancy and his violin.

She was rapidly growing into a girl, nearly seventeen now, who knew what she wanted and meant to get it. She said one day:

"I help you a good deal with your school, don't I, Mr. Yancy?"

"Yes, you do. You're a good girl, Katie."

"I want to learn music. Will you teach me?"

"Well. Yes, I could teach you how to read music."

"I want to play!"

"All I can play real well is the violin. You wouldn't want that, and—"

"Why wouldn't I?"

He smiled a wintry, crab-apple smile.

"The violin? It's not ladylike. You know that."

"Why isn't it?"

He had bushy white, wild-haired brows. The light in his uncertain eyes seemed to focus and grow almost bright.

"Now, you look here, Kate Haveril. There are things a lady should do and things she mustn't." And so forth, the schoolteacher lecturing.

Kate heard him out respectfully. The next day she started learning the violin.

She kept it secret the best she could. When her brother Richard discovered and made the news general at the supper table, Kate's face turned crimson under the looks swiveled on her. All that a reluctant Mr. Yancy had said, and more, was spoken to her in thoroughly direct manner. The idea of a girl, almost woman-grown, too, playing a fiddle!

If it was a shocking thing, the next move of Kate Haveril's was far more shocking. Mr. Yancy took to his bed, really ill. They had to cast about for a teacher to fill out the school year. Kate said she would do it, take the pay, too. She did. And throughout the wide-sprawled neighborhood many a good woman threw up her hands in what was termed holy horror, and asked what the world was coming to. A female schoolteacher! And, as the wise ones foresaw, it wasn't long before little Kate was spoken of as that Kate Haveril, or that Haveril girl. The wild one, you know. The teaching one. Fiddling Kate Haveril.

Her love for her music grew apace with budding understanding of what it truly meant and could mean; her voice came out stronger and dearer and tenderer, lovely. She played the violin well enough; she played the organ; she could play anything, hand organ or accordion. She was going to be a music teacher! She was going to be a musician!

Wild Kate Haveril!

Well, she did grow to be a bit wild. She was eighteen then; she had torn Jesse Bodine and all young love out of her heart two years ago. She was still the wild-rose girl that Jesse had thought her; she was still budding, though she held herself in full bloom; she was, and even the disapproving agreed that she was, the loveliest girl to look at in all Pleasant Valley. You just had to remember, though, that pretty is as pretty does. And never lose sight of the fact that there is a wicked loveliness given by the devil to his chosen ones.

Of course she went to every dance within a radius of forty miles; even that afforded talk. To top the matter, she seemed to go each time with a different boy; who ever heard of such a thing? Worse, it was said that, whether in square dance or schottische, mazurka or heel-and-toe polka, she flirted perfectly outrageously. She drew attention to herself, the way she always had a flock of fool young men clustering about while she made up her mind which one could have the next waltz. And the way she waltzed! "You knew Robbie Tate, that folks said was going to marry Patty Russel? Well, that's off now they tell me; she's roped Robbie in; he was the one took her to the dance over to Hope Valley. And the dance before that, the one over to Sandy Bar, she went with Ches Terril that used to spark Marian Sales. They say Marian cried her eyes out."

Kate was nineteen. She was still teaching down in the valley; she was going to start in giving music lessons. She grew into her first intimate friendship. Again she disturbed the serenity of a serene folk; she was forever with Sarah Fairbanks. *Mrs.* Sarah Fairbanks, the young widow.

The young widow who, it was rumored, was going to marry again; to marry one of the Bodine boys this time.

Kate's mother was bewildered, frightened, distressed.

"Katie, come here. Katie, I know you're a good girl and always will be a good girl. But *why*—" *Why* did Kate teach, like a man? Play a fiddle? *Why* did she have to take up with that Sarah Fairbanks?

Kate flared out in defense of her new friend. Was it a crime that Sarah was young and pretty still? Was it her fault that she was a widow? She hadn't poisoned her husband, had she? Was she supposed to turn into an old hag on a cane because he died? Should she veil her face and wear black all her life? Should she shut herself up in her big house and keep all the curtains drawn? Should she just sit with folded hands, unless allowed to do a bit of needlework, until she died?

Mrs. Haveril couldn't answer all these and a string of other questions; she could only feel, at the end, that it would be more ladylike if Sarah Fairbanks *did* do those things.

And through her new friend, Kate met a new young man, too, and came close to marrying him.

Sarah Fairbanks was only twenty-three to Kate's seventeen, and was never meant to be any man's tombstone. She had more property, more money and nice things, thanks to the foresight of the late Mr. Fairbanks, than any other girl in the valley, and did her excellent best to surround herself with light and color, music and dancing and all the gaieties which she considered within bounds; she had catholic tastes and exercised them. When on a picnic sponsored by her, Kate was engineered into meeting Drill Bradway, it was just that birds of a feather were drawn together, said Sarah.

Sarah went ahead and married Jesse Bodine's brother Jim as was expected, and some said this and some said that, as is customary, and only the two young people knew what sort of bargains they had got, and no doubt they themselves didn't know for quite a time. And Kate and Drill Bradway began keeping company.

There was a dash to him, yet a steadiness, too, and no one denied his good looks; they made a handsome pair. His father was a man of means, an old-timer who had acquired broad lands, who of recent years had owned the village store and blacksmith shop. Altogether, Drill Bradway was a young man of whom most, Kate's parents with the rest, approved. He was still a little happy-go-lucky, but boys will be boys. He'd be a steady man. In fact, both Kate's mother and father were not only tremendously relieved but inclined to be proud.

Then, all for no reason on earth, so it was said, Kate discarded her new Romeo with less than a flick of her fingertips and long-lashed eyes, and was seen driving in the livery stable top buggy with a scandalous newcomer; no one knew much of him beyond that he came from nowhere, he drank and played cards, and he didn't seem to have an interest in life beyond that which he could extract from some sort, any sort, of musical instrument. He fiddled and banjoed and made music on a comb with a piece of paper; that's all he was good for, just music.

After the marriage of Sarah and Jim Bodine, Kate saw a good deal of the Bodines. She grew fond of both girls, Luella and little Molly, not so little any longer, and they of her. She saw Luella married, and Molly thinking about marriage. She saw the Bodine household disintegrate. Jesse's mother overtaxed herself, gave her own welfare scant consideration when during the winter she virtually gave her all to a neighbor woman stricken with pneumonia; Mrs. Bodine died in the early spring, the second after Jesse's departure. Her husband died not very long after, as the result of an accident; a team of young horses ran away when he was driving it into town the first time, a wagon wheel crashed against a rock at the road-side and he was pitched from the seat. His sides and back were injured; he never recovered fully. With the deaths of the parents, the departure of Jesse, then Jim with Sarah, the old place passed into a new phase. The younger Bodines sold it and moved into the village.

It was at that time that Kate jilted Drill Bradway and began smiling at her latest beau. And then there came into Kate's life upheaval and explosion.

• • •

Her parents by now should have known her, as folks said later; but then they never did. High spirits like hers are not properly subdued by putting them into a bottle and popping in the cork with sealing wax applied. If you put an iron band about a growing thing, it doesn't just stop growing, whether it's a lusty young sapling or a cucumber in the garden; it grows in some other direction.

At last the family, after council, laid the law down to Kate Haveril. They began with her treatment of Drill Bradway, and spared none of their own opinions or her feelings. They proceeded from Bradway to the good-for-nothing scalawag she was being seen with now, and were a thought less sparing than before.

Kate didn't say a word. She stood very still, her soft pink cheeks going pale, her lovely soft eyes, large and laughing at first, slowly going dark and hard. By the end her face was white, her eyes were blazing—and her lips were shut tight.

That night she ran away.

Having done most of the things a girl could do to be unladylike and bring disgrace on her name, she now did the culminating thing.

She ran away. To set the crown on it, she whacked off her glory of hair and purloined a suit of her brother's, even to the pants, and was gone no one knew where. Most folks could guess where. Another girl gone to the devil.

And most folks, her own included, even misunderstood why she had gone. It was not because she was angry or even defiant. They chose the wrong words. They meant only to be stern, but they let themselves go, and said things they should never have said. They hurt her; they hurt her terribly. So she went away to be by herself.

Kate became Kit.

At first she hadn't any idea where she was going. It didn't matter. She had some money, for during all the time she had taught school and had had her little music classes, she had saved against the day when her scant savings would come in handy. Tricked out as a boy she'd get along somewhere, anywhere.

She headed south. Her first ride was with a man in a wagon, going the thirty miles to Go-long for a Moline plow. She went still farther south because she heard of a town, and there was another ride afforded her by a teamster hauling hay to the larger town. And she saw the first of many wagon trains going west.

Nineteen, she passed without trouble as a pretty boy of fifteen or so. For one thing, who on earth would ever suppose a girl would do a thing like the one she was so brazenly accomplishing? The suspicion never even came close enough to be a tangent to the round of any man's thoughts.

She found herself moving westward, and soon

began consciously to travel west. The West was calling, lusty and strong, in all young blood. She knew her moments, many and many of them, of dread and homesickness and downright grief and humility and regret; she hugged remorse tight to her breast many a lonely night in some bare shakedown, and cried her eyes out; she awoke and clapped her hands to her mouth to stifle screams in an unfamiliar darkness; in her dreams over and over again she was going home, running up the dear little path through the trees, running into her mother's arms. . . .

It's easier to be valiant in the sunshine. Fears belong to the unknown, anyhow, and that is what the dark is. With every dawn she was drawn along, forced along, called along westward.

There were chores which she could do for her board and keep; on a farm she could feed the chickens, gather the eggs, help in the kitchen at times of boiling kettles whether canning day or washday or hog-killing day. And when once in a blue moon there was talk of a dance, she could fiddle! They could never get enough dancing with that boy Kit at fiddle, banjo or infrequent organ.

She helped a storekeeper in one little town for four months. She learned how to wear her clothes, ragged shirts and coats, loose, shapeless trousers, as a shield against detection. She kept her hair as short as most boys, which was to say almost any ragged length so long as it didn't curl up from the shoulders. She learned to cast her voice in its lowest possible register when she spoke; sometimes a man laughed and said: "Whoa, there, Bub! What's going on with the voice? Changing, huh? Growing up to be a real man! Say, any whiskers yet?"

And she was careful, very careful, about her long-lashed eyes.

Westering, at last with a vague purpose, she traveled the roads of those many others who meant with their eyes to see the blue of California's skies and the gold of California's fields which they had so long seen in their imaginings. And one day more than a full year after she had run away from Pleasant Valley she came to a little new clutter of log cabins which had just been given a name, just recognized by its own haphazard builders as more than a temporary camp; from one of the families they named the place Crabtree Settlement.

And so it was next door to the inevitable that Kit Haveril met April.

"Hello," said an astonishingly pretty, blue-eyed girl flowering into her early 'teens.

"Hello," said Kit.

April smiled, and Kit had never seen a sunnier, sweeter smile; and Kit smiled back.

April had a basket on her arm in which she was carrying some eggs from the Crabtree farm to the store; Kate, of late Kit, newly arrived, came around the corner in time to come close to bumping into the pretty egg-bearer. That first "Hello," April's, was almost jolted out of her, and the smile came naturally as greeting to a pleasant, friendly face; Kit's response was quite as natural. And, though a bit shyly at first, they fell to talking.

"I met the nicest boy at the store today," April told her mother. "His name is Kit. He is looking for some sort of work to do, and I told him maybe papa would let him help with the chores or something."

Long ago Jesse Bodine and Kate's brother, Ransome, had gone on their way. They wouldn't have known Crabtree Settlement of this date. They wouldn't have known little April, grown into this April of fifteen. Time had made its changes, all for the better this time. The first log cabins still stood but were used only as outhouses—woodsheds, tool sheds, smokehouses and the like. Other, larger and more painstakingly planned homes had grown up. The Crabtrees, always planning, come another spring, to go to California, were ranchers now and prospering; everyone knew old man Crabtree. There other ranches in the hills; a silver mine was operating not a dozen miles away; the stage passed this way, so there was a station; altogether there were close to a score of dwellings, which meant that a general muster of men, women and children, the very old and the very young, would bring out close to seventy or eighty souls. Crabtree Settlement began to take pride in itself, like Temlock's Cross Roads. "It's a great country. Yes siree."

Kit Haveril worked for Mr. Crabtree for nearly six months. When asked her name she had answered simply, "Kit." Folk weren't great hands at wanting a string of names; when they asked for a name at all it was simply for a convenient handle; something to call a man by, that was all; not all about him and where he came from and where he was going and why. They weren't concerned with all that; there was no such thing as "background." If a man said his name was Red or Slim or anything of the kind, it satisfied. Of course if there were two Slims or Reds around you'd have to distinguish as Slim or Red Smith, or Jones.

Kit was just Kit.

April was Ben Bolt's sweet Alice reincarnated. All she was made to comprehend in this complex world of so many things was love and loving kindness. An angry voice, a clenched hand, a hint of cruelty terrified her. An unkind word brought the tears to her eyes just as a smile brought her own smile, which had a warm, tremulous glory about it. She was, soft little thing in a harsh pioneer existence, like one of those tender blossoms which grow among the rocks of iron mountains, like the floral daintiness acquiring visibility from the soul of a thorned cactus. And as in one way she had worshiped Jesse Bodine almost from the first sight of him, so did she in quite another way love Kit Haveril. But she was as shy as she was gentle; and the wayward Kit, thinking of herself and her new little friend as two girls, did not stop to consider that April was thinking of them as boy and girl.

April garnered eggs and fed the chickens, and Kit split kindling and milked the cows; April swept and cooked and Kit teamed; April helped with the house and Kit with the stock. April and Kit played checkers together; on two occasions they danced together. And, what both enjoyed most of all, in the evenings before bedtime, with the household gathered in what light the pine fire gave, they sang together. Folk in other cabins came to their doors and windows and listened.

Artless little April was in love, and others knew it. Her mother for one, her father for another after her mother had poked him. Well? Her parents could only say that April was a grown girl now; and this new young man Kit, though young yet for marrying, was a nice boy. And still others knew; not Kit, never dreaming of the possibility of such a thing.

Then one day Kit was startled half out of her wits by the sudden discovery of the truth. For an uncertain time she was panicky; she came close to running away again, quite as she had run away from home.

It was one of the few times that she and April had danced together, April wearing her prettiest, frilliest little dress, ribbons in her curly hair and a glory of light in her eyes. Kit, very gay, looked down into her little dance partner's upturned face—and of a sudden understood.

This time Kit Haveril, the boy, didn't run away.

"April, dear," said Kit while they were dancing.

"Yes, Kit?" said a rosy April, and looked shyly up, almost breathless.

"I must have a good talk with you. Soon. There won't be a chance tonight, but tomorrow. In the morning I am going into the edge of the wood; you'll see me take the team out and the sled. I want you to meet me there."

"Oh! Why, of course I will, Kit!" and April snuggled closer in Kit's arms and involuntarily Kit's arms tightened about her.

. . . The horses nodded in the midmorning sun; it was late September now and the sunshine was like thin gold leaf. The sky was unclouded but had turned a steel gray-blue, and in the shade the air was like the edge of a silver knife. Kit smiled at her little friend in a queer way which baffled April; Kit seemed somehow far older this morning and altogether a wiser and superior creature.

"I am going to tell you a secret, April. I wouldn't

tell anyone in the world but you, and I'm not even going to ask you not to tell, because—"

"Because you know I wouldn't anyhow! You know, Kit, that I wouldn't do anything at all that you didn't want me to. Don't you, Kit?"

"You are going to be surprised, April. You are going to be glad, too, for now we are going to be better friends than ever." Slightly she opened her boy's shirt at the throat. "You see how white I am, April? Almost as white as you."

"Whiter!" gasped April, confused. "Milky white. I didn't know men were like that!"

"Maybe they are not," said Kit.

At the end of the disclosure April Crabtree turned both scarlet and very pale, and there was a moment of silence and confusion for the two girls. Then with a little cry that could have been either of joy or grief or both commingled, April ran into Kit's arms and hugged her tighter than she had ever done before.

Kit, too, cried a little that morning.

CHAPTER VIII

THE MAN WHO BROUGHT THE STAGE IN

Hang Town, Yankee Jim's, Cold Springs, Shirt Tail Canyon, Murderers' Bar, Columbia, Chinese Gulch, Gold Hill, Yellow Jacket! Just names in the ears of Jesse Bodine and Ransome Haveril; just names at first, then, as they drew onward, these places, envisioned, were like many colored beads on a golden string; like little tinkling, chiming bells. And at long last they were tangible, material places of fact. Some were to live and grow and expand; some were to dwindle and die and vanish; some, in later years, as though ashamed of their youthful behavior, were to hide under new, assumed, and more mannerly names. All at the moment were gathering places of all sorts and conditions of men, almost exclusively, though with here and there a fair sprinkling of women. The women were not of all sorts and conditions but of two clearly defined classes: There were the sheltered ones, the ladies. There were those others.

Yellow Jacket was clamorous, strident, hectic more often than not, a rough town, a hot-blooded town, a man's town. To Yellow Jacket's way of thinking, if you liked the town, Welcome; tend to your own business and let other folks tend to theirs, and make yourselves at home. If you didn't like it just exactly the way it was, get to hell out of there. Some that didn't like it and didn't tarry, remarked that there were three places, Heaven, Hell and Yellow Jacket.

Today the stage came into Yellow Jacket with its six horses at the dead run. Shouts went up: "Stage coming!" Men who had never seen Long Peters bring the stage into town stared, marveling, at the racing horses, the wildly rocking coach. Men used to Long Peters stared, too, today. "Runaway!" a man yelled. The crowd that always gathered at saloon doors, along the wooden sidewalk, in the rutted roadway between small frame buildings, was stilled, watching; those in the road scattered to get out of the way before the stage swung around the last bend to come to hotel and stable. That bend was taken on two wheels; never, or so it seemed, did a lumbering coach come closer to turning over.

That was the day Jesse Bodine came to Yellow Jacket, Jesse and his friend Ransome Haveril.

Twenty-four running hoofs pounded up such a thick volume of dust that it was hard to see coach and driver when taut reins and screaming brakes brought the stage to a rocking standstill. But from the men standing closest, from others hurriedly crowding up, other shouts went up. For Long Peters hadn't brought his stage in today and would never bring in another. From the strap he had buckled about him when starting the last lap, down the mountain, Long Peters, half on the seat and half off, hung dead. Dead, too, was the express agent, inside the coach where he had been lifted to draw his last breath, and so not immediately to be discovered though his absence from the high seat was.

The driver sat still a long moment, his hands slowly relaxing on the reins as men surged about and held the trembling, sweat-wet horses; he just sat and looked about him and down into the faces lifted to his. He was a young man, lean and dark and quietly masterful, silent in all this clamor, unperturbed, inscrutable.

A large, powerfully built man, with the stamp of authority upon him, shouldered through the crowd and stopped with his hand on the wheel while he looked straight up into the driver's dark, steady eyes.

"What's all this?" he demanded. "What's happened?"

The driver had removed his broad-brimmed black hat rather than lose it on the run into town; and had sat on it; now he drew it from under him, knocked its crumpled appearance back into shape and put it on. Then he climbed down from his high seat.

By now the stage doors were open and other men got out, Ransome Haveril among them, Ransome with one arm in a sling made by tying two big bright-red bandanna handkerchiefs together. Another passenger, a small excitable man dressed like the small storekeeper he was, Henry Trimble of Peck and Trimble's General Store poured out full information, saying every now and then in the run of his talk, "My God, boys, it was terrible!" and all the time wiping sweat away.

"Who was it?" a voice shouted. "That damn greaser Joaquin Murietta?"

"Might have been," said Henry Trimble. "Might have been the Bedloe gang. They was all masked; you couldn't tell. Five of 'em I counted; I think there was three-four others; under cover, you know, and shooting all together. They got Long Peters, and they got the new express agent, and the stage is all shot full of holes, and this stranger here got it in one arm, and if it hadn't been for him and the man that's driving for Long Peters they'd have got us all, I reckon, and the box, too. We brought the box in safe."

Sheriff Dan Comstock, the powerfully built man with the stamp of authority upon him, had a pair of hard, icy-blue eyes which some said were as good as guns, and these he had kept steadily trained upon the lean, saturnine young man coming down from the driver's seat.

"Looks like you're welcome, stranger," he said gravely and quietly, and then added, "Like I say, you're a stranger in Yellow Jacket."

The young man regarded him, his bulk, his badge and his blue eyes. For the first time he spoke.

"You mean you don't like strangers here?"

"I said you're welcome."

"Thanks. My friend with his arm tied up needs a doctor. Where'll I find one?"

"Take your friend in the hotel. Doc Dabney will be around somewhere. Mind saying who you are?"

"I'm Jesse Bodine."

"I'll remember."

Jesse Bodine started to move away, but the sheriff detained him with a question.

"You wouldn't know any of the outlaw gang if you saw them again?"

"I wouldn't know their faces because of the masks they had on. But one of them—he was the leader, I guess—I'd know his voice if I ever heard it. I'm sure of that."

"What kind of a voice?"

"You can't describe a man's voice, can you? I'd just remember if I ever heard it again."

Jesse Bodine moved through the crowd which stood aside for him, watching him pass, and came to Ransome.

"How bad is it, Ransome, do you think?" he asked.

Ransome managed a crooked smile; it twisted his young mustache and beard awry. He was pale and looked sick, and pain haunted his eyes.

"Not bad, I guess, Jess. But I'm sort of groggy; I've bled like a stuck pig. Lucky you got us along in a hurry. Get me a drink, Jess."

"Right away. And a doctor, too. Take it easy, Ran."

They went up the rickety steps, across the wooden sidewalk and into the front room of the Gold Hill Hotel. Jesse eased his friend down into a rocking chair and stepped through the swing doors into the hotel's bar. The place was empty, not even the bartender having stayed behind when all hands surged out to see with their own eyes what was wrong with Long Peters.

Jesse went behind the bar for bottle and glass and carried them to his friend.

A voice said irritably, "Dammit, you're a cool hand, stranger." The bartender had bethought him of his responsibilities and had returned just in time to see a man with back turned to him walking away with a bottle of liquor.

"My friend needed a drink," said Jesse. He poured generously and handed the glass to Ransome. Then he proffered the bottle and a ten dollar gold piece to the bartender.

The bartender was taken aback, seeing who it was. He gestured with both hands like a man waving away something distasteful.

"I didn't get a good look at you, stranger. I didn't realize you was the man that brought the stage in. Your friend will need the whole damn bottle from the looks of him. And the drink is on the house."

"Thanks," said Jesse Bodine.

Ransome drank deep and was comforted. The landlord came hurrying in from the street and led the way without delay to a small, shadowy bedroom down the hall and at a corner of the building. He and Jesse Bodine lowered a shaky Ransome Haveril down to the bed.

"I'll get Doc Dab here in two shakes," the landlord promised, and hurried away.

Jesse stepped to the curtained window, pushed the curtains aside and looked out upon a section of the street. Men on horseback were already pouring out of town in a gathering flood, headed toward the mountains, toward the bridge across Cottonwood Gulch where the holdup had been attempted. He estimated that more than a score of riders, all armed, nearer forty of them perhaps, were hell-bent to overtake the fugitive bandits.

Taller by an inch or two was Jesse Bodine than when two years before he had turned his back upon Pleasant Valley, his face toward an unknown Yellow Jacket. In some things he had changed; in some he remained and would always remain the same. Sinewy and poised, there was the look of purpose in him; it might be that he did not yet altogether know what that purpose was, but he was going to find it, to achieve its aim. He had sloughed off the first phase of his youth along with the beloved old muzzle-loading rifle of boyhood's days; about his lean middle was the cartridge belt of the country, and from it sagged the two heavy Colt revolvers which he had used so coolly, so efficiently, with such deadly skill today.

Passengers on the stagecoach, he and Ransome Haveril had paid their way with gold which they had made working for a cow outfit where a long valley just over the mountains had invited cattlemen and their feuds; they wore the high-heeled boots of the Western cowboy, the guns and the showy checked shirts. Ransome with his new silky beard and roving eye, Jesse with his young lean hard face and the look of an eagle about him, had drawn many the shy, bright feminine eye and certain other eyes, too, perhaps more feline than feminine, and bolder. And now, of a sudden, they were on the rim of being part and parcel of Yellow Jacket and its far-flung environs. And already they were being talked about among the stragglers in the street and at many a convenient bar.

Jesse Bodine, for one, arrived at a time that seemed made for him. California, young today, and lusty, was younger then, raw and primal. Nor was it any babe in arms; it was well out of swaddling clothes, had long rebelled from any sort of apron strings, had even passed through what might be spoken of as its uncertain 'teens, and now roistered and strove and strutted in its young, violent manhood. Already the first frenzied days of Gold! Gold! were done with, and, in place of helter-skelter camps, towns had sprung up among the mountains, down in the valleys, along the Pacific. There were still ranchos so vast that a *vaquero* might ride all day without crossing an imaginary boundary line, the old Spanish grants and already some new American holdings. There were towns so sleepy and placid and good-humored that men didn't bother any more carrying their weapons abroad except, of course, in case of a pretty definite argument to be settled. So the golden California sun shone down on much green fertility and quiet labor and peaceful pastime. But there were, too, the mountain towns, wild and tumultuous and, some of them, at times lawless. From Sonona along the Mother Lode to Hang Town, Coloma, across to Nevada City, San Juan of the North—mountain towns, mining towns, hell-roaring young towns populated by young men.

When Doc Dabney came to attend to Ransome's wound, Sheriff Comstock came with him. Doc Dabney was young, though his full beard made him look older, and the sort of life he led added a semblance of further years; he was moderately drunk on arrival, such being his habitual condition when not dead drunk. Sheriff Comstock, likewise a bearded man who wore his imposing yellow whiskers in two forked prongs to make one remember the man who had murdered Uncle Joe on Buckeye Creek, had impressed Jesse Bodine as being a man in his forties and was only twenty-eight.

The song that the earth was singing hereabouts was the Song of the Young Men.

Doc Dabney, humming a bawdy little song, got his eyes nicely focused, stiffened his back and went to work. He was not without skill and he had had ample experience with this sort of disorder, but he didn't seem to know the meaning of gentleness and didn't care the snap of his black-nailed fingers for a little pain. Ransome, his arm bared with the flaming lips of his wound showing where a bullet had drilled its way through the flesh, winced a little, then grunted between set teeth, then let out a yell and damned Doc Dabney uphill and down dale. Doc Dabney never missed a beat of his dirty little song.

Ransome was properly bandaged, just the same, and ordered to bed or else to sit still and get busy making up some fresh blood; he was a fool not to have tied up his arm better; he had lost more blood than there was any sense losing. The thing for him to do now was eat lots of half raw meat and fill himself up skin-tight with whisky. Dabney shut his little black bag, demanded his fee of five dollars, but did not bother to give Jesse back any change out of his gold ten, and lurched down the hall to the hotel bar to prove the worth of his own prescription by downing a generous sample of it himself.

"If there's anything you boys want," said the sheriff, following the doctor out, "just say so. This town's right grateful to you."

Jesse got his friend to bed and brought him strong hot soup and black coffee from a Chinese restaurant across the street. It was midafternoon when they had come racing into town; it was early, blue dusk with the first stars out when the self-appointed posse that had stormed out to the Cottonwood Bridge came straggling back empty-handed, jaded and disgusted—and thirsty. Ransome partook of more soup, this time followed up with a good stiff hot toddy, and dropped off into troubled sleep. It was dark when Jesse Bodine, freshened from a thorough wash of hands and face at the washbasin on the back stoop of the hotel, stepped out to see what the town was like by lamplight and candlelight.

He had combed his long black hair straight back and wore his hat on it at an angle. He had dusted his high black boots and had shaken out his red-and-black checked shirt, whipping the dust out of that, too. As he strode along the creaking plank sidewalk, the two Colt revolvers bumped at his lean hips. He mingled with other young men who, like himself, expressed their youth in the way they dressed, the way they wore their side arms—spurs, too, some of them—and the way they walked.

He glanced interestedly in at every door he passed; it was a fresh, pleasant summer evening and most of the doors stood hospitably open. A saloon, a little shop of one sort or another—eating places, jeweler, watchmaker and goldsmith, general store, post office—saloon again, two saloons to any one of the other sort of place. Inside were coal-oil lamps with silvered reflectors; their light straggled out across the sidewalk, weakened toward the middle of the road, but was met there by the dim light from across the way. Early as was the hour, there was a busy hum throughout the main street of Yellow Jacket, a hum that was due in the natural progress of the evening to grow into a louder hum and before the night was over to swell into a roar. In nearly all of the saloons there were gaming tables of various sorts; a little early for them to be busy yet but somehow they all seemed securely and smugly patient for the inevitable hour when dice would roll and cards would rustle and wheels would spin. They were hungry tables but knew they would soon be well fed.

Jesse Bodine stepped in through one of the saloon doors and went to the bar and called for his drink. He didn't exactly want it; whisky had played a small part in his life and that small part had caused him to regard it shrewdly and a thought suspiciously; he drank now as an excuse for crossing the threshold away from the sense of being alone and into a warm company. The man behind the bar scarcely glanced at him; setting forth bottle and glass he was raking in Jesse's silver dollar, one of his few remaining ones, when a voice boomed out:

"Hey there, Blackie! Don't you know who your customer is?"

Blackie, well named, glanced up briefly.

"No, I don't," he said. "Why? Ain't his money no good?"

"It's Jesse Bodine!" And Jesse wondered how the man with the booming voice knew; later he discovered that many knew, having had the information more or less directly from Dan Comstock.

"Who'n hell is Jesse Bodine?" asked the bartender plaintively.

"He's the man that brought Long Peters' stage in today! Where was you anyhow when the stage come in?"

Blackie promptly shoved the silver dollar away from him.

"It's on the house, Bodine," he said as if by vote. "Drink hearty. Sorry I didn't see who it was."

"I'll pay for mine, thanks," said Jesse in that quiet way of his. He wasn't being nasty about it; he was simply negotiating a deal in the customary manner. He added, having no desire to appear discourteous, "You don't owe me anything."

"Have it your way," said Blackie, a fair man.

Jesse downed his drink and called for a cigar; he was passed the box of fat black torpedolike things with very ornate red-black-and-gold bands about their bellies, the best the house afforded.

Later he stepped into other saloons, and generally asked only for a cigar. Most men knew who he was; he was the man who had brought in Long Peters' stage. Already he had a small reputation; he, after both Long Peters and the new express agent had been shot down, had fought it out with the highwaymen and had brought the stage in. So men took stock of him; their eyes measured him.

He heard them speak of the holdup, some in angry voices, some casually as of any bit of interesting news. Some held that it was Joaquin Murietta's work; others laid the thing at the door of a man named Bedloe; both names he had heard mentioned by the little storekeeper who had been a passenger along with him. The consensus was that the desperadoes, no matter under whose bloody banner they went, were safe away this time. They had swooped down from the mountains; they had sped back into the mountains; the mountains with their thousand dark ravines and hidden valleys and caves would protect them.

Starlight, lamplight next, music now. Loud music it was, music with a quick beat like running feet, blatant music. It, like everything else here, was lusty and tumultuous and young, whether from accordion, fiddle, cheap piano—piano, rather, which had been cheap before it sailed around the Horn—or from the huge new-fangled wheel which was a sort of music box. And into some of the larger places of nocturnal entertainment came the girls of the camp.

He saw a crowd of men surging into one of the larger and gaudier saloons, the most flamboyantly ornate in Yellow Jacket, the Silver Mirror it was called, and eased along through the swing doors with the surge and jostle of the throng. Behind the long bar was the glass that gave the place its name, a vastly long French mirror in a gilded frame that had come up from San Francisco only at the cost of infinite labor and care and an inordinate sum of money. The room was big and barnlike; at the farther end was a slightly raised stage of sorts; half a dozen girls were very much in evidence.

They were bright, pretty young girls, Jesse thought; girls of many nationalities, American, Mexican, French. A whole boatload, so it was said, of French mademoiselles had arrived through the Golden Gate only two weeks ago; San Francisco, woman hungry, had gobbled them up like hot cakes of a frosty morning. Just the same, the

Silver Mirror had reached out across hills and plains and had snatched a sample of them for the delectation of Yellow Jacket.

At the moment of Jesse's entrance the whole bevy had gathered about one man, like bees to the honeycomb. He was a tall man, tall even among so many other tall men, red-headed, red-bearded; there was red dirt, the dirt of the mines, on his heavy boots. He wore his battered old hat on the back of his head, and there was a leaping blue fire in his eyes. His coat was thrust back to right and left; his vest was of black and white cowhide with the hair still on it; he wore two big gold watches like gilded turnips, and the watch chains crossed, and were made of nuggets strung on copper wire. The man, with the girls all about him, was talking.

"Roll up, gents, and name your poison," he shouted. "If you know me, you're welcome, and if you don't, you're welcome anyhow, but by God, if there's a man here that don't want to drink with Bud Weaver, let him git out! Me, I'm Bud Weaver, and I ain't ashamed of it, and tonight I'm weaving it wide. Gents, tonight's my night to howl!"

And howl he did, like a prowling timber wolf, and the girls about him and clinging to his arms added their shrill "Yee's!" and "Yippee's!" and men all through the room, yielding headlong to the contagion, laughed and shouted and stamped.

Bud Weaver cut his howl short off and extended both long arms commandingly and called for "Silence!" and got it on the ebb of diminishing tolerant laughter.

"I'm a-singing you a song," said Bud Weaver, and did so. The song was:

> "Oh, my name's Sam,
> And I don't give a damn;
> I'd soon be a nigger
> As a pore white man,
> I play my fiddle
> And I drink my dram.
> Some folks don't like it
> But I don't give a damn!"

Again his long-armed gesture silenced the room, quieting what might have been a mighty gust of applause. Men, in a community craving amusement, were amused.

"Rightly," he said, "my name ain't exactly Sam; it's Bud Weaver. But I don't give a damn just the same. I was a cow hand—"

"Sing it, Bud!" someone called. Bud bowed and obliged.

"Oh, I'm an old cow hand, from the Rio Grand'—"

But he drew it short; he had a speech to make and meant to get along with it.

"I was a cattleman," he said this time. "All my

119

life I was a cattleman. Then I heard tell of this country, and I come along with some of you other boys to get me a carpetbag full of gold. Well, I got it now; I've worked like a damn mule and I got it, and it's right over yonder in the bank at this minute. Most of it is; I've held out plenty for tonight. Tonight the Silver Mirror the same as belongs to me." He turned his elongated frame slowly, seeking the proprietor; on focusing upon a swarthy, sleek-haired, long-mustachioed man at the far end of the bar, he challenged, "Ain't that right, Jake?"

"Whatever you say, Bud," nodded Jake.

"Thank you, Jake," said Bud, very polite. "Like I say, boys, tonight is my night to howl and I'm hell-bent on doing it proper. Tomorrow morning I go to the bank and get my money, and I stomp the red dirt off'n my boot heels and take a stage and go down into the Big Valley to buy me the damndest cattle outfit you ever heard a man talk about in his dreams. This morning I sold out my claims to Big Copeland for a hundred and forty thousand dollars. That goes into my outfit, and the lovely mountain city of Yellow Jacket won't never see me no more. And now gents, make you wishes known!" And for peroration he gave them a second wolflike yowl that made the first seem like the whisper of a summer breeze.

Bud Weaver was well liked, not a man better liked in Yellow Jacket; that was one thing. For another thing, such an invitation as his made other quick, if transient, friendships. Nothing was clearer than that the Silver Mirror was all set for an evening of high festivities. Or, if anything whatever was clearer just then to Jesse Bodine, it was that he had at long last come into port where he wanted to be, where a man could fill his hands with wealth like a child gathering wild flowers, where a man in rude clothes with the soil still on his hands and the red dirt on his boots, could spend like a king.

But of a sudden, with sounds of hilarity beating against him, like waves against an insensate rock, he lost all sense of the roisterers, his attention riveted elsewhere. His eyes came to a chance meeting with another pair of eyes bent steadily upon him from across the room, and he saw a man he remembered, a man one did not forget though seen only once, and even after a long lapse of time.

It was the gambler, Claude Purcell, the man who had forcibly drawn his attention more than a year ago, that day at Temlock's trading station; Ransome Haveril, too, had noted him, demanding, "Is he a minister?" Since that day many names of people had chimed along with names of towns in Jesse Bodine's ears; Joaquin Murietta whom he had heard mentioned today, and the Bedloes; Lola Montez, still echoing, and her little protégée Lotta of today, Rattlesnake Dick, Sonora Jim, Claude Purcell.

It struck Jesse Bodine that in any crowd, even with men jammed so closed about him that he could scarcely breathe, this Claude Purcell would strangely seem aloof, an individual alien to the others. He was clad now as at Temlock's in long black coat, highly polished black boots, high silk hat. But it was not his garb that drew attention here in a place of all sorts of outlandish dress; where other men were ruddy or tanned almost to blackness, his thin face was white. Men said that the sun had not shone on Claude Purcell once in ten years; certainly he never appeared in public until dark. His trade was plied by night, or else, if by day, in closed rooms.

But there was still something else. It was his eyes. Never had Jesse Bodine looked into eyes so dark and magnetic and penetrating.

A very faint smile touched the gambler's lips. He came straight across the room to Bodine and put his hand out; his slender fingers, tipped with perfect nails, were cool and strong against Jesse's warm hand.

"Howdy, Mr. Bodine," he said in a pleasant, quiet voice. "I'm glad to see you again."

"Again?" said Jesse.

"I was making a trip by stage. You were at Temlock's place that day. Your friend was with you then, too; the man with his arm in a sling today."

"I remember seeing you at Temlock's," said Jesse. "I didn't know you had seen me."

The gambler remained for a few more gravely civil words, made no reference to the part Jesse had played in the affair at Cottonwood Bridge, and turned away to speak with someone else, leaving with Jesse the queer impression that he was to see Purcell again, since somehow, for whatever reason, the gambler had been studying him and intended to see more of him. When Claude Purcell left the room Jesse Bodine's eyes followed him.

CHAPTER IX

THREE SIXES IN THE GAMBLER'S CABIN

Meantime Bud Weaver, who had set out to have the time of his life, was going splendidly. He was a man of strong constitution and could drink like a horse, and that was the way he was drinking. And already, not satisfied with the pyramiding expenses piling up for his holiday as men lined up at the bar three deep to drink his health over and over again, he was freely dispensing largess with his own hands. The girls admired his watch chains, did they? He told them with profane emphasis that he was glad that they did; as for him he was sick and tired of the sight of common, raw gold; he wouldn't touch an ounce of it again ever in his life with a ten foot pole unless it was made up neatly into nice clean shiny coins. He ripped both chains from their moorings; they seemed to come up by the roots, the dangling timepieces like tubers; he stripped the nuggets from their copper chains and pressed them into the eager, rosy palms itching for the touch of the sordid ore so newly riven from the dirt. After he had given away the watches, too—two of the girls wore them ostentatiously about their bare necks—he dusted his hands off.

"Now suppose you ladies step up on the platform and entertain the gents," he suggested in mild jovian thunder. "Sing, dance, anything! You've saw the show girls, some of you, down in San Francisco? Well, then!"

They "Yee'd!" and "Yippee'd!" and scampered to the low platform, and men craned their necks to watch. One of them, with a pure, sweet, liquid voice, was singing "When the Roses Bloom Again" as Jesse Bodine, mindful of Ransome Haveril alone in his room, went out and returned to the hotel. He found Ransome asleep, a bit restless and flushed, but certainly just as well left alone as companioned. So Jesse returned to the street.

The sidewalks were empty now, save, here and there, for a solitary figure or a small group passing from one saloon or gaming house to another. There was a brilliant galaxy of stars, some of them seeming to burn like steady fires upon the dark ridges of the mountains, and the frogs yawped down in a marshy place and the night was filled with beauty. Already the subdued hum of voices had grown in volume; it was though Yellow Jacket were a sprawling, loose-limbed giant thing muttering in its sleep.

Not ten steps from the hotel door Jesse met the gambler, likewise strolling and seemingly aimless. His hands were under his coattails, his head was back as if he were remarking within himself upon the beauty of the starry sky, he was slowly smoking a cigar.

He stopped for a word.

"How is your friend Haveril?" he asked.

"Asleep. I guess he's doing all right."

"Not a doubt of it. Dr. Dabney says it's a good clean wound with no bone broken, no major blood vessel torn. A day or two of rest and he'll be as good as new." They strolled along a few steps. Purcell said: "If you have nothing in particular to do, no special place to go, I'd be glad to have you stop in at my cabin for a chat. I'd like to get to know you better, Bodine."

"Thank you, sir," said Jesse. "I'd be glad."

The gambler's cabin, a neat two-roomed affair of logs, stood slightly aloof, like Claude Purcell himself, at the north edge of the town. Young Bodine, vaguely flattered yet also vaguely distrustful, since he failed to understand why he should awaken any interest in a man like Claude Purcell, was faintly ill at ease at first on entering the gambler's sitting room. To the younger man the place reeked with elegance; this was the first time in his life he had ever set his foot on a carpet. Yet the carpet was there, a rich, expensive Turkey red, and his dusty boots were perforce making marks on it. There were four mahogany chairs, a mahogany table with marble top, a lamp with a sparkling fringe of prismatic crystals about the glowing shade.

Purcell proffered a box of cigars; the two sat and stretched out their legs; for a time the gambler gracefully made conversation. What Jesse already knew, that he had to do with a man of some degree of culture, was further impressed upon him. He saw a shelf with books on it; there was a stack of newspapers; he made out a copy of the *Atlanta Constitution* on top.

"I wonder what I've got that Claude Purcell wants?" he kept thinking.

Presently Bud Weaver and his night of howling was mentioned. That faint smile touched the gambler's clean-cut lipline.

"Bud's a good sort," he said. "This country needs more men like him, steady and honest and capable and industrious. And though he hasn't thought it all out for himself, he's one of the leaders of a new movement out here. These men have been raping the land to rip the gold out of it; it's time that men developed the land. They're beginning to turn into the fertile valleys, to build up big ranches, to live like civilized human beings. Bud is dreaming a bigger dream tonight than he knows."

Conversation drifted. Or perhaps it was rather that it seemed adrift while being smoothly and adroitly steered. Mr. Purcell who, it appeared, knew every town of any size or interest—that meant money and gambling, poker preferably—in the state, spoke interestingly and held young

Bodine's attention, for Jesse wanted to know all that he could of the wonders and opportunities of California and estimated that no man could better inform him than Claude Purcell. Once Purcell asked casually, "Do you care for poker yourself, Mr. Bodine?"

And Jesse was swift to wonder: "Is that it? Has he got it in his head somehow that I've got money?"

"I do like to play poker," he said frankly, "but I'm no great hand at it yet."

Purcell smiled.

"I'm glad you added that 'yet.'" He leaned forward, gently brushed the overlong ash from his cigar, was still a moment and then said gravely: "You've got it in you, Mr. Bodine, to be a great poker player. As great at poker as I am; perhaps greater." And he sat back and began speaking of other chance matters.

"For the most part," he was saying, "you'll find Yellow Jacket a quiet and peaceful spot; men are busy here and mind their own business and so keep out of trouble and the making of trouble. Your coming chanced to be at a rather noisy time, what with the stage robbery attempted, and now the farewell party of our good friend Bud Weaver. On most occasions however—"

He really didn't get quite all of the word "however" spoken, but bit the last syllable clean off. Without warning and quite soundlessly, his door was flung open and three men stepped into the room.

"Hold it the way it is now," said one of the men, the one slightly in front of the others. He was a small, very dark man; he looked to be of Latin extraction. He, like the two larger, blonder men close behind him, looked full of determined business, as did the weapons in their hands; the three pairs of eyes were hard and menacing and suspiciously watchful.

One of the three kicked the door shut. Neither Jesse Bodine nor Claude Purcell stirred. They were smoking; as it happened each at the moment was holding his cigar in the fingers of his left hand; the gambler's right hand was on his chest, fingers fanlike with his thumb in his vest arm-hole; Jesse's right was out on the table idly fingering the rim of an ash tray.

"What do you boys want, Mike?" asked Purcell, speaking as quietly as he had spoken all evening.

"You know what we want, Purcell. And we're going to get it."

"Money, I suppose?"

Into Mike's dark face came a hot, blackish-red flush.

"We ain't no damn thieves an' you know it, Claude," he said, harsh and surly. "An' it ain't your money we're after. It's Charlie King's. No," he added, slowly, "it ain't Charlie's no longer. It's

Mrs. King's now, Charlie's widder. Her 'n her two little girls'."

"So Charlie King is dead? I'm sorry," Purcell lifted his brows; he shook his head and did look sorry. "What happened to him?"

"You did," said one of the men backing Mike up; he shifted restlessly; he kept his heavy, big-barreled pistol trained on the gambler's upper chest. "You played him poker not two weeks ago, over to Grass Valley. Charlie lost nine thousand dollars to you. Him and his old woman was savin' that, gettin' ready to move and take their youngsters back home, back East. Charlie couldn't go home and face 'em. He got drunk instead; he stayed drunk day and night; finally he shot himself."

"Mr. Bodine," said Purcell.

"Yes, Mr. Purcell?"

"You keep out of this. Understand? No matter what happens, you keep out."

"All right," said Jesse.

"You're damn right he'll keep out!" said Mike. "Unless he wants his guts shot full of holes."

"So," mused the gambler aloud, "Charlie King loses some money to me in a poker game, then goes out and gets drunk and shoots himself, and you boys come all the way over here from Grass Valley to bellyache to me and ask for Charlie's money back?"

"You got it, Purcell," said Mike.

The gambler shrugged.

"It's a new one on me," he said, and shook his head again and seemed to sigh over the thing. "I remember when I was a boy, and we used to play marbles for keeps, there was always some watery-eyed, leaky-nosed boy who wanted his marbles back when he lost. I wouldn't have said that you boys graded up that way."

There was anger in Mike's eyes and in the eyes of his two companions, and Jesse Bodine felt that three fingers fairly itched on the triggers of their guns. The third of the trio spoke up now for the first time; it was as though all three meant to go on record as pressing equally the case of the late Charlie King.

"You got a reputation as a square gambler, Purcell," he said. "How you got it, I don't know. There ain't no such animal. You're as crooked as the rest of your lot, which is to say as crooked as a dog's hind leg. You didn't win Charlie's money; you cheated him out of it. And me, for one, I'd just as leave you made as much of a move right now as to wiggle your ears; that'd be all the excuse I want to blow you clean to hell."

Claude Purcell did not oblige, he did not stir a muscle as he sat looking thoughtfully at his visitors.

"So Claude Purcell had to cheat to win from a man like Charlie King, did he?" he asked at last. "That's nonsense. Still, have it your way. It's nine thousand dollars you came to get, isn't it? Gentlemen, I'll raise no argument. You have the drop on me and the game is made and I lose; your three sixes top my hand. Will you go on your way quietly now, accepting my word that I'll send the money over to you within ten days?"

They jeered at him for taking them for fools.

"Your word," said Mike, "ain't worth a grain of fool's gold with any of us, Purcell. We'll take the money now. And don't say you ain't got it, because we know better or we wouldn't be here. Cough up and make it lively."

"I've a notion to see you in hell first," said the gambler equably.

"You'll be there a long way ahead of us. Better get another notion."

Purcell sighed. "Perhaps you're right. Yes, I've the nine thousand and you might as well have it now. It's in the other room, in my strongbox. The key is in my vest pocket. Shall I move my hand enough to get the key for you?"

"Keep still!" roared out the man nearest the door. "Don't twitch a finger or I'll let you have it!"

"Last time it was my ears," said Purcell.

"Stay just like you are—both of you," warned Mike, and moved slowly forward. "I'll get the key. Which pocket, Purcell?"

"Lower left vest pocket," said Purcell.

Mike drew so near that his coat brushed the

gambler's, and all the while kept his gun trained upon the higher portion of the vest mentioned, and all the while his two companions were as watchful for treachery as two old tomcats eying a promising rathole. But what happened next was too swift for any of them.

Even Jesse Bodine couldn't have told how a small silvered pistol got into Claude Purcell's hand as the gambler fairly exploded into incredibly fast action. He shot Mike square between the eyes; he shot one of Mike's companions through the bared, brown throat; he shot the other man three times, once high up through the chest, then again through the chest as the man stood rocking on his feet, then between the eyes as he had shot Mike. Before Mike's body struck the floor both other men were falling. And not a man of the three had fired a single shot.

Jesse Bodine found himself on his feet, his own gun in his hand, staring in shocked bewilderment. Slowly Claude Purcell rose from his chair, the sluggish smoke dribbling out of the short barrel of his gun. There was a very slight narrowing of his cold, hard eyes, never another hint of expression on his hard white face.

"I'll step along and tell the sheriff about it," he said. "He likes to keep law and order operating in Yellow Jacket, and most of us here are with him in that."

Jesse Bodine moistened his lips; they had gone harsh and dry.

"Shall I come with you? If you want a witness—"

Purcell shrugged and dropped his gun down to the table.

"My word is enough with Comstock. If he wants more, well, he can come back with me and see how things stand here. It's a clear enough case of self-defense. But you won't want to stay here with this company. We'll just close the door and leave things as they are."

They walked back toward the heart of Yellow Jacket, and there was a hollow sound from the wooden sidewalk under their heels. The gambler asked a man or two if he had seen Comstock; Jesse returned thoughtfully to the hotel to look in on Ransome Haveril again.

This time he found his friend awake and sitting up in the chair by the open window, rocking back and forth in pain, and cursing fretfully.

"Where you been, Jess?"

"Nowhere. Here, I'll make you another hot toddy."

"Yes. Make it strong as hell. In another minute I'd have been biting my arm off. God, it hurts!"

He drank half a tumbler of hot whisky in hot water with sugar, and drew a long grateful breath. Then he crawled back to his bed and shut his eyes.

Jesse sat in the chair, not rocking but tensely

still, and looked out into the night where there was a slice of earth and sky between the corners of the hotel and the adjacent building. He wondered: Had Purcell cheated the way those men said he had? He wondered: Was there a strongbox in the next room, and was the money in it, and was the key in Purcell's pocket? He wondered: Where did that gun come from that all of a sudden was in the gambler's hands. And he wondered through it all: What does Claude Purcell want from me?

After a while Ransome dozed off again and Jesse Bodine, of less mind now for sleep than ever, sat on in his chair for a long time. In the end, restless, he tiptoed out and strolled along the sidewalk. He judged it must be about three o'clock, yet Yellow Jacket's many saloons weren't thinking of time. He turned toward the Silver Mirror, attracted by the thunderous shouts coming from that direction. Bud Weaver, he supposed, was still making merry mad carousal. He was right. And he was just in time to be treated to a curious and interesting sight.

Down the street, coming toward him at some little distance beyond the Silver Mirror, were two figures walking down the middle of the road. One was a very tall man; he could make out that much even in the poor light of the hour. The other, far slighter and shorter figure, could have been almost anything; Jesse Bodine's first eerie impression was that the bigger man had captured and was convoying a sheeted ghost, for surely there was a flutter of white and he could not know on the instant that it was the flutter of an angrily expostulating little man's nightgown. Then a crowd of men came surging out of the Silver Mirror, shouting and laughing and stamping, a crowd at the top of hilarity, and obscured his view. Coming closer, he got the explanation.

Bud Weaver had run out of ready cash; he had arrived with sudden unexpectedness at the moment when he could not find on his person anywhere, no matter how he rifled his pockets, a nugget or a coin or so much as a pinch of gold dust; and this had happened when he felt he had only started to celebrate. Inspired, he had marched off to the cabin where the banker of Yellow Jacket lived; he had done the direct thing in the direct way, and now, in high good humor, despite the little man's yanks and tugs and seething expostulations, was jabbing the nose of his gun into the small of the little man's back and ordering him to open his bank and produce what was Bud Weaver's. And this time Bud wasn't contented with a paltry thousand dollars; he carried his heavily weighted carpetbag when he drew the crowd back into the Silver Mirror. Jesse Bodine saw him vanish through another flutter, that of the bright dresses of the young ladies of the place.

Jesse Bodine passed on beyond the outer fringe of the town and into a rutted road and, quitting the road, climbed a little way up the flank of the rocky hill. He sat in the silence on a flat stone well above the town and let his eyes traffic with its dark outline dotted with dim lights; then he looked beyond it at the rugged mountain ridges and, beyond them, at the curve of the star-sprinkled sky. He took sober stock of this place, what he could see of it by day and night, what he could sense of it.

He knew that it was not all mad merriment like tonight's, for these men were hornyhanded with the labor of their days; it was not all banditry and such violence as had taken place in the gambler's cabin. There were the mining claims where strong, purposeful fingers clawed the soft, yellow, mighty gold from the bosom of the earth. And, beyond the reach of his physical vision but strongly vivid in his mind's eyes, were the valley lands and the peaceful, busy towns. There were the enormous cattle ranges, mile after mile of them, there were the all but limitless ranchos that had come as careless grants from a king across the water who had never seen them, who did not in any sensible sense own them, the lands of the Spanish grandees. He had heard almost as much rumor of these as of the wild towns. He knew that Americans were beginning to trickle down into the fertile valleys, too; there was Bud Weaver with his dream of a small kingdom all his own. He looked at the sleeping world with the eyes of a young conqueror biding his time, with the eyes of an eagle sailing high over all of it, looking far and wide for its prey. The time would come when the eagle would fold its wings and drop—and spread its wings again before it struck, and unsheathe its iron talons.

He, like Bud Weaver and others before him, dreamed of his own kingdom.

And he, unlike Bud Weaver in this, thought that he began to see another way of coming swifter and straighter to his heart's desire.

He got up, a little cramped and stiff from sitting, and returned the way he had come. The sky along the eastern horizon was paling slowly, steadily; the stars were waning and losing their glory in the coming glory of a new day, and the air was sweet and clean, fresh from the mountains with their pines, on the little newborn breeze. He breathed deep, very deep, and held his body straight, his head up.

He went to his room and slept, sitting in the rocking chair by the window with the gentle stir of air fanning his face. He and Ransome slept for hours. It was he who woke first. He went out to the stoop to wash; the water was deliciously cold on his hands and face, on his bared arms and chest and neck and head.

He returned to the street, hunting a place that should be open by now where he could get a good hot breakfast. The sidewalks were all but deserted; the sun was well up, genial and warm, but the town quiet. The vendors of one sort and another were in their places of business; the night's roisterers had gone their way to their work somewhere or to sleep. He saw one still figure sitting on the edge of the sidewalk, legs hanging down to the street, shoulders humped over, hat drawn forward over a concealed face.

The man looked up. A pair of heavy-lidded and red-rimmed eyes turned up to him, then drifted away. Near the man's feet, empty in the dust, was an old carpetbag.

"I'm waiting for the Silver Mirror to open up," said Bud Weaver wearily. "I left my watches there for safekeeping. I bought 'em back from those girls last night, and gave 'em to Jake to keep for me. A man can't tell what time it is with no watches, can he?"

It seemed to Jesse Bodine that surely by now every shop and saloon in town must be open. He looked toward the Silver Mirror; it alone was closed. That struck him as downright queer.

Just then a cheery call came from across the street where a man, the cook no doubt, looked out of his little lunch counter.

"Hi, Bud! Better come over and get a cup cawfee. It's on the house."

Bud Weaver shook his head and winced and shut his eyes tight a moment.

"I'm waiting for Jake to open up. I left my watches at the Silver Mirror. I want to know what time it is, and there ain't a damn watch in this town I'd trust but mine." He glanced at the sun, seemed about to shake his head at it but refrained, merely wincing again. "I wouldn't trust the sun itself against them watches of mine."

The lunch counter man came across the road, drying his red hands on a dirty towel. He was laughing as he said:

"Why don't you open it yourself, Bud. You've got the key yet, ain't you?"

"Me? What are you talking about?" Nonetheless he fumbled in his pockets and found a long brass key. He looked blank. "How'n hell did I get it?" he demanded. "I didn't kill Jake for it, did I?"

"You bought the Silver Mirror from him," laughed the other man, and winked broadly at Jesse Bodine. "Don't you remember?"

Bud Weaver thought it over a long time. He didn't question, he didn't deny, he didn't argue.

"Well, I'm damned," was all he said.

He got stiffly to his feet, knocked his hat brim back and went to the saloon, key in hand.

"I want to see what time it is," he said as he opened the door and went in.

CHAPTER X

THE YOUNG SPANISH DON AND THE MINIATURE

Such was Jesse Bodine's introduction to Yellow Jacket, such its welcome to him. Already, despite his youth, he was a hard man; Yellow Jacket was to make him harder. He came here a dreamer of dreams; Yellow Jacket was to induce his greatest dreams. He was wide awake to life, he was wide open to its suggestions. He learned, learned, learned. He learned from Claude Purcell, from Bud Weaver, from men laboring on their claims, some sticking like glue, some forever darting to fresh fields, away on the breath of the slightest rumor like leaves in a gale. He was avid to learn; he meant to come to grips with life with an equipment that would give him better than the even break which was better than most men got. He was like a young knight buckling on his virgin armor, testing armor and steel in every possible way before he pulled his visor down.

From the first he belonged to this country and it belonged to him; they were two of a kind, aces red and black.

And here, too, Ransome Haveril fitted every bit as naturally, but in a different way. His wound

143

healed rapidly, his strength came flooding back, his eyes brightened and his heart lifted. He and Jesse had a cabin together on the edge of town, like the gambler's; it seemed set there just for their use. Two old miners, the oldest men in Yellow Jacket, had shared it for years. Of late they had got tired of drink and game and carousal; they had had enough. They had somehow saved a goodly share of all the gold that had come their way. They seemed to change, folks said. They got on each other's nerves; they started quarreling one night, the first quarrel, and left Yellow Jacket, not speaking to each other, the following morning. Their cabin became Jesse's and Ransome's.

Ransome made friends on every hand, and news and information of all sorts flowed to him; he it was who brought Jesse Bodine word of newly discovered possibilities of Cold Creek. Within a week the two were working their own claims there, instructed in the use of tools, by other men, red-shirted and shaggy-bearded for the general thing, working above and below them. For a time they worked hard from dawn to dark, swinging with pick, heaving with shovel, moving boulders out of their way and sending them rolling, to land with a great splash in the creek bottom, squatting over the pans in which they washed their gold. They returned nightly to their cabin, walking wearily like old men, tired in every muscle down to the bone. The saloons and games had no call for them then, though sometimes Ransome would heave himself up after an hour's rest and would say, "I'm going for a drink; come along?" and would go alone for what company he could find. He soon returned, to flop down on his bunk and fall fast asleep.

And after a month they felt like old-timers here in Yellow Jacket. They knew everyone, they had learned their way about. And they estimated that they had done well. Granted that they had not turned up an individual nugget worth a thousand dollars, despite always a secret high hope, as they recalled tales heard; that sort of thing had been done on occasion. But in a snug hiding place under one of the hand-hewn puncheons of their floor, their joint pile of dust and watermelon seed and a few small nuggets satisfied them. At the end of the month, having promised themselves to wait a full four working weeks, they weighed in on Harry Trimble's scales; and, though they did not find themselves exactly rich, they did find themselves far richer than they had ever been before, and felt like millionaires. When they cut the pile in two, each had close to four hundred dollars.

Ransome's eyes glistened and Jesse's grew profoundly thoughtful.

"Man!" cried Ransome. "Just greenhorns, we can knock out ten, fifteen dollars a day apiece!

That's just run o' the mill, too, and one of these days . . . !"

How a man could let himself go!

They trimmed each other's hair; they scrubbed, and Jesse shaved while Ransome trimmed a beard of which daily he grew prouder and fonder. Ransome went to the store—they took that Saturday afternoon off, and all Sunday, too, a thing which many others did—and bought new boots and hat, a flaming red shirt, half a dozen socks, an elegant looking pair of pants with stripes. Jesse fared forth in his turn, and all that Ransome could see new was a tall and shiny pair of black boots.

Early that night Ransome started out to do the town. He dropped in at every saloon and amused himself with the various games, roulette and faro and chuck-a-luck; he met up with his friends for much talk and laughter and the necessary trips to the bar; he opened wine for the camp girls at the Silver Mirror. And he made new friends.

Tonight he was to cement a new friendship which was to have far-reaching effects not only in his own life but in that of certain others, Jesse Bodine's among them. He was seated at one of the Silver Mirror's small tables, a dusky bottle and glasses between him and the prettiest, youngest and altogether liveliest of the Silver Mirror girls, a golden-haired blue-eyed Southern miss with the dulcet drawl of Georgia in her languorous

146

speech, when a newcomer to Yellow Jacket dawned on his view for the first time, on the girl's for but the second time. She emitted a small smothered squeal.

"Misteh Ransome, suh, you just look yondeh and see what I see!" crooned Peaches. "Ain't he a lovely ma-an? Will you get him foh me, Misteh Ransome?"

Here was one who had ridden far that day, a young dandy from one of the Spanish ranchos lying farther south in the valley-and-hill country. Already Ransome had discovered that men dressed pretty much as their tastes and imaginations suggested, money for sartorial barter permitting, but here was a new note. The boots were the smallest and tightest and of the highest heels ever to come Yellow Jacket's way, and shone until they were as good as Claude Lorraine mirrors; the hat had a low crown, a very broad stiff brim, an ornate silvered band; about the man's waist was a scarlet silk sash thrust into which were two ivory-handled pistols and an ivory-hafted, long knife. The man had a small dark face and wore about his brown throat a gold chain from which hung an oval locket as big as a silver dollar; his jet-black eyes were of the most expressive sort; a tiny mustache as black as his eyes, was twisted upward to end in needle points. It was the last sigh in grace when the man moved.

"What is it?" grinned Ransome.

"A very grand Spanish don," said the enthusiastic Peaches. "He came once befoh. He is Don Philip Something-or-Other from La Fiesta. He will see me and then he will come oveh to ouah table—and you will offeh him a drink, won't you, Misteh Ransome, deah?"

The young don, as his liquid eyes swept the room, could not have failed to see Miss Peaches, so did she crane her creamy neck, into such a luscious smile did her welcoming red lips part. But he did not appear to remember her. He moved straight to the bar, whipping his pantaloons idly with his soft-leather gauntlets, and paid her not the slightest attention.

Peaches pouted. Ransome laughed. Also he protested.

"Look here, you're having a bottle of wine with me. How about turning those great big eyes and that man-murdering smile my way? Here's happiness, Peaches."

"I don't care," pouted Peaches. "He just didn't see me. He said such nice things to me the otheh time; he told me my eyes were brighteh than stars and that when he rode at night and saw the stars he would always be remembering me. Only that the stars weren't as pretty, because they're not so nice and blue. And his voice when he is talking to you and saying things like that is just like singing."

"With him, maybe that's all it was, just a song," Ransome teased her.

"Misteh Ransome!" She set her hat at a defiant angle, a monstrous pink hat, parasol size, with a drooping ostrich feather. "If you was a Southe'n gentleman you wouldn't say such things!"

"Only from as far south as Kentucky," chuckled Ransome.

It was a couple of hours later that he found himself talking with the young don, and then only as the sequence to a small but intriguing accident. It was when the Silver Minor's piano was being thumped by a mournful looking, droop-eyed and droop-mustached, wan, thin man, and the bevy was on the platform, singing and cavorting for the delectation of the roomful of men, and when Ransome and Don Felipe Moraga were packed elbow to elbow in the throng. Ransome felt something strike his hand with a light tap and, looking down, saw that it was Moraga's chain and locket. The clasp had somehow come open; only Ransome's quick, lucky gesture saved the bauble from slithering on down underfoot.

The locket flew open in his palm and, as a man will, he looked closely at what it had immured. Within was a miniature, beautifully painted; and Ransome, always with an eye for feminine loveliness, gasped out, under his breath, to be sure, yet audibly for the man jammed against him,

"Lord! She's the prettiest thing a man ever saw!"

Just then Don Felipe's delicate, well-kept hands were softly applauding what was going forward on the stage, and his lips and eyes were gay with his smile, so he gave the man at his elbow only a modicum of his attention, saying absently:

"Pardon? I thought you addressed me, Señor."

"Your locket," said Rasome, and held it up, still open. "It fell."

Don Felipe took it quickly then, and closed it with a snap. He strove to bow after his own graceful fashion, from the hips, but in the press had to do with an inclination of the head, and even then knocked his wide hat awry on a taller man's shoulders.

"Thank you, Señor," he said courteously, but with no warmth in his tone. His eyes on Ransome's now were cold and unfriendly. "And you said, Señor?"

"Just that she is mighty beautiful, the girl in your locket."

Don Felipe's eyes narrowed and he looked as arrogant as all his ancestors. Clearly he was of a mind to take offense, and he fairly bristled with whatever it was going on inside a mercuric soul. For an instant he was at a loss. In the end he said briefly:

"It is my sister."

That, of course, was to stop all talk. Ransome

had no doubt that he lied, but let it go at that. Just the same the image of the girl, lovely like a dark flower, remained pictured in the eyes of his heart. He had meant what he had said.

The number on the stage was over and the girls were coming down and Ransome was moving away when Don Felipe's voice, softer now and without malice, stopped him.

"I am ashamed that I spoke as I did, Señor. I cherish that locket with my heart. I did not make you understand that my gratitude is for you, all of it."

"That's all right," said Ransome lightly. "Glad I noticed it."

"Might I be permitted to make my amends in a glass of wine, Señor? A good wine or even a bad one, or a glass of *aguadiente*, washes away bad memories, no?"

"With all the joy in life!" cried Ransome Haveril, and forthwith the two drank together.

One drink led to another. They went out of the Silver Mirror arm in arm, bent nowhere in particular, just seeking other pastures. They introduced themselves and shook hands: Mr. Ransome Curtis Haveril from Pleasant Valley, formerly of Kentucky; Señor Don Felipe Antonio Maria Moraga, of La Fiesta. And they explained each to the other his reasons for being in Yellow Jacket.

"Tonight, Señor, I am in Yellow Jacket just for

fun!" Don Felipe's eyes twinkled and the feet in his small tight boots began tapping. "I ride the sixty miles from La Fiesta to play! *Bueno*! They are gay here on a Saturday night; cards to play, music to hear—and *las muchachas* to dance! I have brought some money in my pocket; later, *vamos a ver*, I am going to play the poker!"

He spoke English well-nigh perfectly, but it was an English softened on a Latin tongue. He did not say "in" but "een"; not "sixty" but "seexty"; and with him "dance" was a-l-most "thance." When he cursed, as he did and fluently when his high heel got itself snared in a broken plank in the sidewalk, it sounded like love-making.

They were drawn to each other, these two; they sat in a dim corner of a long barroom and smoked together and drank together, and liked each other better all the while. It wasn't long before Ransome could refer to what all the while remained high in his thoughts, the girl in the picture. The little Juana Moraga! Juanita! 'Nita!

"*Es verdad*, Señor Haveril! It is nothing but only the truth! She is my little sister. When I told you that, you laughed inside of you; you said inside: 'He is a liar. It is his *novia*.' For our birthday last May—for we have the same birthday in May, 'Nita and I, though there is a difference of eight years between us; she is only sixteen now and I am already twenty-four!—but that day she gives me this locket! I wear it at all times. She is

152

like an angel, the little Juana, and her brother is sometimes a bad boy, and needs a little angel over his heart to make him be good again!"

He laughed softly and lifted the miniature to his lips.

And that sort of thing struck Ransome Haveril as strange, hardly conduct befitting a man full grown, but he made allowance for Spanish blood.

"I've heard talk about the old Spanish grants," he said, with a purpose in the back of his mind. "Bigger than all get-out, they say. They say each man's place is like his own kingdom, sort of. And I've heard of the Spanish towns, like Monterey."

"*Amigo!*" cried Don Felipe. "You are going to come along with me to visit us at La Fiesta! You are going to see one of the oldest and finest ranchos, and the best horses in California! My mama and papa will be glad when I bring you to them and tell them, 'This is *mi amigo* Ransome Haveril.' You are going to see! And we are going to have a fine barbecue and a dance and horse races, and you will see the bear fight the bull! Monterey? Maybe we are going there, too." He bunched his fingertips and blew a kiss. "Monterey is a town to love, Ransome. And I have many friends there. And pretty girls! Yes, you are going to come along with me. *No?*"

"Come with you? There's nothing I'd like better, Don Philip," said Ransome. "I've never seen one of your big California ranchos." And he kept telling himself that he had never seen a prettier girl than Don Felipe's little sister.

Later, as conversation wandered, Bud Weaver's name was mentioned. A cloud darkened young Moraga's countenance.

"I have been hoping to see Mr. Bud Weaver," he said, and was frowning. "I know him but little personally, but from what everyone says of him he is a fine man. Just the man that all of us at La Fiesta wanted for a neighbor. You see, Señor, this Bud Weaver was to buy a ranch adjoining ours; he even had an option on it. He did not come as he had promised; we found that out. And now, here in Yellow Jacket, I have heard an explanation. They say that he celebrated his departure from Yellow Jacket too soon; that now his money is all gone." He shrugged and sighed and fell to drumming on the table. Ransome wondered why, if he did not know Bud Weaver personally, he should show such concern; why, indeed, knowing him or not, it could make so great difference to Felipe Moraga.

Don Felipe read his look and explained again. His voice, though not lifted, was angry.

"There is another man who wants the Rancho Monte," he said. "He will get it now that Bud Weaver cannot. He is a man I do not like, Señor; nobody who knows him likes that man. I am going to tell you who he is, and I only can hope that he

154

is no friend of yours or of any friends of yours. It is a man named Breen, Willard Breen. Hackamore Breen, they call him. Do you know him?"

"Here I thought I knew everybody in Yellow Jacket and I never heard of any Willard Breen."

"Oh, he does not dwell here; he is almost a newcomer to our country and is always on the go, looking for something; he has much, much money, they say, and I suppose it was the ranch he was always hunting. Until he found El Rancho Monte. But he comes here often; when there is a big poker game, there is this man Breen, and there are many big poker games at the Silver Mirror. He is in town tonight, because I saw him." Again he sighed and drummed on the table. "Tomorrow, like me, he will be riding south, I bet you. To try to be a neighbor to the Moragas! Maybe someday I am going to have to kill that man, *amigo*!"

On the sidewalk again, smoking their cigarettes and idling, Ransome saw Jesse Bodine walking alone and headed, as Ransome suspected, toward the Silver Mirror. Ransome called and Jesse stopped.

"Meet up with a friend of mine, Jess," said Ransome. "He's Don Felipe Moraga from the big Fiesta Ranch, sixty miles south of here. I'm riding down with him to see his place tomorrow. Don Philip, this is my friend and pardner, Jesse Bodine."

They shook hands, Jesse gravely as was his

fashion, measuring as best he could this new "friend" of the gregarious Ransome's, Don Felipe with a warm smile.

"Ever heard of a fellow named Breen? Willard Breen?" Ransome asked.

Jesse nodded. "Yes. He's playing poker tonight at the Silver Mirror; Claude Purcell told me of him. Why?"

"Nothing. Don Philip just mentioned him, that's all."

"And you, Mr. Bodine?" Moraga asked. "You are playing too?"

Again Jesse nodded.

"That is what I should like to do!" cried the young Spaniard. "I have brought some money with me, five hundred dollars." Then he laughed deprecatingly and shrugged. "With Claude Purcell in the game, one knows who wins!"

"What do you mean by that, Mr. Moraga?" Jesse Bodine's voice sounded cold.

"Oh, I don't mean what maybe that sounded like! Not that there is anything that is not upright and honest in Mr. Purcell's game! He has a name for being a square gambler. But he has a skill at the game that no other men seem to have."

"Still you want to play?"

"But what is money for! It is for amusement, surely. *Bueno*, to sit in a game with Mr. Purcell, a thing I have never done, would be, I think, something to remember! Yes, yes; I would like it."

"And you won't mind," laughed Ransome, "if your friend Willard Hackamore Breen sits in too?"

Moraga looked at him very soberly.

"Maybe God is going to deal a Moraga all the high cards tonight," he said, and seemed devout. "To win all that *cabrone*'s money, ah, that would be like a good dream turning out to be the real thing!"

"The game ought to be starting pretty soon," said Jesse Bodine.

So the three went along together to the Silver Mirror. Jake Epperson who had been proprietor that night when Bud Weaver had taken over, who had vanished clean away from Yellow Jacket, was again behind the bar—his bar. For it appeared that again he was proprietor here. The three got a part of the story a minute later when Jake ushered them into a small back room; Claude Purcell was there already, leaning back in his chair. So was Bud Weaver, who wanted to play; so was Breen, the man whom Don Felipe did not like.

Bud Weaver was talking:

". . . and after all, I reckon the luckiest thing I done that night was to buy this place. I didn't want it but, hell, all the rest of my money faded, and anyhow I woke up next day owning the best barroom in town. Howsomever, Jake's back in town and back behind the bar. He's got the Silver

Mirror back and I've got the cash, or part of it. And that's how come I'm horning in tonight with you boys."

When he had finished, Claude Purcell got to his feet and made the necessary introductions. Jesse Bodine shook hands with Willard Breen and with Bud Weaver; Ransome Haveril followed suit. Don Felipe grasped Bud's hand but only bowed a stiff little bow to Breen. Breen smiled, then touched his small, tight brown mustache and wiped the smile away. He was a young man like the others, Purcell being well away the oldest, somewhere in his late thirties; Breen was lean and sinewy and brown, his eyes a sharp, cold blue, his dress that of a Western cowboy. He impressed both Jesse and Ransome distinctly unfavorably. He was a crafty man, or his constantly narrowing eyes belied him, and a cruel, or that cruel, thin-lipped mouth under the neat mustache meant nothing.

"Count me out," Ransome Haveril said when they drew chairs up to the table. "I'll watch a couple of minutes, if you don't mind, then move along." He clapped a hand on his new friend's shoulder. "I'll be looking in on you later, Don Philip," he promised.

"Where I come from," said Willard Breen coldly, "a man either sits in to a game or finds his fun somewhere else."

It was as good as a slap in the face not only for

Ransome but for his friends, as good as saying bluntly: "I don't know you, and some of these others do. How the hell do I know what tip-offs you'd like to give?"

Don Felipe flushed hotly and started to speak; even the quiet Jesse Bodine stared angrily; but Claude Purcell settled the matter, saying in a businesslike way:

"Mr. Breen is right, boys. It's a custom here in Yellow Jacket, and no offense meant."

"I'll go," said Ransome promptly. But he hung on his heel long enough for a steady glare at Willard Breen. Breen, for his part, didn't even look up. Ransome went out just as Jake Epperson came in with cards and chips; a roustabout at his heels brought whisky bottles, water and glasses, setting them down on a small side table where already there was a box of cigars.

Jake pulled up his chair, fingered the chips in front of him and invited cheerily:

"Name what you'll take, boys. Chips are free as long as you pay for them." Then he laughed. That was always Jake's way of starting a game, Jake's little joke.

"I'll take a thousand bucks to start with," said Bud Weaver. "Just to grease my play."

With Jake banking, the game started. With six men playing, with one of them Claude Purcell, with both Willard Breen and Bud Weaver evidently very sweetly heeled, the affair seemed to promise pleasant moments for all, and a profitable evening for the fortunate.

Jesse Bodine lost every cent he had that night. When he arose from the table and stretched, shortly after midnight, he was, so far as money went, as clean as a hound's tooth, but in his eyes was a shining light. It was the light of eagerness, of battle lust. Tonight he was through, but there were to be other nights, many of them. And he told himself that he had got his money's worth, in an evening's entertainment and in something else that would abide with him."

Long before he had shoved his last chip into the pot he had seen young Moraga shaken free of his ultimate peso. The young Spaniard never was and never would be a poker player; he rode his hopes too hard; once in on a hand he could not throw down his cards but had to keep seeing the bet every time the pot was boosted. He was too impulsive, too mercuric, too reckless.

"Too bad, Moraga," Willard Breen had said with that damned smile of his as it fell to his lot to rake in a nice little stack, Moraga's last. And the young fellow's eyes flashed dangerously as the hot color stained his cheeks again, and there was the glint of his teeth as his lips curled back from them, and for the second time he was about to speak under Breen's lash. But he said nothing. He smiled and shrugged and to the others said:

"*Gracias, caballeros*. It was good fun, no? And now I will go and look for my friend Señor Haveril."

Before Jesse Bodine was forced out he had had his run of luck, and he had played his cards shrewdly enough, and had won more than he had ever won in his life; at one time he was better than a thousand dollars ahead. But then he ran afoul of the saloonkeeper, Jake Epperson, who took him down for fully a quarter of his stack. He won small pots after that; no sizable one. Then he ran into Willard Breen looking for him. Jesse had estimated Breen at holding a full house at best; he himself had four sevens. Breen showed four queens.

That little smile of Breen's hurt a man more than a blow. And there was nothing to do about it.

When Jesse stood up, Breen said generously: "No reason why you can't stick around a while and watch, Bodine; you've sure paid for a front seat ticket. I've learned a lot of what I know about the game, watching old-timers at it. Am I right, Purcell?"

"Going, Mr. Bodine?" asked Claude Purcell. "Will you do me a small favor?" He drew a small morocco-bound memorandum book from his pocket, and a filigreed gold pencil; he tore out a leaf and wrote a few words in a fine, copperplate hand. He tendered this to Jesse, saying, "Will you glance at this memo as you go, and, if it's all right, hand it to Chris? You know him? He's tending bar in Jake's place."

Wondering, Jesse took the paper and went out; as he closed the door he heard Breen suggesting that, with but the four playing now, they cut the joker in. This was being done as Jesse closed the door.

He looked curiously at the note. It was written to him, and said:

"If you'll hand this to Chris, he'll stake you to a thousand dollars. That's in case you'd like to come back into the game. And if you lose you can take your time paying me."

He crumpled the note in his hand and went on his way. Again the gambler puzzled him, vaguely disturbed him. Why on earth should Claude Purcell want to lend Jesse Bodine, almost a stranger, a thousand dollars?

"He isn't Santa Claus," he muttered to himself. "What have I got that a man like Claude Purcell would want?"

He returned to the door and looked in.

"All taken care of, Mr. Purcell," he said. "And I was to say thanks to you. Good night, boys."

He strolled out into the open air, thinking. Just the glance he had had back into the card room afforded food for thought; he had seen the way Bud Weaver was looking across the table at Willard Breen; there was naked, red murder in Bud's eyes, and small wonder. All night Breen had been jeering at him from behind a thin mask; any man could see how those two hated each other. There was jovial, obvious, straight-from-the-shoulder Bud Weaver who had had his heart set on the Monte Ranch and who a few days ago had counted it as good as his own; there was the other man who hungered for the same beautiful acres and who now in his turn counted them in his pocket because Bud Weaver had to make a fool of himself with his money. There you had Breen topping Bud's hand time after time, raking the chips in with slow, tantalizing fingers, smiling that damned small-mustached smile of his. Hackamore Breen said with a chuckle, "I'm buying me a ranch tomorrow; every dollar I rake in now helps to buy another herd." Bud Weaver winced so that all could see. And so Jesse Bodine left them.

Bud Weaver lost twenty thousand dollars before three o'clock, and kicked his chair back and went growling to the bar. The bevy came fluttering, but he damned them out of his sight and got drunk alone. The next day he would go to the store, outfit himself again and once more turn his back to the valley lands, his face to the rocky hills where gold was.

In the end, with Jake Epperson saying sourly that he had enough, the spoils were pretty nearly evenly divided between Claude Purcell and Willard Breen. Breen came out of the card room

163

laughing. Claude Purcell seldom laughed. Never over a poker game.

Jesse Bodine had waited for the game to end and saw them come out when in a little while it would be day. Seeing his chance for a word alone with the gambler, he took it.

"That was mighty nice of you, to offer to stake me, Mr. Purcell," he said.

"Why not come over to my cabin with me?" asked Purcell. "We'll make a pot of coffee. I'd like a talk with you, Mr. Bodine."

The next day, then, these things happened:

Bud Weaver locked his hard hands about a pick handle again.

Willard Breen rode nonchalantly southward and bought El Monte Rancho, thus at last becoming the Moragas' dreaded neighbor.

Ransome Haveril bought a horse from the only man in town with a horse for sale, the man who cared for the stage horses, and rode away with Don Felipe for a week's visit at La Fiesta.

And Jesse Bodine found out what Claude Purcell wanted.

CHAPTER XI

IN THE CARD ROOM AT SHINGLE JOHN'S

After that night when men spoke of Claude Purcell it was more often than not to mention Jesse Bodine, too. It was to say that Purcell and Bodine were here or there together; that they were in a lallapalooza game over at Hang Town; that the two had played in the newest, swankiest gambling palace in San Francisco.

At first it was Claude Purcell and Jesse Bodine. Time rolled by—weeks, months, a full year. Then it was Claude Purcell and Duke Bodine.

Duke Bodine. The name suited him. He dressed the part. Up and down the string of rollicking mining camps and towns, down to the coast as far as Monterey, there was no more carefully dressed man than Duke Bodine. Black suited him; he stuck to it from glossy black boots, long-tailed black coat, trousers sometimes with a faint stripe, sometimes gray, but nearly always black, black flowing tie, a broad-brimmed black hat. He wore a large diamond on the little finger of his left hand. He had paid three thousand dollars for it from the winnings of a poker game in the extravagant city which so short a while ago had been Yerba Buena.

He was even taller now, but at last had come to his full stature, and was still lean and sinewy; quicker of thought and more deliberate of speech than ever. Duke Bodine the gambler. Young men, newcomers to the West, looked at him as he had looked at Claude Purcell at Temlock's Station.

He and Purcell had had a long talk that night after the game at the Silver Mirror; Duke Bodine was the result.

Claude Purcell had said to him over their coffee in Purcell's cabin: "Mr. Bodine, I make it a rule to respect each man's privacy, and I have no desire to enter yours unwelcomed. If I seem to grow too personal at any point, you have but to say the word and I'll draw off."

"Go ahead," said Jesse Bodine.

"I think that already you are fully aware of this fact: Money, in almost limitless quantities, is to be had here in California, and by any man who wants it. And all men do want it. And you have realized that there are two ways to get it. One is to go out into the mines, drag the gold up out of the earth. The other way is to let other men do that—and hand it on to you. In my time I have tried both methods. You know which I have chosen."

When he paused a moment, Jesse Bodine again said his quiet, "Go ahead."

"The gambling fever is always in men's blood," said the gambler. "In the blood of all men to some extent. Here, in California, every man you meet has the betting urge strong upon him. Men go to their mines; they work like mules; they stay sober and keep away from towns; they come in with their gold, and insist immediately on spending wildly and on hitting the gaming tables. Of course all play to win. But most play, even more than that, for the sake of the game. And for the most part, Mr. Bodine, they do many other things far better than they play poker."

A shadowy smile came to the firm line of Jesse Bodine's lips.

"Like me, you mean."

"*Not* like you, I mean. Such men will never learn how to win at poker; they can't. You can." One of his own rare smiles touched his lips and warmed his cold eyes slightly. "I warned you I'd grow personal, remember! Well, then: All you lack is experience. You are a born poker player. You asked why I offered to stake you to a thousand dollars tonight. To have you play with it and lose it, either to me or Hackamore Breen. To have you come to me and let me stake you to another thousand." He shrugged. "I am well heeled, Mr. Bodine; a thousand or ten thousand wouldn't matter. I wanted you to play for bigger stakes, to get the one thing you need—experience. You have more intelligence than most, and poker is not a game of chance. These sums would be tuition you were paying at the right school."

"And then, Mr. Purcell?"

"I'll grow personal about myself. I have a good deal of money; I want a good deal more. I am not going to stay out here all my life; the things I want most are the things the eastern and European cities can give me. I am planning to open up several gambling houses. When I clean up on them I am going to take my winnings and say an eternal farewell to this new, raw land. I am looking for a man like you. Let me assume that I know more about cards than you do; let me pass along to you some of the knowledge I've gleaned; play with me and other men a few times so that I can watch your game. Then come in with me."

To Jesse Bodine came a glow and a thrill and a sense of a high honor done him. Already he had seen in Claude Purcell something of a superman; from now on the gambler was to him a sort of young god.

Literally, he went to school to Claude Purcell. The two were seen together in many far places, were heard of in many big games. Purcell dissected every game after the session, win or lose; his talk had to do not only with the values of hands—the chances of the draw, whether to a pair, two pair, threes or a bob-tailed flush—but with the "styles" of the men they played with. No detail connected with poker playing was too slight to be noted. Before one of these games he said: "You watch Captain Randall; he's one of the biggest players in the country. Watch him without letting him know you are watching. If you ever see him scratch his jaw with his thumbnail, go after him! He'll be bluffing then. He's been doing that for years; he doesn't know it himself." Jesse Bodine remembered and watched and got his chance; with three tens in his own hand he took six thousand dollars away from the captain in a single pot. The captain didn't have the full house that others thought he had; his thumbnail had betrayed him.

Things like that, all sorts of things, Jesse Bodine was taught and told by Claude Purcell. And now he was Duke Bodine, the gambler's stanchest friend and admirer, but, he thought, his own man. A man with a three-thousand-dollar diamond on his little finger, and fifty thousand dollars in a safe place. Duke Bodine, the gambler.

And Duke Bodine, like most men—like Claude Purcell himself, and like Bud Weaver—was counting his present as only a stepping stone to the thing he wanted.

He had his eye on the Lazy Creek Ranch.

The Lazy Creek, the Monte which Hackamore Breen now owned, and the Moraga rancho, La Fiesta, were like three sleeping giants with their heads on one pillow, their monster forms spreading out in different directions. And Duke Bodine had seen the three ranches, a guest of the Moragas at the suggestion of his friend Ransome

Haveril, and had fallen in love for the second time in his life—this time with the Lazy Creek Ranch.

"It's mine," he said in his heart. "It's lying here asleep, waiting for me. And it won't be long."

So the weeks passed and the months, and a full year.

During this time he and Ransome Haveril saw little of each other. Ransome stuck with their claim when Jesse pulled out and went his way with Purcell. The claim continued to disgorge its golden treasure and Ransome began saving; he, too, meant some day to withdraw from the rough mountain country, to live in one of California's "little cities." But first of all, when he should become a man of means, he was going to marry little Juanita Moraga. Twice a month, regularly, he was a welcome visitor at La Fiesta.

Another man than Duke Bodine wanted the Lazy Creek Ranch, and likewise meant to have it, and already accounted that he had his hooks in it; this man was Hackamore Breen. What happened was Breen's doing. It gave Bodine the ranch, came close to bringing Hackamore Breen his death, and made Bodine an enemy. This was the way of it:

Lazy Creek Ranch had been aforetime Las Hermosas, a grant of many indefinite acres extending some twenty odd miles in sprawling length, encompassing two lovely valleys, extending up into mountain ravines, and had belonged to one of the old Spanish-Californians. Along had come one of the gringos, a trickster from the East with holes in his pockets, a smooth tongue in his mouth and rascality in his head, a young man named Frank Brewster. He was plausible, and the Spanish-Californian was a generous and trusting soul. Brewster, in no hurry yet losing little time, accomplished his aim. He married the Spanish-California gentleman's daughter and soon got his hands in the old gentleman's coffers. The ranch was already being robbed right and left by other plausible crooks whom the old Californian trusted; it wasn't long until Brewster had gotten it into very grave difficulties; things went anyhow, bad to worse; and in the end the family was dispersed, the ranch sold for a penny—and Brewster himself turned out to be the owner. That was some ten years ago.

Next, he grew dissatisfied. He had killed the cattle for their hides and tallow or had sold them off; the ranch was falling to pieces; his wife had at long last left him and gone to her mother's people in Monterey; Brewster was nicely trimmed by a cleverer crook than himself. During these ten years the ranch had been idle, deserted. Now he wanted to do what a few more months would force him to do willy-nilly, to get what ready money in hand he could and hie him to newer if not greener pastures. He had heard of Duke Bodine's interest and sent word to him that he was ready to sell and knew that terms could be arranged.

A meeting was arranged. Duke Bodine was in Yellow Jacket when he received the word from Frank Brewster. The message exuded an atmosphere of haste and secrecy. Bodine was to come alone, to meet Brewster that night in the card room which was to be kept private for them at Shingle John's saloon in the little valley town of Shingle. It was near dusk when Bodine got this word and in the first dark he was on horseback, riding south.

Blue night hung over the ranges, and a wind sighed down through the hills; there was the faint, far call of coyotes; save for that, the night was still. And the stars were as golden as the Mother Lode's veins, yellow lamps in the deeps of the sky, shining down on pine and oak studded slopes, and the black cottonwoods in Long Wolf Valley where it wound among the Mañana Hills; where Mañana Creek went spilling along, molten ebony mostly and at times fluid silver, to Mañana Town; and then it became Lazy Creek in lower Lone Wolf, whispering in a slow, lazy bend about dim-lit Shingle. Duke Bodine forded the creek, splashing silver drops and creating meshes of fine spray, and rode through the quiet to Shingle John's.

Shingle John, a gross, sullen man, his hair down to his shoulders, his beard a dark brown mat, was alone in his bar. He had small eyes, inordinately bright, and turned them expectantly on the young man stepping in; Bodine had not removed his big-roweled Mexican spurs, and the clanking of them outside had heralded his entrance. Further, Shingle John knew of his coming and was awaiting it.

"You're Duke Bodine, I take it," he said.

"Is Frank Brewster here?"

"Shore, he's here. Been a-waitin' for you for two hours." He jerked his head toward the rear of the room where there were two doors, both closed. "He's in there." He spat deliberately. "He ain't alone, though." He had a leering sort of grin which made even a stranger want to slap that hairy face of his. "Hackamore Breen's there, too, now. Beat you to it, he did, Bodine."

"Thanks," said Duke Bodine. Rather than ask, he'd try both doors. But while his spurs were clanking down the long empty room he knew which room, for he heard voices. They were angry voices, one Brewster's, one Hackamore Breen's. He heard his own name and knew that they knew who he was, as though the spurs had announced, "Here comes Bodine." His hand was on the latch when he heard the first shot.

He whipped the door open. In a small, lamplit room with the lamp a dull glow like a sickly little moon through a bluish, smoky mist, Frank Brewster was falling backward, and as he toppled, Hackamore Breen poured the second and third shots into his body. Brewster made a strangling sound and melted to the floor as though his bones had turned to water.

It was sheer murder; the murdered man hadn't even pulled his belt gun up out of its leather.

Hackamore Breen whirled, his face evil with rage and hate, and the murder spewing its venom into his soul; the fuller light from the barroom flashed in his eyes. Already with nerves at stretch, quickened to the ultimate within him, he saw the look stamped on Duke Bodine's hardened face. But quick as he was, Bodine was a small fragment of a second quicker. Their two shots rang out like one, yet in less time than a man can register, a bullet can travel such a short distance as lay between them. Hackamore Breen's aim was disturbed and his bullet flew wild as he fell close to where Frank Brewster's dead body lay.

"Well," muttered Shingle John, "you've killed him."

"Any objections?" said Duke Bodine, hard and cold.

"No. That's to say, in a way I h'ain't and then ag'in in a way I have. He had it comin', Hack Breen did; so did Frank Brewster, for that matter, an' it's jest as good both of 'em is dead. But you've shore messed up my place like hell and all."

Duke Bodine holstered his gun and stepped into the card room to stoop over the two fallen men. No more than a glance was needed to tell him that it was all over with the man he had come here to see; Hackamore Breen's second or third bullet had crashed into Frank Brewster's brain, almost dead center between the eyes. As for Breen himself, it was a different matter; he had taken Duke Bodine's shot somewhere in the upper body and might live or might die. Much no doubt would depend on what attention he got. Bodine turned his back on Hackamore Breen's white agonized face and wild eyes and went out of the card room.

Shingle John followed him.

"Look here, Bodine. You got to lend me a hand—"

Duke Bodine went to his horse and sat a moment meditatively still in the saddle. Frank Brewster was dead, so there would be no immediate purchase of the Lazy Creek ranch. There would be heirs of some sort popping up in time to put in their claims; there would be the long, involved court procedure to follow. And so the Lazy Creek, which had seemed to him as good as in his hands a few minutes ago, seemed now far away and out of his reach. Thanks to Hackamore Breen.

What now? Stay overnight in Shingle? He was of a mind to ride elsewhere. It was forty miles or more back to Yellow Jacket—nearer forty-five.

So it would be something like fifteen miles to ride on to the Hacienda de la Fiesta. The Moragas would never turn a traveler from their wide door, no matter the man or the time of night. Further it was likely that Ransome Haveril was at La Fiesta, and Bodine had not seen his old friend for three or four months. That determined him.

Through the silent night he rode for more than two hours, with the good, fertile soil of La Fiesta Rancho underfoot, before he reached the ranch headquarters, itself like a small village. He saw the starlight glint upon the horns of cattle beyond count; more than once his approach put to flight a herd of wild horses. It was well after midnight when he saw the dull red of tile roofs and the lighter shade of sturdy whitewashed walls, looking gray by night. Beyond the main building, across a little tributary of the Mañana Creek, were the barns and corrals, the smaller adobe houses sheltering the army of retainers, Indians for the most part, *vaqueros* and those many hangers-on tolerated by the bounty of the old Spanish-California families. Not a light shone anywhere; the place lay fast asleep under the stars.

He stabled his own horse, then opened the gate in the white wall about the old home and walked quietly along the narrow walk flagged by earthen bottles forced neck down into the ground so that their bottoms made a walk-way, and to the wide oaken door set deep into the three-foot-thick adobe wall. There was a bellpull; he set his hand to it, then hesitated to awaken the sleeping household. Then for the first time he saw a light; someone was carrying a candle from one room to another. He gave the cord a pull and heard the jangle of the bell within doors.

A face looked out of a window; a voice called, "*Quien es?*" Who is it at this time of night, and what do you you want? One question asked, others implied.

It was Señora Moraga, Doña Luisa as everyone called her, wife of the Moraga patriarch, mother of Don Felipe and his angel sister Juanita, and of fourteen other sons and daughters. She was on her way, modest in voluminous black shawl, to the kitchen, to prepare something for Señor Moraga who could not sleep for the terrible agony of a toothache. She welcomed Duke Bodine in with a deprecatory wave of her hand and a maiden's blush for shame at her costume, and hurried away for more suitable dress and to announce the glad news that Señor Bodine was honoring the Moraga home with his presence.

Left alone with the candle in the large main *sala* of the place, with ancestral paintings looking down at him from the whitewashed adobe walls —paintings so well done that they set one wondering about the itinerant artist who must have made them—Duke Bodine did not have long to wait. Don Antonio—that was Señor Moraga—

hastily forgot his toothache, if only briefly, dressed and came to welcome his guest with both hands. Presently his wife returned and renewed her own and reinforced her husband's welcome.

There was a patio and in the patio a staircase which led up to a balcony, and their voices floated out into the patio, up the stairs and to other ears. Here was company! Little Juanita was one of the first to hear and to come wide awake and creep out on the balcony to peep down and listen, and then to scurry for her clothes. She awakened her sister Maria; the two of them brought their oldest sister, Teresa, up on her elbow, demanding sharply if there was a fire somewhere. One by one these and others after them, until the whole household was astir, came down the stairs or from some other part of the house; with the rest were Don Felipe and his *amigo* Ransome Haveril.

Very formally Duke Bodine was presented to those of the flock whom he had not met before. All shook him by the hand, all made him welcome in the sincere way that was theirs; they made him know that they were truly glad that he had come to them. They made a great ring about him, smiling at him, and the girls especially looked at him with big eyes. How handsome he was and how nice, and how beautifully he dressed and carried himself! *Muy caballero*! Even the little angel 'Nita, who was already heels over head in love with his friend Ransome Haveril, regarded him with shining-eyed approval. She, though one of the first to descend the stairway, had taken time to put her long earrings on; she was astonishingly pretty in them, with her lovely little dark face, her wealth of black hair and enormous liquid Spanish eyes.

It remained for Ransome Haveril, when he and Duke Bodine had shaken hands, to ask, "What brings you here this time of night, Jess?"

Both Señor Moraga and his señora spoke up quickly, some words in English when they remembered, more in Spanish, either when they forgot or could not think of the English for it, to offer their guest their hospitality before such a thing was thought of as explanations. Did one need to explain, then, why he came to see them? Juanita and little eighteen-year-old Rosa scampered into an adjoining room, to hurry back with wine and cakes and cigars. You would have thought Duke Bodine was the king come to see them!

A hush filled the room when Bodine had finished telling of the occurrence at Shingle John's. But the silence was but of a shocked moment's duration, shattered swiftly with exclamations. These in turn were stilled by the commanding hand which Don Antonio uplifted. His were troubled eyes.

"Señor," he said gravely to Duke Bodine, "I do not wish any man's death, but for you, for us all, it would be a good thing if that man Breen dies tonight. He has come among us to make trouble; he has made trouble already. If there is any good in that man I do not know what it is. There is much that is bad. If he lives, take care!"

They talked, all together there, for upward of an hour. Bodine learned things of Hackamore Breen which he had not known before. Breen once had come wooing one of the Moraga girls, little laughing, Rosa, only two years older than Juanita. Rosa had laughed at him behind her fan; that had been all at first. Then one day she saw him beating a horse; Hackamore Breen's eyes were like a devil's, his lips were retracted from the white glitter of his bared teeth; for a flash of time he was the incarnation of bestial cruelty released in an orgy of wanton wickedness. The girl had fled, horrified, screaming for someone to come save the poor horse. After that she had never laughed at Hackamore Breen, even behind her fan. She had never let him so much as see her face from that time.

Then Breen had looked toward little Juanita; she, who had heard the story from Rosa's whitened lips, avoided him as she would have shunned a snake. He was persistent; he sought after Maria. He wanted to marry into the Moraga family. Maria would have none of him; she had a way of lifting and shaking her long skirts at the sight of him, of lifting her dimpled chin and drifting away.

Even then, they realized later, Hackamore Breen was trying to acquire some sort of an interest, any sort to begin with, in the big Fiesta Rancho. But the Moragas, though always outwardly courteous, would have none of him. He had grown, they knew, to hate them; as he had punished a horse that had angered him, so would he punish a Moraga.

Now he had bought the adjoining ranch, one of those three vast holdings which lay like giants broadly extended, with their heads resting among the hills as upon a shared pillow; and now already he was making trouble. For there was a grave vagueness concerning boundaries, and La Fiesta and El Monte appeared to overlap; and Hackamore Breen put claim to lands which had always been Moraga lands.

"You see, Señor, these ranchos in the beginning were grants to our first *Californios* from the King of Spain. Freehandedly he gave lands by the running league. How mark them off? Like this, Señor: You put a *vaquero* on a good horse, and he rides three miles or six or ten or twenty, off to the north; and he stops where there is a great rock or tree or some good landmark; and that is one end and corner of the rancho. Then he rides off to the side a league or two or whatever it is that the king has said, and he stops at another landmark, and there you have two corners of the rancho. And he rides again for the third corner, and on back to where he started, and that is the way of it. So it is not strange, is it, Señor, that at times one *vaquero* in his riding has gotten a mile or two out of his way? These are natural mistakes and need make no trouble; they are to be settled over a bottle of wine—by friends. But with a man like Señor Breen? Never!"

At last the family withdrew, leaving the two friends, Bodine and Haveril, together for the private talk they would be sure to want. The two drew their chairs closer together and looked at each other and smiled.

Ransome Haveril clapped his hand down on Bodine's knee.

"Well, Jess! It's a sight for sore eyes, to see you again, old-timer. It sure is! And I hear great things about you! *Duke Bodine,* huh?"

"Tell me about yourself, Ran."

"Doing great, Jess. Yep, me too. Remember the day we first talked about leaving Pleasant Valley and striking out west? That was a great day for us, huh, Jess? Yes, I'm doing fine. Last week I bought the store in Mañana; I'm going to make money hand over fist. And then—"

"Marrying soon, I guess," said Duke Bodine.

Ransome laughed. "Damn it all, Jess, if ever I could just once get that girl alone for two minutes! How the hell can a man ask a girl to marry him when there's always her brother or her sister or her papa or mama or her aunt hanging around?"

It was Duke Boditie's turn to laugh. "I imagine the señorita knows what you want to say anyhow. And I guess you know the answer! Congratulations, Ran."

"Thanks. Maybe you're right. But, look here; there's something else I want to talk about. I was down in Mañana this morning, looking at my new store. A man came in and we got to talking. He was a stranger to me but I've heard of him. Yarcum, his name is, Rance Yarcum, and he used to be a sort of peddler and now he's a pretty slick customer, so they say. And what he told me, Jess, makes me think Hackamore Breen did you a pretty big favor and saved you a heap of money when he killed Frank Brewster—most likely he saved you the trouble of killing Brewster yourself!"

"What are you driving at, Ran?"

"Last night, according to Rance Yarcum, he had a run-in with Brewster, and Brewster sold him the Lazy Creek Ranch!"

Duke Bodine was frowning. "But Brewster sent me word—"

"Brewster was getting ready to leave the country. So he sees a foxy play. He sells the Lazy Creek to Yarcum, sells it cheap, too, but gets the hard money. Then he fixes to meet up with you; he'd have sold it to you, too, for whatever he could get, then flit for somewhere else—and let you and Rance Yarcum figure out who owned the Lazy Creek! I'm dead sure of that, Jess."

"I'll be damned," said Duke Bodine softly. Then the quick lights came back into his dark eyes and that shadowy smile of his drifted across his lips. "Where is this Rance Yarcum now?" he asked.

"Headed straight as a string out to San Francisco. He was pretty glad and gleeful, Yarcum was, over what he'd done, and he felt like telling the world about how smart he was. He has scooped in the Lazy Creek, but not to keep; not Rance Yarcum. He says there's a man in San Francisco he can sell to at a profit in ten minutes after he finds him. And he said, also, that he was going to have a talk with Hackamore Breen about things; he figures that Breen still wants the Lazy Creek, and that if he gets two gents bidding against each other—"

"But he must have known that Breen wasn't in San Francisco?"

"He's knows that Breen's headed there—was, I mean, until you shot him. You see, there's a wench in Hackamore Breen's life; it's common talk around here that he's gone wild-crazy over a song-and-dance girl that's turning things topsy-turvy, and that he can't let her be. You've heard of her, I guess; everybody has. It's the new chief entertainer or what the hell at the Golden Palace. They call her Lady Kate."

Duke Bodine nodded absently. Yes, he had

heard of Lady Kate. As Ransome said, everybody had. New as she was in the young, roistering city, she had struck a note that carried far. But he had nothing to do with Lady Kate. Or so he thought.

Except in so far as she might in any way be connected with Hackamore Breen, and only in case Breen lived and came gunning for trouble. He stood up, took a couple of steps toward the window, stood looking out into the starlit night, then turned to say:

"Thanks, Ransome. I'll be off at daybreak. If I can't overtake this Rance Yarcum of yours on the way, I'll get him in San Francisco. If you'll explain to the Moragas—"

His words were cut off by a pistol shot and the splintering of glass. Both he and Ransome Haveril leaped for cover, then ran to the door. A bullet had come so close to Duke Bodine that his flesh had shivered and he had fancied he felt the wind of its passing against his cheek.

No other shot was fired. Presently they heard running hoofs; the sound was that of a horse down in the shadows by the creek, going fast. They came back and closed the door; no use following with the fugitive so well away.

"I reckon Hackamore Breen ain't dead yet," muttered Ransome. "That was a close call, Jess."

"Breen wouldn't be in any shape to ride after me—"

"Breen has men on his pay roll that do things like that for him, Jess. Better watch out."

Duke Bodine shrugged. Of course he would have to watch out. But already his thoughts were back with Rance Yarcum. San Francisco.

. . . San Francisco. Duke Bodine and Lady Kate.

CHAPTER XII

DUKE BODINE AND LADY KATE

Rance Yarcum proved to be a hard man to locate, and it was not until after more than a month of persistent search that Duke Bodine came up with him. During that time Yarcum's movements seemed erratic; at times Bodine felt as though the man were dodging about just to avoid him. The truth of the matter was that Yarcum had gone straight to San Francisco, looking for the man with whom he thought he might do business; learned that his man had gone "to the mines," indefinite destination; had gone on, looking for him, through Sacramento, to Nevada City, back to Dry Town, to Hang Town, along the string of mining camps as far as Columbia, then again to the young city at the Golden Gate. And there it was at last that Duke Bodine came up with him.

To find a man in the City might have seemed like locating the needle in the hay, for already San Francisco was truly a city, a place of phenomenal growth, young in years but full grown; Duke Bodine found it a glittering Phoenix after its last rising from ash heaps. For a full six times in less than two years it had burned to the ground, only to burgeon again with the rapidity of a field of mushrooms. Like everything else in California, more than most, it was extravagant. In the year of the golden discovery it was a congregation of some twenty-five thousand men living in shacks and sheds, lean-tos and canvas shelters; less than a year later it sheltered, in one way and another, double the number of dwellers. It roared on through those first wild years, piling thousands and thousands and still inrushing thousands and tens of thousands. Houses, so-called, were thrown together in a few hours. They burned like tinder, once a fire started; everything went up in roaring flame, even the sidewalks, since they were made of planks. It burned and was built again; burned and was rebuilt; burned and was rebuilt, over and over. Until at last it was the San Francisco through whose teeming streets Duke Bodine now sought Rance Yarcum. By now there were buildings which men swore no fire could raze, built with brick walls three feet thick, with heavy, double iron doors and windows; and there were edifices of granite fronts; and there were the "palaces" on the hills housing the new country's money princes. And Duke Bodine, going up and down, had informed himself to some extent of his quarry's habits, what hotel he stayed at, what restaurants and bars he favored. So the day after Rance Yarcum's return Bodine found him. Odd, it was, too, the way the thing came about.

It was a chill, foggy night in San Francisco, with

the fog lying in folds above the vague housetops, hanging like curtains down into the streets so that the lights were like dim, uncertain stars. Duke Bodine had drawn near the wide double doors of the Golden Palace, one of the several places where he might come up with his man, when a showy carriage drawn by two ornately harnessed fine black horses pulled up at the edge of the high plank sidewalk, and a woman's voice from the carriage's dark interior called softly to him:

"Mr. Duke Bodine, isn't it?"

He lifted his hat and bowed; he hadn't the faintest idea who it was, even when a head was put out through the door, for all that he saw was an enormous black hat with a sweeping ostrich plume curling down over the brim and brushing a cloaked shoulder; the face, the eyes, the mouth were to be guessed at rather than seen. The voice was hauntingly pleasant, a lovely voice; it belonged, he supposed, along with all the rest of the finery, hat and cloak and glittering equipage, to one of the town's light ladies.

"May I have a word with you, Mr. Bodine?" asked the voice, and he thought that its owner was smiling, and that quick, light laughter lay behind the words.

"Certainly, Ma'am," said Duke Bodine politely, and stepped closer.

He could see her eyes now, large and laughing as he had thought they would be, and could make out her smiling mouth, though none too clearly. He felt sure that he had never seen her before.

"I am Lady Kate," she told him, and he knew that she was watching him shrewdly.

Duke Bodine was not impressed, was not interested. He had heard much of Lady Kate, as had everyone else during the last six months or a year. She was a public property. The sort of woman in a degree that Lola Montez was, he thought. Beautiful, undeniably. Talented. A very clever woman. And as hard as nails. He knew how she had sung and danced in scores of mountain camps, and how men had gone wild over her and had thrown gold at her feet; and how, laughingly, tossing them kisses from her fingertips, she had had a little negro boy, all decked out in gold braid, gather up the spoils and carry it off to her dressing room. She did not even sully her white fingers with it! Men might have been angered; instead, they cheered her and cast more gold. A wealthy woman now, without doubt, despite the extravagant parties which she was always giving some celebrity or another. The mistress of General Bright-Hampden, rumor had it.

So all that Duke Bodine did when she had as much as introduced them to each other with her, "Mr. Duke Bodine, isn't it?" and "I am Lady Kate," was bow again.

She laughed softly; something seemed to amuse her. Then she sat back, the big black hat and sweeping ostrich plume being swallowed up by the carriage's interior, and he thought that it was just some whim of a spoiled beauty that had caused her to address him, and that this was the end of an abortive adventure, when she said from her place of vanishment:

"It is just possible, Mr. Duke Bodine, that I am in a position to do you a small favor. Someone mentioned to me that you were here; people do talk so, don't they? And mentioned also that it was common knowledge that you are looking for a gentleman named Yarcum. Mr. Rance Yarcum, recently owner of the Lazy Creek Ranch over in the Mañana country."

"Yes," he answered. "That's so. Do you mean that you know where he is?"

"If you would care to ride with me?" said Lady Kate. He could make out that she was making room for him, gathering her skirts closer.

"Thank you. This is very kind of you."

He got in.

"Drive on," commanded the lady, and the restless black horses were off at a lively trot.

"You will think me very bold and unmaidenly," said Lady Kate very, very demurely, so demurely that he sensed a mockery which he could not understand.

"Not in the least," he retorted, and strove not to be stiff with her, though he had never had any idea that she was not bold and unmaidenly. One did not get to be a Lady Kate by hiding her blushes in seclusion. "I think you are most kind."

"Will you tell me about yourself, Mr. Duke Bodine? Your reputation makes of you a terribly romantic character, you know. Oh, I have heard such tales of you! I am almost afraid to be alone with you!"

"You are laughing at me all the time, Lady Kate," said Duke Bodine quietly. "Just why, I don't know. That, of course, is your privilege. But, may I ask, where you are taking me? To wherever Rance Yarcum is?"

"You are not afraid that I am kidnaping you, Mr. Duke Bodine?"

He wondered why each time she called him that, Mr. Duke Bodine; and it seemed to him that, ever so slightly, she stressed the "Duke." Was that what she was laughing at, the title men had given him?

He answered her light question lightly:

"Kidnaped by so glorious a lady as your reputation makes you?"

"They tell me that you are the most fortunate— or is it skillful?—gambler in the West; above Claude Purcell, even. Isn't it a lovely ring that you are wearing! I've heard of that, even. I saw it flash there on the sidewalk."

The carriage swayed and lurched with the horses' swift trotting; he felt the gossamery brushing of her gown against his hand. The dark within which he was so intimately enclosed with her was faintly fragrant; he could not tell what perfume she used, but it was as lovely and as feminine as she herself seemed to be; it was like the faint breath of wild flowers in Maytime. There had been a fragrance like that somewhere in his life long ago—in Maytime, in Pleasant Valley.

"Not so fast," Lady Kate called to the driver, and the horses were promptly drawn down to a head-tossing walk. To Mr. Duke Bodine she explained gaily: "It is such a short drive, and why hurry through life's pleasant moments? Although, I must admit I am impatient, too, to arrive. Do you know why, Mr. Duke Bodine? You see how honest I am, quite a simple soul indeed! Well, then! I want to see you in the light. Do you know that people say of you that you are the handsomest man in California?"

He couldn't fathom her. He couldn't even begin to make her out. Was she simply made of mockery? Did she strive to make all men realize that they were fools and that she knew it? Or was mockery merely her mood tonight? She was, he thought, like San Francisco itself, hidden now in its flounces of ocean mist, as mysterious as that.

He was not given to badinage with women, not trained to it. Long ago there had been a girl in his life. She had gone out of it and no other had entered. He had filled the emptiness with his ambitions. But he was a hard man to discomfit, either by man or maid. He bowed toward her, making a slight, graceful gesture with the hat which all this while he had held in his hand.

"I cannot keep up with you, Lady Kate," he told her. "Your wits fly far too fast for mine. You see, I am still concerned with something which you said just now, when you spoke of my ring. Shall we go back to it?" He had drawn it from his finger; she caught a subdued gleam as he extended it toward her. "Will you accept it as a small gift from one who has not words to thank you for your kindness?"

For an instant he hoped that he had upset that perfect poise of hers; he could have sworn that she had, barely in time, smothered a gasp. Then she put out her hand for the ring; he felt her gloved fingers, their touch most daintily light, brush his. She was laughing again, quite gay.

"Lovely!" She lifted her hand for him to watch. "Can you see, in this dark? I am wearing it! It is on my thumb, over my glove. Is it a very lucky ring, Mr. Duke Bodine?"

"It is lucky now, to have you wearing it!"

"Is it my pay for the little kindness I am doing you, taking you to where Mr. Yarcum is?"

"I didn't think of it that way."

"You have friends among the old Spanish-Californians, haven't you? I believe you know the Moragas of La Fiesta quite well? Have you lived with people like them so much that you have acquired their ways? One has but to admire anything they own and, presto, you are begged to accept it as a trifling gift. This ring, now; I know it must be valued at several thousand dollars!"

"To Lady Kate, I know, several thousand dollars is nothing."

"Funny, isn't it, that you and I, though we've heard of each other so much, have never met until now? You have never seen me, even? You have never been interested enough from what you have heard of me to come to hear me sing?"

"I have been very busy," said Duke Bodine. For more than once he had been in some town where she was to appear, and had played poker the night through.

"Too busy for women?"

"That is how it has been," he told her.

She leaned back among her cushions and for a time was very still, secretly still, he thought. There was no sound just now save the click of the horses' hoofs; they had turned into a newly cobbled street. He knew now, or thought that he did, what direction they were taking. Ahead he could barely make out the hill upon which the nobs had created them their abodes, extravagant young palaces such as extravagant young money kings should conceive.

Once he thought that he heard her sigh.

"General Bright-Hampden is a very dear friend of mine," she said abruptly. "He has generously loaned me his house. Just now he is somewhere in South America where he has shipping interests. It is to his house that I am taking you. Several gentlemen are dining with me tonight. Mr. Rance Yarcum is to be one of them."

The horses strained up the hill to a pair of wide iron gates with a lantern at each side. The gates stood open; beyond, Duke Bodine could see the subdued glow of lights outlining the three-storied house. The house door, too, opened at the sound of the carriage's approach; a white-haired negro in livery hastened down the steps to assist Lady Kate to alight.

She caught up her skirts and ran up the steps, calling gaily, "Come on, Mr. Duke Bodine," and had passed into the light of the hall before he reached the threshold. She did not fully turn her head; all that he saw of her face was the curve of her cheek, her enormous black hat with its flaunting white plume obscuring the rest, as, with her skirts still gathered up in her two hands, she said over her shoulder from the first step of the broad, curving staircase, "Caesar will show you into the drawing room."

He knew the sort of thing to expect upon entering the home of General Bright-Hampden. Lady Kate's glistening highheeled French slippers carried her upward upon red Turkey carpet; Bodine, conducted by the mildly pompous negro, set his own fine black boots upon the same

Turkey red; the pictures on the walls were reasonably good and looked down upon him from wide, gilded frames; the lights were brilliant, shining through the pendent prisms of the ceiling clusters; the furnishings were solid mahogany.

Caesar conducted him to an open double door and announced sonorously, "Mr. Duke Bodine, gentlemen!" The first man Duke Bodine recognized in a small group standing about a table, glasses in their hands, was his friend, Claude Purcell.

Purcell greeted him warmly.

"I didn't know you were in town, Duke," he said, his cool tapering fingers shutting down firmly on Bodine's. He didn't evince so much as a flicker of surprise; it not being his custom to betray his thoughts. Another man might have demanded, "You, Bodine! Here at Lady Kate's?" but not Claude Purcell. He simply added, "Know everybody here?"

Duke Bodine glanced at the other faces which had turned at his entrance. He thought that one of them must be Rance Yarcum; he had never seen the man but here was one who fitted the description: A small, wiry, dark man who dressed loudly, was to speak loudly in a moment or two, and who looked shrewd and alert, a peddler of old, a sharp trader always.

"I'm a stranger to everyone here but you, Claude," said Duke Bodine.

"That won't do," said Purcell with his hint of a smile. "Gentlemen! My good friend, Mr. Duke Bodine. He wants to meet you all. Duke, Captain Robert Leigh; he is English and a friend of our absent host, General Bright-Hampden." Captain Leigh, blue eyed and boyish looking, bowed stiffly. "Mr. Bodine, Mr. Rance Yarcum." Duke Bodine had been quite right; it was the small, sharp looking man who ducked his head and stepped briskly forward to offer his hand in a queerly tentative sort of grip. "Mr. Bodine," continued the gambler, "you have heard of Mr. William Coburn, our important mining engineer and owner." Mr. William Coburn, florid and bald and given to an explosive manner of speech, nearly wrung his hand off, very glad indeed to meet Mr. Duke Bodine. Then there remained, "Señor Alfredo Moraga," white-haired, quietly distinguished looking. This Señor Moraga turned out to be a brother of Don Antonio of La Fiesta.

"Mr. Bodine, you've come just at the right minute!" cried the explosive Mr. William Coburn—plain Bill Coburn to a thousand "friends" of all sorts and conditions. He lifted his glass high, slopping out a few drops of the pale bright contents. They were drinking champagne, for as soon as the tall ships came sailing through the Golden Gate, San Francisco became a champagne town—in more senses than one. "Just in time, Mr. Bodine, to drink a toast with us.

Gentlemen, to our absent hostess, who will surely not keep us waiting much longer! To the flower of California, Lady Kate!"

Caesar, the dignified negro, filled Duke Bodine's glass. Bodine joined the rest in the chorus of "Lady Kate!" and their glasses flashed up, tilted and flashed again, and came down emptied.

Presently Duke Bodine and Claude Purcell were slightly withdrawn. Talking together as the small group disintegrated Purcell asked casually, "What good wind blows you this way, Duke?"

"I want a word with Yarcum, Claude. And I'd like it as soon as possible, as I don't know what's ahead for the night, and I'd like to settle something with him before any sort of interruption. How well do you know him?"

"As well as I want to," said Purcell. "I don't like the man. But, I know him well enough to get him in a corner for you to talk with if that's what you want."

"He owns the Lazy Creek Ranch. I'm after it. So is Hackamore Breen."

"The Lazy Creek?" Purcell lifted the thin dark line of his brows; it was as good as a shrug. "I didn't know you were going in for real estate, Duke. Better look San Francisco over, if you are. There's still a chance here to buy a likely property in the morning, sell it in the afternoon and make a fair stake."

"It's not that, Claude. You know I've always

meant to go in for ranching, when things were ripe."

"Like our friend Bud Weaver?" smiled Purcell.

"Not like Bud Weaver, I hope. I'd await another opportunity to talk with Yarcum but for one thing; as I've said, Breen wants the Lazy Creek, and Breen's a friend of Lady Kate's. For all I know he may show up and get the first shot at Rance Yarcum."

"I didn't know that you knew the lady, Duke."

"I don't. I never saw her until tonight. There— Yarcum's looking this way."

Purcell was quick to catch Rance Yarcum's roving eye, and drew him across the room with an almost imperceptible back-tilted gesture of his head.

"Duke wants a word with you, Rance," he said carelessly. "I'll leave you two to your better acquaintance." He moved away to join the captain and Señor Moraga.

"I want the Lazy Creek Ranch, Mr. Yarcum," said Duke Bodine. "I know about what you gave Frank Brewster for it. I'll give you that and ten thousand dollars on top of it."

Yarcum's shrewd face grew shrewder. He pulled at his lower lip, simulating profound meditation.

"There is hardly time to discuss a thing like this tonight," he said after a moment. Measuring the extent of Duke Bodine's interest, that was what he was trying to do. "Tomorrow morning—"

"Now," said Duke Bodine. "A little thing like this doesn't take time. I'm ready to hand you the money now; that'll take one minute. You can jot down a receipt, guaranteeing delivery tomorrow of the deed; that'll take a minute. If we get busy at the same time, it'll be one minute for both."

"Make it an extra fifteen thousand instead of ten—"

"Certainly." Duke Bodine unbuttoned coat and waistcoat, unstrapped a broad money belt, thereby disclosing the weapons he wore underneath it, and stepped to a small table in an alcove. Rance Yarcum goggled at him; his thoughts could have been read by a child: Why in the devil's name hadn't he asked an additional twenty thousand instead of fifteen?

"Look here, Mr. Bodine—"

Duke Bodine turned slowly. His face was as void of expression as was ever Claude Purcell's in a poker game with the ace wild and the blue sky for a ceiling, but in his eyes there was a look that made a man think unpleasantly of unsheathed knives.

"I believe we have just made a trade, Mr. Yarcum?" he said coldly. "You asked your extra fifteen thousand and I said, 'Certainly.' You have a scrap of paper and a pencil, haven't you? If not, I have."

"All right, all right! Well, then, I paid Brewster twenty thousand—"

"You paid Brewster about half that. Brewster sold to you for what he could get in a hurry; next he was going to sell the same place to me for what he could get, but Hackamore Breen killed him first. Personally, I think Breen was a thought hasty in killing him offhand like that. A man should be given a couple of minutes to square himself. Here's twenty-five thousand dollars, Mr. Yarcum."

"Make it thirty thousand—"

"All right. We needn't quibble. Here's thirty thousand."

Yarcum was sweating visibly when he got the few lines down and signed. He took up his money, counted it shrewdly but in haste, and hurried back to the table for more wine.

Duke Bodine stood, the scrap of paper twisting slowly in his fingers, staring out through the window to which he had stepped from the alcove. The fog trailed its ghostly veils about the face of the City; now and then he saw lights which seemed to swim waveringly as they faded and died out; the curve of the bay, its islands and high-masted shipping were lost in the night. He would have seen none of it all had the full moon hung in a clear sky over it. He was seeing the Lazy Creek Ranch as he meant it someday to be. He drew a long breath. "I've been homesick for that sort of thing. It's like coming home."

He was snapped abruptly out of his musings. Caesar at the door of the drawing room was announcing,

"Gentlemen! Mr. Willard Hack'more Breen!"

CHAPTER XIII

THE LADY IN RED

No one here had heard a word of the meeting of Duke Bodine and Willard "Hackamore" Breen at Shingle John's. And that was because Duke Bodine had told no one but the Moragas at La Fiesta, and Ransome Haveril, none of whom had traveled far afield since the happening, and none of them was given to talk involving a friend; and because Hackamore Breen, for his part, had thought best to leave Duke Bodine out of his account of it. There was a dead man to explain, Frank Brewster. The thing to do, Shingle John willingly conniving, was to tell the tale in such way as to keep Hackamore Breen in the clear. Thus: Breen, regaining consciousness, fired a couple of shots from the gun Shingle John obligingly pulled from the dead man's holster, then said, sure, he had killed Brewster, after Brewster had tried to shoot him. Self-defense, and no need for folks to go poking their noses into a private matter already disposed of.

So now, when Hackamore Breen came into the room, and stiffened at first sight of the man who had come so close to killing him there at Shingle John's, and when the several men present saw the way he and Duke Bodine stood stone still, looking at each other and saying never a word, there was a long moment of tension. If either man had so much as moved a finger it is altogether likely, so ready were both for violence, so watchful for it, that in another moment they would have finished in a blaze of gunfire that other argument begun in smoke.

And then Lady Kate made her entrance.

For the first time Duke Bodine saw her clearly and in a bright light. He had known all along that she was beautiful; her loveliness now was a revelation. Briefly she took his breath away. Attired like a princess who was vibrantly young and glorious and daring; she wore a red gown that was like a flame, that was low bodiced over her milk-white breast, that wrapped tight about her slim waist, that flowed about her like a cloud that an ardent sunset had stricken into fire. Her hair was piled high, and there was a sort of coronet of pearls about it. Her mouth was red and laughing and defiant, her eyes were bright with soft laughter, and yet there was a light in them that was not soft. She wore jewels as though someone had dared her and she had snapped up the dare with a vengeance. She had been saying over and over to herself when she chose her dress,

"Red, red, red! A flaming lady for you, Mr. Duke Bodine!"

It was not for nothing that she had sung and

danced before gatherings of all sorts. She paused a second in the frame of the wide doorway, and she willfully dramatized herself. She put her head back and lowered her lids and laughed her welcome, with both bare white arms extended. Her eyes swept the room; none but Lady Kate knew that her gaze was, most of all, for Duke Bodine.

She read the look on his face, for he was at no pains to mask it. She saw a spontaneous, leaping admiration; she knew that, if for but a fraction of a second, he had stopped breathing. She had wondered. Would there be recognition? There was none. Never in his life had his thoughts been further away from little Kitty Haveril than they were at this moment. He saw in Lady Kate of California nothing at all of the Wild Rose of Pleasant Valley.

And yet, "She looks so young!" was the thought that came, after the first impact of her loveliness, to Duke Bodine.

First of all she put both slim white hands out to Hackamore Breen and gave him a smile which, though all were free to see, was warmly intimate, for him alone, somehow a secret smile. Instantly Duke Bodine remembered: Some said that the heartless Lady Kate had had a heart after all and that she had given in to Hackamore Breen. At any rate she singled him out now, if for but long enough for the embrace of a smile and the clasping of hands, and Breen's still rigidity vanished instantly. She said warmly:

"Willard! It's nice seeing you. I heard of—of your accident. You are all right now though!"

Hackamore Breen reddened. Duke Bodine would be hearing that! And for the moment, gone too swiftly for him to avail himself of it, he was at a disadvantage, not finding the right thing to say, saying nothing. Lady Kate looked curiously at him, then passed on to her other guests. They came forward to take her hand, to kiss it, some of them; Purcell kissed it, Captain Leigh certainly bent low over it and may have brushed it with his slight mustache. Señor Moraga kissed it ardently while he pressed his left hand to his heart.

Lady Kate turned smiling to Duke Bodine last of all.

"Hello, Duke," was what she said. "My, but you're looking fine. Such a long time since I've seen you! California does agree with you, doesn't it?" She gave him her hand and he held it in his, loosely clasped, very still. She laughed softly and exclaimed, "I do believe your eyelashes have grown longer! Why, Duke, they're like a girl's."

He kept his silence. If his heart leaped, then stood still, no one of them knew. If as swiftly and as vividly as a flash of summer lightning there came to him a memory like a picture—Pleasant Valley, Maytime, a girl—only Duke Bodine knew.

He relinquished her hand and stepped back and looked at her, unsmiling.

"You have changed, too," was all that he said.

If she was disappointed, if she was hurt, if somehow the fun had gone out of the thing or if she did not care, she gave no sign of any kind.

"Yes, we have both changed," she said, and turned to the others.

Yes, they had both changed, neither knew how much until each saw the change in the other. Each in his own way, they had grown hard.

"You two have known each other then?" exclaimed young Captain Leigh, and perhaps scented romance; he was, in his fashion, a romantic young man. "I mean somewhere else— far away, maybe, and long ago!"

Yes, Captain Leigh, very far away, very long ago. . . .

Caesar, parting the heavy portieres of the doorway at the far end of the drawing room, announced:

"Dinner is served, Miss Ladykate."

Lady Kate took Señor Moraga's arm and led the way.

At the table, gaiety was forced and spurious; it hid like a shy thing, and for a time not even frothing glasses could bring it forth. Duke Bodine and Hackamore Breen faced each other directly, Duke Bodine on Lady Kate's right, Breen on her left. Why she had placed them thus only Lady

Kate could tell, and even her motives may have been clouded. Perhaps she meant to tease one of them, or both. It could have been that she, who had experienced so manifoldly since the old Pleasant Valley days, wanted to see how this fresh experience would affect her, to sit between a man whom she had once loved and a man whom she loved now. But one thing she did not know, and it could either have enhanced the situation or made it impossible, and that was that the two only a little more than a month ago had done their earnest best to kill each other.

But she, like the rest, felt the tenseness of the moment and, without understanding it, did her best to cope with it. With the years and the varied experiences they had brought her, she had become a very clever young woman and had adroitly used men as stepping-stones.

And, after the first brief spell of uncertainty, all her guests lent her their aid. No longer did Duke Bodine and Hackamore Breen glare at each other.

It was Breen himself who caught up the tempo from Lady Kate and salvaged the dinner hour from becoming the gloomy affair it threatened to be, Willard Breen, not the Hackamore Breen that Duke Bodine had known. For of a sudden Breen showed the other that side of him which, it would seem, he had saved for what he judged "polite society." He spoke well, when he gave his mind to it; he was not devoid of a certain amount of easy culture nor without that indefinite quality called charm. A natural ruggedness melted when he smiled as he did now at their hostess, and he became almost suave. Very skillfully he set himself the happy task of coming to Lady Kate's aid; once he even said pleasantly, "Am I right, Mr. Bodine?" and transferred his smile to the man he so thoroughly hated, and received Duke Bodine's nod and affably spoken affirmative. And from Lady Kate he received a glance of gratitude and perhaps—so at least Duke Bodine suspected—the soft pressure of her hand under the table.

And so, after the bad start, everything galloped along splendidly and an excellent meal was done full justice to, and General Bright-Hampden's champagne flowed freely and to excellent advantage. Laughter was going around and a glow of well-being had quite dissipated the earlier chill when Lady Kate stood up.

"Please, gentlemen!" she cried at them. "You must sit down again and finish your wine. Now! I can tell just what you are all about to say! You know that I have to run now, because I am to sing at the Golden Palace, and you are all going to escort me there! No, you are going to wait here for me until I come back. Most of you know your way to the General's card room, don't you? And I know that wherever Mr. Purcell and Mr. Duke Bodine are, a poker game isn't far off! And I seem to have heard rumors of Mr. Bill Coburn winning an enormous pot at Dry Town on a bob-tailed straight! I don't know so well about Captain Leigh, but a Spanish gentleman like Señor Moraga is always willing, like the Barkis that Mr. Dickens tells us about! And you, Willard?" She looked smilingly at Breen.

"But you must permit us to hear you sing tonight, Señorita!" exclaimed Señor Moraga.

Lady Kate laughed and blew him a kiss from her fingertips.

"When I come back, then. I will sing for you alone, Señor!"

"Kate—" said Breen, and started toward her.

"No, Willard, not this time. Please." Then her eyes drifted, low-lidded, lazy, to Duke Bodine. "I am going to ask Mr. Duke Bodine to escort me. Will you, Duke? And at the same time promise you'll return here immediately to these other gentlemen?"

Duke Bodine's eyes were narrowed, too, as he and she looked at each other. After a moment he bowed and stepped to her side, offering his arm.

She waved gaily to those watching them go, and she and Duke Bodine passed through the drawing room and into the hall where a little negress in a starched white cap and apron was ready with Lady Kate's hat and cloak and gloves. Then the two passed out through the front door held open by Caesar. The carriage was at the steps; Duke Bodine helped her in, then went around to the other side and got in to sit beside her. The driver cracked his whip and they were off.

Duke Bodine could scarcely see her now in the dark, but could not but be intensely aware of her nearness; again that tender fragrance like Maytime in Pleasant Valley was around them; he felt the lacy brushing of her sleeve against the back of his hand, as light and gossamery as a wisp of San Francisco mist.

He heard her sigh as she settled back. Neither of them said anything. The horses' hoofs clacked merrily, and there was the grind of the carriage wheels.

He heard her sigh again; she had stirred restlessly.

"Always so silent, Mr. Duke Bodine?"

"I don't know what to say," he answered her, his voice flat and toneless, carrying no message of its own.

"I was thinking of something funny," said Lady Kate, a soft chuckle in her voice. "When you started west that time, do you remember I said that you'd be coming back sometime in style— with a coach and six white horses, or something? And when we meet again, it is I who appear in the carriage!"

"Yes, I remember. It's a memory as of another world, another life."

"You haven't turned out to be a great talker, have you?"

"No. I haven't even thanked you properly for tonight. Taking me where Yarcum was, I mean. It meant a great deal to me. You see, for a long time I've had my eye on the Lazy Creek Ranch. Yarcum beat me to it a while back. Thanks to you, it's mine now."

"The Lazy Creek! I've heard of it. It's near La Fiesta and El Monte, isn't it? I'm sure Willard has mentioned it to me. Why, he was after it himself at one time!"

"Yes."

"And he still does want it?"

"It's mine now," Duke Bodine told her the second time. "If I knew how I'd thank you properly."

"Oh!"

They fell silent again. Duke Bodine listened to the sound of the horses' hoofs and the grind of wheels, and looked through the night toward the city below and the bay beyond; a little wind was blowing, the fog had thinned, some scattered stars gleamed through. He felt queerly disturbed, and of a sudden the world seemed a queer sort of place and not altogether real; uncertain and unstable, not altogether profitable. He was not at the moment conscious of any regrets, of any desires; even it seemed of slight importance that now the Lazy Creek Ranch was his. It was a piece of the whole setup, uncertain and unstable and not particularly real, not greatly worth while.

Nor was the girl beside him altogether an earthly reality. Darkness and silence had engulfed her. If he should put out his hand to touch her, would she prove to be as insubstantial as the wreaths and flounces of mist?

"I have heard much of you," she said quietly after a time, "you and Claude Purcell. I haven't heard anyone speak of Ransome. Do you know where he is? Do you still see him?"

"Yes. We have remained friends. I expect to see him in a few days. He is at the Moraga hacienda, La Fiesta."

"You will tell him you have seen me?"

"Don't you want me to?"

"I am shrugging my shoulders, but you can't see, can you? My big brother Ransome, that I used to be so proud of, used to worship so! Then one day he just—just went away. You went your way and Ransome went with you, and in my turn I went my way—I'm just shrugging, Duke Bodine."

Duke Bodine got to thinking gropingly of that Maytime of a long ago, of a day when a boy and girl and bickering Buckeye Creek had the world to themselves, when the boy dared think of kissing the girl, but dared no further. What was it that he had had in his heart to say to her? "You're just like a wild rose, Kitty." And a cold wind had come blowing through the trees and the skies had thickened to a black storm, and they had fled to a sort of cave in the creek's bank. Maytime fancies were blackened by murder, gone with the blotted-out blue sky. A man had murdered for a small buckskin pouch of gold dust and had kicked his life out in death's dance at the end of a rope. And for a time young Jesse Bodine had been lost in a maze; he had harbored a dream then of which he had told no one. It was not of a golden coach and six white horses, but of someday owning his own lands, vaster than all he could see from a high place on the rim of Pleasant Valley. And there was to be a noble house on a wooded knoll—and a girl like a wild rose . . . And next? A thin, fine golden chain and a pendent locket, discarded, winking in the sun.

. . . With narrowed eyes he watched the way of the wind with the thinning wisps of fog. He thought of ashes being wind-blown.

To Lady Kate he said: "We're almost there. You asked me to promise to go back to the house on the hill. I'm not sure that I care to do that. My business with Yarcum is done for tonight."

"There is always poker," she reminded him crisply.

"Yes. There is always poker."

"It's a small thing. Yes, still shrugging! But you promised."

"All right."

"Ransome Haveril hasn't fallen in with thieves too, has he?"

"Thieves?"

"Men like Claude Purcell. Crooked gamblers."

"Claude Purcell is my friend. He is as honest, as square-dealing a man as any I've ever known."

"An honest gambler!" She laughed her scorn at that. "Water that is not wet; a light that sheds darkness; a snake that walks upright on its tail! Honest gambler! You fool! Or are you only a fool, and nothing worse?"

"There is nothing worse," said Duke Bodine, very cool. Her sudden flash of heat had startled him; he couldn't understand it; he could only strive to ignore it. He had thought to let it go at that with his close-clipped, "There is nothing worse than a fool." But he added after a pause, and therefore was the more deliberate, "Unless it be a man like Hackamore Breen."

"Willard Breen is a very dear friend of mine," she said hotly, and he knew that she was glad to be done with repression; he sensed, too, that there was some sort of turmoil within her and that she was not a girl given to throttling every emotion.

He answered her in a coldly impersonal way; he said:

"So I gather. That's why I warned you."

"So it's a warning then? Thank you, Mr. Duke Bodine, I don't need it. Furthermore it's a slander. Willard is fine; yes, fine is the word. Maybe you have heard that I am to marry him?"

"He is a damned scoundrel," said Duke Bodine, very cool.

"Perhaps you don't understand when I use the word *fine!* He wouldn't stab a man in the back!"

"Ah, that's just what he would do! That's the sort Hackamore Breen is. Anyhow I've told you."

"Oh!" The ejaculation was like the flicker of flame. Then Lady Kate gathered her skirts about her; the carriage was coming to a stop in front of the Golden Palace. Duke Bodine stepped down and offered to help her, but she brushed his hand aside. A small crowd gathered at the door of the Palace lifted hats and clapped hands; she bowed and smiled and passed inside. Duke Bodine stepped back into the carriage and, a man to keep a promise, was returned to the house on the hill.

CHAPTER XIV

DEATH SITS AT THE CARD TABLE

Caesar escorted him to the General's card room which had already been made invitational with cards and bottles and glasses. Chairs were set and some of the gentlemen had already removed their coats and rolled up their sleeves. Duke Bodine nodded when Bill Coburn asked whether he wanted to be dealt in, and the game began.

There were six men playing, Duke Bodine, Claude Purcell, Captain Leigh, Bill Coburn, Señor Moraga and Hackamore Breen. Already, having been eager to escape, Rance Yarcum had taken his departure. It could have been that he wasn't altogether comfortable in the presence of Duke Bodine and Hackamore Breen at the same time.

At the outset the same sort of tenseness dominated the atmosphere that had prevailed at the beginning of Lady Kate's dinner. Again Duke Bodine and Hackamore Breen, dispensing with pretence, clashed even in an angry silence; when at times their eyes met they were cold with hatred that was like a frozen fury which would thaw at the first flash of fire. Now instead of using steel they thrust at each other venomously with every hand of cards that made a thrust possible. So much was obvious immediately.

Then there was another factor which lent its force toward a further tightening of nerves, though this manifested itself later on. Bill Coburn, massive and florid, was as outspoken a man ordinarily as his appearance led one to expect, and Bill Coburn at no time was at any particular pains to conceal the fact that he equally disliked and distrusted the gambler Claude Purcell. Altogether it would have been a hard matter to think of these several men sitting over a game together in any outer semblance of amity were it not for some such condition as obtained tonight: They were all here as guests of the colorful Lady Kate, and not one of them meant to budge until she came back.

Well, whenever trouble is in the offing it would appear that an impish fate is quick to do its part and chip in with further irritants. Thus, at the round table Señor Moraga waved Caesar away with his wine bucket, and demanded brandy.

"With a fair lady present," said Señor Moraga in his mother tongue, "it is different, and wine is to be taken to toast all loveliness; I never knew the time, *Caballeros*, even when I was a young man around the town, that we ever drank brandy out of a lady's slipper! Horrible to think of, no? But at man's work or man's play, a man's drink! *Salud y pesatas, Caballeros!*"

Health and wealth! A fine toast for a poker

game. Coburn approved the brandy idea; so did Hackamore Breen. Claude Purcell never drank at all, and Duke Bodine drank but sparingly. Captain Leigh, a sentimental look in his eyes, stuck to wine. Bill Coburn, a good drinker, had already during the early evening taken as much as would do most men for the twenty-four hours, and his color was high, the stain of a flush running up his high forehead to spread pinkly over his baldness. And Hackamore Breen was already hot with anger. These facts fate had added gratuitously.

Captain Leigh didn't last long. He was not the seasoned poker player the others were; he hadn't been in California long and didn't realize how big the stakes such men as these were bound to be playing for soon, and had only a couple of hundred dollars on him; he was a fine, likable chap and a dead-game sport, but inexperienced. Slightly embarrassed, on withdrawing, cleaned out, he was obviously of a half mind to apologize for having bothered them.

"Sit down, my boy, sit down and watch the game!" boomed Bill Coburn heartily.

"I don't like an outsider looking on," said Hackamore Breen at his surliest.

"Oh, shut up, you," Coburn snorted. "Let Leigh do as he damn well pleases. I'll tell you, Leigh! Go in yonder to the piano! Give us some music and those rousing old songs of yours! How about 'The Roast Beef of Old England'? And, on the table in there, there's a stack of newspapers that came in from Boston only last week." He chuckled and peeked slyly at his cards. "We won't keep you waiting long; I'll clean up here in short order."

Captain Leigh did stroll away to the piano, and for a little while gave them music—no rousing British ballads, as Bill Coburn had suggested, but music like moonlight on rippling waters.

. . . There was a sizable jack pot which no one could open. They sweetened it all round and drew new cards. Hackamore Breen, under the gun, passed. Moraga, next, passed. Bill Coburn opened; Purcell boosted him; Duke Bodine saw Purcell's bet; and this time Hackamore Breen came in and raised Purcell's boost. Swiftly the pot grew fat.

Moraga withdrew, muttering soft Spanish oaths; Coburn slammed down his cards, Purcell withdrew. And with a pot of over fifteen hundred dollars between them Duke Bodine and Hackamore Breen unsheathed their knives.

Breen had called for three cards; Bodine had called for three. Bodine had gone in with a pair of jacks and had drawn the other pair; four jacks with five men playing. He raised Breen and Breen raised him back.

Poker would not be poker but only pure mathematics wedded to psychology were it not that in poker, as if life, pretty nearly anything can happen. Duke Bodine went out on a limb with his four jacks. Just the same, and before the limb broke altogether under his weight, a sense of being wrong warned him; he did not know why he began to entertain doubts; perhaps it had been the twitch of a muscle in Breen's face or a gleam in his eye, or something else. At any rate he called Breen, and Breen put down four queens and raked in the pot.

Neither man said anything; at first Duke Bodine did not feel anything. It was just a pot lost, that was all, an old, old experience. But Hackamore Breen had a trick of jeering at a man, without using words, and could sneer without lifting a lip. He could make a man feel an unspoken insult like a whiplash across the cheek.

The game went on with Duke Bodine dead set to pull Breen down. Bill Coburn shook a couple of kinks out of his tongue; he had gotten where he didn't give a tinker's dam what he said or who heard it or what the hearer chose to make of it.

"Damn you, Purcell," he said once when Purcell had won from him pretty heavily, and, on Purcell's deal: "I don't know why the hell I play with you. A man ought to know better than taking chances with a professional gambler."

Claude Purcell, used to things like that, was unruffled and let the remark pass. Again Hackamore Breen held his peace, as far as words went, but that damned sneer of his again spoke for him. And when, shortly after, Claude Purcell raked in another big pot, Breen asked with stressed innocence—as though he had forgotten!—

"Who dealt that mess anyhow?"

Purcell had dealt.

Duke Bodine did not turn his head to look at his friend but watched him out of the corner of his eyes, from under those lowered, long-lashed lids of his.

Claude Purcell's expression, or lack of it, was unaffected; he did not speak.

The game went on. They had been playing a couple of hours. Señor Moraga played with finesse and acumen, but was inherently reckless. For a time he did well and ran ahead of the game. But he underestimated Bill Coburn, who by this time gave the impression of being deep in his cups, and unwary; Coburn, craftier than he looked, took the old gentleman down the slide for over a thousand dollars. Señor Moraga sighed and curled his white mustaches and poured himself another small brandy. But the twinkle never left his eye.

There came a hand which seriously engaged Duke Bodine and Purcell and Breen and Bill Coburn. The cards were running high; Bodine and Breen each had called for three cards, Purcell and Coburn two. Purcell was in with a couple of hundred dollars when he decided that he did not like the look of things. Breen had raised, Coburn had come in—and Purcell put his hand down, rose and said, "Deal me out the next hand."

Caesar long ago had departed to wherever it was that Caesar betook himself at this time of night and this stage of a game, and Purcell wandered away for a cigar and stopped for a word or two with Captain Leigh who, in the front room, was looking out a window at the lights of the City and at a glittering bay from which the wind had swept all fog.

"Damn that Purcell," growled Coburn apropos of nothing in particular.

Duke Bodine boosted the pot. Hackamore Breen, glowering over his cards, took his time. Then he came in and shoved another ten dollars along, on top of Bodine's and, sitting back, said:

"You know what these gamblers are, Bill."

Coburn made his bet, covering Breen's and sweetening the pot fifty dollars. Then he said, "Huh, Hackamore?" as though he hadn't heard. And Breen, still with that intangible sneer of his, still whipping the man he hated, over Purcell's back, said measuredly:

"Hell, we all know Purcell's as crooked as a broken stick in a puddle of dirty water."

Duke Bodine came in. He boosted Coburn a hundred dollars. And then they went to it hammer and tongs, the three of them out for blood. Before they were done, it was the best pot of the evening.

And Duke Bodine dragged it in with a straight flush.

Then he looked up from the table, straight into Hackamore Breen's cold, angry eyes.

"You're a liar, Breen," he said.

"Gentlemen! Gentlemen!" shouted Señor Moraga, a note of horror in his voice. "Think what you would do! Remember we are here tonight the guests of a lady—*Jesus, Maria y José*!"

Both Duke Bodine and Hackamore Breen sat very still in their chairs. Bill Coburn moved softly, shoving his chair back soundlessly and sliding out of it and stepping nimbly aside. For it seemed to Bill Coburn that he could already smell powder smoke, and he had no desire to stop any wild bullets.

And there sat Duke Bodine and Hackamore Breen with only the small round table between them, their hands in full sight with the cards they had just played, their bodies rigid, with never a muscle twitching, their eyes like cold, polished gems in their deadly stare. It was one of those dynamic moments when a man knew that if he so much as moved a finger it behooved him to move with the ultimate degree of precision and rapidity.

Suddenly the room was profoundly still; it was as though the place fairly reeked with silence.

There was a tall grandfather's clock standing at the side of the door through which Claude Purcell had just now passed for his cigar and a word with Captain Leigh; not a man of them had so much as noticed it until now, and now not a man could have escaped awareness of it. For through the hush came its steady and measured tick-tock, tick-tock, tick-tock, and the sound seemed to grow louder and clearer, more distinct and emphatic; it was like the beat of a measured tread, like the slow march of fate. It was like what in reality it was—the grim and relentless and never-staying counting-off of the seconds of a man's life. Though every clock in the world since the first was conceived has made it its cold, casual and calculating business to announce the steady onward march of Death for all things, itself included, still it has at the same time proclaimed joyous tidings—young lovers, eager for each other's arms, men awaiting a sure good fortune, have heard its assurance that the golden moment was approaching, be it near or far. This clock was different now. It was saying the one thing only: "One of you men, maybe more than one, who hears this tick-tock, tick-tock, tick-tock, will be here in full sight of me presently, and won't hear anything or see anything or know anything, because he will be dead."

At long last Hackamore Breen's lips twitched into his habitual sneer, and he spoke. His hands remained where they were, very still on the table.

"Were you talking to me, Bodine?" was what he said.

All knew that he knew without asking.

He had heard the clock.

"Yes," said Duke Bodine.

He knew what Hackamore Breen was about. The man was as deadly as a rattlesnake, but just now as wary as a cat walking a limb above a pack of hounds. Breen was simply sparring for time; he must have been thinking that if his hand flashed ever so swiftly to his gun there would almost instantly be two dead men, not just one, sitting at the card table.

Claude Purcell, Captain Leigh close at his heels, had come to stand in the open doorway; Duke Bodine, without shifting his eyes from Hackamore Breen's darkly flushed face, could see the two of them clearly reflected in a large mirror on the wall.

Purcell spoke coolly.

"I think I heard my name," he said.

"Damn it!" exploded Bill Coburn. "Let's go slow here, boys! Lady Kate's apt to be back any minute now; we don't want the damn place a shambles when she gets here!"

Captain Leigh, looking troubled, exclaimed: "Both Mr. Purcell and I heard what was said, and it's one of those things that can't be left hanging in mid-air. I, for one, took it that we were all gentlemen playing together here." He was looking curiously at Claude Purcell. Then he transferred that bright stare of his to Señor Moraga. "You,

Señor," he said, "have heard what both Mr. Coburn and Mr. Breen said. You, I understand, have known Mr. Purcell well and long."

Señor Moraga surprised them all then. He drew himself stiffly erect and said very distinctly without raising his voice unduly:

"Yes. I played tonight with the others simply because, as one of a lady's guests, I stifled my own personal feelings rather than risk offending her." He gave them a high Spanish shrug; his eyes were cold and bright and contemptuous. "I have long known Mr. Purcell for what he is, no gentleman but a cheat at cards and—"

His words were the last he was ever to speak. They were like shears cutting the tension of restraint and releasing destruction snipping the thin thread of his own life. Claude Purcell, without a word, whipped forward his right hand from behind his back and shot Moraga square between the eyes. The shot licked out with the deadly quickness of a rapier's flash, and equally swift were the actions which followed it.

Hackamore Breen thought to have his chance made to his hand and moved with a swiftness akin to Purcell's, throwing himself sideways in his chair, snatching his gun up out of the leather holding it so loosely, firing across the table, the three movements welded into one. But again he had to do with a man keener and quicker and steelier-nerved than himself. His shot and Duke

Bodine's rang out while what seemed a whole fusillade thundered through the room, and Hackamore Breen spilled to the floor while Duke Bodine, with no worse than a bullet hole through his sleeve and a burn along his forearm, sprang to his feet.

He leaped up and whirled in time to see what was happening. Moraga, falling, was just striking the floor. Bill Coburn, shouting wrathfully, did his best to kill Claude Purcell and would have succeeded save for the gambler's cool brain and ruthlessness. In a flash Purcell leaped to the side of the door and, passing, shoved Captain Leigh between himself and the menace of Bill Coburn's smoking weapon. Purcell vanished from sight and Captain Leigh staggered a few wild steps, then sat down on the floor, shot by Bill Coburn.

"Leigh! Leigh!" said Coburn. "My God, man! I—"

Captain Leigh wasn't listening, wasn't looking at him. He had turned the other way, and saw Claude Purcell across the drawing room, about to be gone for good. Leigh called after him.

"You—Purcell!"

Purcell glanced over his shoulder and would have run out into the hall. But Captain Leigh, still sitting, had managed to get his own pistol into his hand. He lifted it, calling his warning:

"Purcell! For killing Moraga—"

His weapon finished the sentence for him. When in another second Claude Purcell would have been safe away, Leigh's first and only shot brought him down. An amazing play of expression at last came to the gambler's face; Duke Bodine, running to him and stooping over him, saw it. Surprise, bewilderment even—then a flash of terror.

"Mr. Purcell!" Duke knelt beside him and partly lifted him from the floor.

"He has killed me. I—I am dying."

"Those things they said about you—I know they were all lies!"

"You fool!" said the gambler, and in that look of his, at last so freely expressive, along with fear now was the final jeer of contempt.

Then Lady Kate came running in.

CHAPTER XV

AT LAZY CREEK

Lady Kate's face was as white as death, her eyes were enormous with horror. She saw Claude Purcell die. Duke Bodine stood up, and she stared at him speechlessly and saw that his face was frozen; it told her nothing.

Neither of them spoke for a long while; then he said tonelessly:

"You had better not come in, Kate."

But she pushed by him and hurried to where Captain Leigh sat propped against a wall. His hand was pressed against his side and his fingers were red; the pistol on the floor close to his knee still sent up a thin, grayish-blue wisp of smoke. Smoke hung in the air, the scent of it acrid and sharp in their nostrils.

Captain Leigh, a very gallant gentleman, tried to say something to her; tried to let her know that he, for one, was ashamed that in her absence they had behaved themselves so that a thing like this had happened.

Then Lady Kate, already numbed with horror, saw Señor Moraga lying on his back, unmistakably dead. And she saw Hackamore Breen; he was trying to pull himself up, trying to get his gun again.

Bill Coburn, hurrying to Leigh, went out of his way so far as to kick the fallen weapon across the room and out of Breen's reach.

"Damn it, man," he said thickly, "we've had enough of this."

At last the girl found her voice, but even then she could scarcely speak. She went swiftly to Hackamore Breen and put her arms about him, thus helping him up into his chair again, and said weakly:

"Willard! Willard! Who did this to you? Dear God in Heaven—"

She did not need to be told. Already she knew; she sensed a part of the story even before she saw how Hackamore Breen's baleful eyes turned to Duke Bodine.

"You did this, Jesse Bodine!" she cried out, her voice clear and bright with anger.

Bodine didn't answer her. He stared at her a long, still moment, then went to the table where just now they had been playing cards. Her mouth came a little open; there was a pinched look about her nostrils; her brows flattened down into a straight line over her eyes as she watched him. Coolly he was gathering up the money that was his, pocketing it. Then he turned from her and Hackamore Breen, and went to Bill Coburn bending over Leigh.

"We'd best get him to a bed somewhere, Coburn, right away," he was saying. "Then I'll go scare up a doctor."

"I shot him, Bodine," Coburn muttered. "It was that damned Purcell; he shoved Leigh right into it."

"Purcell is dead," said Bodine. "So is Señor Moraga. Help me with Captain Leigh. We'd best hurry, too, I tell you."

Within five minutes he was on his way down the hill to find a doctor and others to do what needed to be done. He did not return to the house on the hill. Instead, within the hour he was on his horse and riding out of town. He wanted as he had never wanted before to be alone. Well, there was the Lazy Creek Ranch awaiting him.

And to Lazy Creek Ranch he came in the bright morning of the third day. He gave La Fiesta a wide berth, not yet ready for any human companionship, not ready, certainly, to see Ransome Haveril and to have to speak of that Lady Kate of whom they had heard so many tales. Lady Kate of today—little Kitty Haveril of long and long ago.

The world lay quiet about him, a deep-breathing, smiling, peaceful world. The gentle throb of dove notes came to him through the silence, and the valley quail marched in front of him along a broad, cattle-made trail, and he saw deer feeding. Cattle were fat and sleek in the valleys; wild horses tossed their manes and watched him. He came to the creek winding lazily over silver-gray sands and stones, with bending willows on the banks whipping idly in the drift of the current, and he nooned in the shade. The world lay close to his heart that day, and all striving seemed far away, like some restless sea shut from sight and hearing by vast distances.

For upward of ten years the ranch—his ranch— had been untenanted; the stock he saw bore the brands of either La Fiesta or of El Monte. When he reached the ranch headquarters it was to come to a place of utter desertion and largely of ruin. There were the two barns, gray and crooked, with shake roofs sagging like broken-down, sway-backed horses; there was the old adobe home, on a slight knoll above the creek, whose walls in places had already begun to dissolve under the beat of rains and the blast of winds, disintegrating wherever the start of decay had come with broken tiles. Once there had been a flower garden; the earthen walls still stood about it, tile-crowned, and there were a few desolate pear trees, a gnarled olive or two, here and there a straggling, unkempt Spanish rose.

He moved quietly through the big one-storied house which no longer than a decade ago had been home to a family as large as that of the Moragas of La Fiesta. Some floors were of hard-packed earth, others of rough-hewn planks of various widths and thicknesses, and the plank floors sagged in many places. Some windows were broken; at some of them old faded curtains still hung in dreary tatters. Most of the furnishings had departed long ago. either hauled away by the departing family or taken freely by others who had had occasion for them; but there remained sturdy, homemade benches hewn from oak, some of them rudely carved, and a sprinkling of other things—table, bed, discarded leather trunk or cumbersome chest—just enough of that sort of thing to make the place reek with desertion.

He had brought with him a sack of provisions slung across his horse's back behind the saddle, and bivouacked in a large sunny room with a long-vistaed view down the valley—his valley—and a deep, black fireplace for night light and all the company he wanted. And thus began for him a period of time, all too brief, of a splendid isolation. With all his heart and soul, with the very fiber of his physical being, he craved aloneness.

For he had come here like a wounded wolf to its lair, like a stricken eagle to its aloof pinnacle. More had happened to him inwardly at that house on San Francisco's hill that night than he had then realized. Long he had made a sort of god of the handsome Claude Purcell, and he knew now that Purcell had tricked him as he had tricked so many another man until his slippery trail had snaked about him in such fashion as to ensnare his wary feet. "You fool!" had been the gambler's last words to him, along with the undying contempt of a dying man, and fool he had been. He had seen, though in the mirror, how Claude Purcell had murdered Señor Moraga, how he had thrust the gallant Captain Leigh into the pathway of Coburn's spray of bullets, how then he had sought to escape, leaving his *friend* to do what he could for himself. His friend who had taken up his quarrel; who had named Hackamore Breen liar for Purcell's sake. Once he had overheard a man say, "Claude Purcell and Duke Bodine, two of a kind," and had been flattered. Men would go on saying it.

The props had been rudely and ruthlessly knocked out from under his high and shining pride, and he was sick at heart.

And then there was Lady Kate.

He felt dirty. He went down to the creek and stripped and dived deep in a green, shady pool—and saw his body begin to look clean and white again. It was a glorious experience to swim. He remembered how Ransome had taught him.

For a time, alone there in the old abandoned home on Lazy Creek, a place that seemed to him haunted by whispering voice and tread in the dusk and the dark, he set his mind against thinking about her. But he could not for long shut her out, and soon enough he was throwing the gates of his thoughts wide open to her, thinking of her to the exclusion of everything else. He saw her as she was, or at least as he thought she was;

and he thought of her as he had known her so long and long ago when she wore the little pink-and-blue, faded gingham dress, not the flaming scarlet gown of now. He dwelt broodingly on a vanished Maytime and a tender, fragrant young love. "You are just like a wild rose, Kitty!" He sat on his bench, with his elbows on his knees, his knuckles against his temples, and, though he did not groan aloud, something within him groaned. And he knew now how vitally he had loved little sixteen-year-old Kate Haveril, and what a great fool he had been to leave her back yonder in Pleasant Valley, and how brutal he had been, too; and how, ever since then, without knowing it, he had loved her.

He had seen Ransome Haveril turn to this girl and that one during the footloose years, and recalled how he himself had had no place in his life for any of them. "I have loved her all this time and didn't know it. And now I have lost her. And I can never get her back, because she doesn't exist any longer. Lady Kate isn't Kate Haveril. Kate Haveril is dead."

But after a while, remembering his little sweetheart so poignantly, mourning her as dead, remembering the curve of her cheek and the curl of her hair and the quiver of her sweet mouth and the soft purl of her hushed voice, he found himself remembering that other girl, too, the vivid girl with the great hat and flaunting plume and defiant gown. He smiled bitterly. "I gave the little wild rose girl a small fine gold chain. I gave the other girl a diamond."

He had heard so many things spoken of Lady Kate. He winced as some of those rumors, so unheeded until now, recurred to him. It was said that she had been bought and paid for by General Bright-Hampden; it had been said that she was one of those gay ladies who was for sale, but who came high; the most expensive lady to have and to hold in all the spendthrift West. Now men said that she had been Hackamore Breen's light-o'-love, and that so mighty was the spell she had cast over him that he was going to marry her, to install her like a reigning queen at the Rancho El Monte.

Lady Kate married to Hackamore Breen! The thought was like a knife in his side. He stood up, moved about restlessly, went again to his window to stare frowning down the quiet, sunlit valley. Lady Kate for a neighbor, Mrs. Willard Breen, of El Monte!

"She mustn't do it!"

He heard himself speaking the words aloud, and his frown grew blacker. "Damn it, Jesse Bodine, it's nothing to you!" But he had always been honest with himself where it was given him to see the truth. "It is everything to you! You have always loved her; you love her now. Kate Haveril isn't dead at all; she is asleep behind a strange, hard veneer that the years have put over her. The real, true Kate Haveril is deathless. And no matter what life has done to her, she is not for Hackamore Breen."

Twice he and Hackamore Breen had shot at each other with scarcely more than a yard between their pistol muzzles! Ah, but he had not known then of the danger to Lady Kate!

A week passed and he did not leave his own acres save for one night ride to Shingle Town to replenish his larder. He got his beans and salt and flour; more important, he came by a certain scrap of news after angling for it: Hackamore Breen was not only alive, but was making a rapid recovery, and already, the day before, he had returned to his place at El Monte Ranch. There was more than that. He had traveled with a sort of cavalcade— two wagons, men on horseback, two ladies. One was the Lady Kate who, it was said, had done more than the doctor in caring for him, the other a friend of Lady Kate's of an older and scarcely less broad reputation, Big Belle of the Mines.

Jesse Bodine rode home under a glory of stars without knowing stars shed any glory.

Then something altogether wonderful happened. Wonderful things do happen now and then, and then was like now. There returned into his life something which he had forgotten, something which did not truly seem to belong to this life at all, but to some ancient, forgotten one. Whether it was by chance, or whether chance is the wrong word, he did not know. But Jesse Bodine woke from a restless sleep and got up and went to his window to look out and see whether the world he knew was still there. There it was, quiet and showing him a sort of Mona Lisa smile, not quite dark, not quite light, the stars doing their best, Lazy Creek drifting slowly, with silver dimples in the rapids. And, not caring whether it was four o'clock of an autumnal afternoon or four o'clock of a spring morning, he dressed and went out and climbed on his horse and rode up along the winding valley.

He saw a flicker of firelight and, in the firelight, a girl.

He didn't know her in the least. He was merely mildly surprised to find several people making themselves at home, encamped on his ranch.

But she, seeing him, even with shadows wrapped about him, gasped. Her hands went, swift as swallows, to her breast and her eyes grew large, dewy with gladness. There was no longer any sting left; life had wiped her schoolgirl slate clean; she had loved him once and would love him always, but there could never again be any thorns in that love of little April Crabtree.

Then, of course, he knew. He came down out of the saddle and trapped her two hands in his, and a smile came back to his lips and into his eyes that hadn't been there for years.

"April! You! Here!"

"Jesse!"

There are those, scientifically bent, who know about light-years, who know how fast light can travel; but not a one of them knows how fast thoughts can fly. Instants can be long. The two in a flash remembered, and all the while Jesse Bodine was clasping her hands, and he said:

"April! When was it, and where? And just look at you now! Do you know that just about the finest minutes I ever lived through were with you?"

He didn't know that she had once loved him. He didn't know that she had ever known Kate Haveril! He didn't know that she had ever seen Kate. She couldn't conceivably dream that Kate Haveril was so near right now that she was just over the hill. And how could she suspect that she herself, little lovely April Crabtree, was somehow a golden link between Jesse Bodine and the girl who, a boy to her, had been the Kit Haveril of that other time?

Jesse Bodine became almost overnight a sort of Young Patriarch. The Crabtrees, father and mother and Ann with her two babies, and of course April, were glad to pour water on their campfire and come to stop for a time at the big empty house on Lazy Creek. And later still others came, as Jesse began to take the first steps to build up the ranch and stock it and drive his stubborn roots deep down and for all time into the soil. There was a certain to-be-remembered Bud Weaver, a Texan, a man whom Jesse had liked from the first; and Bud, always about to acquire his own spreading acres, was content for the time to come to Jesse Bodine as foreman. He came with money in his pockets, sick of mining, ready to put his funds into stock, to be in a way a partner. There came with him a long, narrow, weary-eyed man with melancholy mustaches, a certain Lonesome Pete, Bud's uncle, likewise a Texan longhorn.

So it began, and others gathered. For one item, there were a dozen Indians, a sort of family clan, assorted *vaqueros*, houseboys, field hands, along with their wives and children and ponies; they constituted almost a small village down in the end of the meadow and, in the course of time, became loyal and were like children whom he must maintain and protect.

Then one day Ransome Haveril got wind of Jesse's return. That was shortly after Jesse had ridden to Shingle and had heard of Hackamore Breen's home-coming, and Ransome had lost no time in coming to Lazy Creek. More, he brought his young friend Don Felipe along with him. True, these two never did quite constitute an integral part of Jesse Bodine's household, but there came times, many times and close together, when they as good as lived under his roof.

There was Captain Bobbie Leigh, too.

Representing a South American firm, that of Begg & Co., in a commercial way, he traveled once to La Fiesta to talk cattle-buying—hides and tallow, rather—with the Moragas. He, like others, grew with time to be such a frequent visitor at Lazy Creek as almost to be one of Patriarch Jesse Bodine's small, loyal army.

So it appears that Bodine drew warm, friendly souls as a magnet draws true steel.

And little blue-eyed April saw one night a vision out of a girlhood dream, and it was a laughing, black-eyed Spanish *caballero*—and Don Felipe Moraga saw her too, and at the same instant, and sparks flew.

But, with so many people to tell about, one must go slowly, not to get them all tangled up like so many fireflies caught in my lady's scarf. Let's take them singly or two or three at the time, as they demand consideration. First of all: Ransome Haveril, sitting gracefully sideways in the high-horned saddle, rides up to the top of the knoll, under shadowy trees and lets out a high yelp with large gratification in it as he spies his old friend Jesse Bodine slouching in the late sunshine on a spacious if dreary veranda.

"Hi! Jess, you old son-of-a-gun!"

"Ran, you ugly father of yellow tomcats! Pile down, and make yourself to home! Look around, Ran! This is my new place, and it's all yours same as mine. Like it?"

Then of course, after a grin and a handshake, it all had to come out—Kate Haveril. Lady Kate.

Ransome went pale and looked sick. Lady Kate? Here in California? His own sister—little Kate Haveril of Pleasant Valley?

"Quit your joshing, Jess."

No, but it was true. Kate Haveril, just over the hill, so to speak. With that dirty double-dealing devil Hackamore Breen. Readying up to marry him, it looked like.

"By God!" said Ransome Haveril, and his face went red, and he came surging up out of the old broken chair down into which Jesse Bodine had eased him.

Then he looked at his old friend's face. Jesse, grim-jawed and hard-eyed, nodded.

"I can't help it, Ransome. That's the way it is. . . . You see, Ran, before we started out together I . . . Well, I did think that maybe someday she . . . Hell! You know. I thought that maybe she'd wait."

Ransome's pallor grew a sort of sick green.

"Jess, I won't take it from you or any other man! She wouldn't be like that! Damn it, you lie!"

"I haven't said anything," said Jesse Bodine, always soft-spoken, never more so than now.

"I know! I know!" Ransome ran both hands through his hair, making it as wild as a porcupine's bristles. Then his jaw hardened, and for once he looked like Jesse Bodine. "They say," he spoke quietly, "that Lady Kate is just a girl of the camps—any man's girl! It's a lie, Jess. And she is with Breen?"

"She has a chaperon, remember," his friend reminded him stolidly, having himself no faith in chaperonage. "Big Belle is with them."

"Coming with me, Jess?"

Jesse Bodine hesitated a thoughtful minute. Then he shook his head.

"Not this trip, Ransome," he said.

Ransome stood frowning a moment. When he spoke it was to say quietly:

"I tell you it's all a damned lie. Just the same I've got to kill him."

But he didn't kill Hackamore Breen that day. First, he saw little April coming out into the patio, bare-armed and lovely and wearing smiles like flowers, and he remembered her and her sister Nellie. Another thing, when he rode hotly over to El Monte, after a quiet pleasant time with Jesse and April, talking of days which to them all seemed so far away, he found Breen away from home. And he found Lady Kate sitting in the yard under a big live oak with Big Belle.

Lady Kate wasn't any Lady Kate at all today, but just a lovely young girl in the careless dress of a country girl in an early California; a ribbon in her hair, bright orange calico, dusty shoes. When a man, riding fast, came clattering into the hard-packed yard, she wasn't at first greatly interested, because men were always riding hard whether coming to El Monte or anywhere else. And she didn't even know the man right away, this stalwart, dark-bearded young man, not having heard that he was in the neighborhood. But Ransome, looking for her, came down out of the saddle like a shot, and caught her runaway hands, and hugged her.

"Kate! Kate! Oh, Kate!"

After all it doesn't seem to be so much the actual words as something else. They thrilled together like lyric strings on the same violin. Blood, so they say even today, is thicker than water; just possibly, perhaps, it was thicker then.

But the magic of the moment was swiftly broken, for he remembered his errand. A man like Ransome Haveril can't very well forget that he is on his way to kill another man when that man is his sister's lover.

"Catherine," he said. After all, though they called her Kate and Kitty and even Kit and sometimes Cathy, her name was Catherine Constance Haveril. "Look. Tell me. Where's that yellow dog Hackamore Breen?"

She blazed out at him:

"You can't talk like that to me!"

"No? Why can't I?"

She sat rigid; her chin hardened. She looked beyond him, beyond the wooded hills.

"I am going to marry him, Ransome. Real soon, too."

"You'll do nothing of the kind! You—Why, Catherine, you can't."

It was her turn to say stormily, "Why can't I?"

"Because—Damn it, Kate, there's Jesse!"

That made her laugh. Jesse Bodine!

"Yes, Jesse Bodine! He's my one real friend, Kate. He'd go to hell for me and I would for him, too. And he loves you, and always has, and you know it."

She gave him a small smile, tight and cynical. What was more, she lifted her brows in two fine, lofty arches.

"Jesse Bodine? Love?" She pretended to be high above all human weaknesses, and reached over and rumpled his hair. "Ransome, you silly boy!"

Then, out of a clear sky, Big Belle broke in upon them. (She had been eavesdropping, and judged it time!) It was Big Belle, by the way, who had given Lady Kate her name, Big Belle who had a boarding house up in Nevada City, who mothered a lot of dance hall girls and that sort; and now she made her entrance singing her own song:

"I'm a Daisy Bell, and a Bell can ring!
    Here's something you can recollec':
If any damn man jus' makes me mad,
    Well, I step out and break his neck!
So hop along, roll along, come along
    For a smile from Daisy Bell,
An' if you don't like the tune of my song,
    Well, gents, go plumb to San Francisco."

She was fat and middle-aged and somehow lovable; that was because, be her shortcomings what they were, she had a warm, true heart. Ransome lighted up at the sight of her, as she came bearing down on him, her broad hand held out, as she said:

"Lady Kate, why didn't you ever tell me you had a brother? You mystery girls make me sick. —Put 'er there, Mr. Haveril!" And she and Ransome shook hands and liked each other.

Then, "I've got to high-tail out of here," said Ransome, giving up for the day anyhow his idea of killing Hackamore Breen. "I'm on my way back to the Lazy Creek. By the way, there's a girl there, name of April. She's just exactly like somebody, Cathy, that we used to read about in that big fat book of fairy tales. No, she ain't my girl, but she—Well, I sort of wished you could get to know her."

Kate, at ease now, knowing that there was no danger of Ransome and Hackamore Breen coming to gunpowder right now, laughed that lovely, husky-throated laughter of hers. Clasping her brother's two hands, her head tipped back, her eyes lifted and full of laughing lights, she said:

"April? That's funny; a funny name, isn't it, Ransome? I knew an April once upon a time—"

"Not this one," said Ransome. "Jesse and me, coming west, met up with her and her folks, the finest. I—Well, I sort of liked her sister Nellie.

But little April, just a little thing you could have slapped over like a mosquito, she was dead in love with Jesse. April Crabtree, her name is, and she's staying at the Lazy Creek now, and—"

"But Ransome! I do know her! I didn't know she was here in California! Ransome! You say she fell in love with Jesse? And—and—"

"So long, Sis," said Ransome, and kissed her forehead. Then he shook hands again with Big Belle, saying, "I'm glad to know you, Ma'am," and went off, clanking his spurs, to his horse.

Lady Kate stared after him. Then he sat down again on the bench under the live oak and was very still, her lips tight, with Big Belle looking at her. And then of a sudden she broke into wild, uncontrollable laughter.

Big Belle came over to Kate's bench and sat down and took her hand and said, mothering her crossly, "You're a great big little fool!"

"Oh, am I?" cried Kate, and snatched her hand away.

"Yes, you are! And I know three things now: One is why you always wear that thin gold chain around your throat, keeping it hid. And the other is why just lately, since that mix-up at Bright-Hampden's nob hill place, you've got a diamond ring strung onto the same chain! And the other thing is—*Hmf!*"

"Tell me! What?"

"You guess," said Big Belle, and this time Kate

did not jerk her hand away. Rather she nestled her curly head against the woman's full, deep breast. Big Belle stroked her hair softly. "Listen to me, little fool," she said very gently, "you better do you some straight thinkin' and do it fast. I kind of smell powder smoke and trouble. Better go get your man, if you want him. Better go get the right one before it's too late."

No, today Kate wasn't in the least the Lady Kate of the carriage, with a great plumed hat and all that.

CHAPTER XVI

LIKE A LEAN, CLEAN ARROW

Little April's heartstrings must have been like those of a rare violin, awaiting a master's tremolo, muted. She throbbed to life; she was in touch with the universe. It must be true that there are those exceptional spirits clad in human clay to whom is given the high gift of an exquisitely sensitive touch with that *je ne sais quoi* that we call, simply, our lives, or, in general, life. She did not know that Kate Haveril was "just over the hill," and she did not know a lot of other things, such as: Jesse Bodine and Kate Haveril were made at God's bidding for each other. But she sensed happenings swiftly to come.

For one thing, Jesse Bodine had long ago given over carrying a rifle, but now had bought the finest new carbine to be had in San Francisco, and carried it with him wherever he rode. He said, when she mentioned it, that there was an old timber wolf he was gunning for. But it wasn't long before she knew the timber wolf was Hackamore Breen.

The morning that he said casually that he was going out to have a good look at the watershed, and went out looking at his carbine in a certain way, she knew what was in the wind. For she had heard a word here, and a word there—Bud Weaver and Lonesome Pete talking at random and mentioning names, even Don Felipe clenching his fists, though he didn't say anything. And she knew what the watershed was—a bit of high ground with a mountain lake bejeweling it and sending its cascading waters down into debatable lands. She vaguely understood how three big ranches, La Fiesta and El Monte and the Lazy Creek, crazily overlapped just there.

April stood out in the hard-packed yard when Jesse Bodine rode away, swaying in his loose-riding style in the saddle. Then she ran to her room, got hastily into overalls and boots, and went down to the barn. One of Jesse's new Indians, grinning white-toothedly and flourishing his hat rather than just removing it, brought her a saddled horse.

After a while she saw, far ahead, Jesse Bodine riding up through the scattering of pines and oaks on a slope which ran down to the headwaters of the creek.

He rode out that day with blood in his eye, looking for Hackamore Breen, hoping to find him trespassing. Only now were "Old Californ's" customs being broken down, annihilated by cold men like Breen. Time was when "Ever't'ing, *amigo*, that is mine is yours, too. You see a fat yearling that maybe somehow belongs to me, and you kill it to eat? *Bueno*! W'y not? There is *mucho* plenty of ever't'ing in the worl', Señor, an' like thees you make me happy." But of late the gringos had come booting in, and they had robbed and stolen right and left, and had broken the rainbow. Now the word "Trespass" was born, so far as young California was concerned. Let Breen plant his damn hoofs this side of the imaginary line, Jesse Bodine was well within his rights to shoot him. And it was high time that someone killed Hackamore Breen—before Lady Kate gave her priceless self into his keeping.

The way that the three big ranches spread out, the Moragas claimed the watershed, and so did Jesse Bodine; but between them there could never be any trouble. But Breen claimed the same territory, and that was different!

Jesse Bodine kept remembering two girls who were the same girl, little Kitty Haveril of Pleasant Valley, Lady Kate of San Francisco and the mining camps. One of the things that could never happen was that she should be befouled by a man like Hackamore Breen. It just wasn't going to happen. And so he kept his narrowed eyes watchfully trained down every aisle through the shadowy pines.

He pulled his horse down to a dead halt and unlimbered his new carbine; it might just possibly come in handy some day to see whether this horse would stand for shooting from the saddle.

He chose a whitish, resinous wound on a pine for a target, and fired; his horse shivered, then stood still. Jesse patted the tense shoulder in friendly fashion; here was a horse to ride. Then he tried again, just truing up on his marksmanship. He selected a ripe pine cone and made a try toward cutting it free from the lofty limb. While the cone was falling he laughed quietly to himself; it was rather good to know that now, after this long time, he still had the trick of such shooting as could bark a squirrel. He patted his horse's shoulder and rode on again, and though the echoes of his two shots were dead among the hills the memory of them lingered on in other ears than his own.

Then, from the brow of the hill, he saw five men. They were on his land, as he figured it, and they were building some sort of fence, a few crazily crooked posts with stripped saplings strung between them, and the fence was across the trail that a man from Lazy Creek would travel, headed this way. And one of the men, not laboring but smoking a cigarette in the saddle while he commanded the others, was Hackamore Breen.

Jesse Bodine slid out of the saddle. His horse, for which he felt a sudden affection, he led into a piny grove offering protection.

Then he stepped out into the open.

"You, Breen!" he called. "Better tell your men to jerk that fence down!"

"Oh!" thought April, her hand against her lips,

grown very still where she watched through the pines.

Breen saw who it was and reached for his gun, a belt gun, having ridden without a rifle today. He yelled back:

"Got you dead to rights this time, you son of a she-coyote!" And he was laughing in his sneering way, his face full of teeth, when he said to his men, "Kill him, and you get five hundred dollars in gold!"

They started shooting. Three of his four men carried rifles. Those three stood out in the sunlight so that Jesse Bodine could see them clearly, and he very coolly and steadily shot them down. One, two, three. It was like knocking over tenpins. He was satisfied if he got them in knee, elbow or ankle, just so that he put them out of the fight, for, after all, he had no quarrel with them. And he knew that today he could shoot the eye out of a gnat sitting on top of Soldiers' Peak, a mile away.

Then, with the corners of his mouth drawn in, in a sort of hell's grin, he shot down Breen's other man, leaving Breen himself for the last, as a man saves his cut of apple pie for after dinner.

"That's just to show you, Hackamore, damn you!" he called pleasantly. "Want me to shoot your eye out?"

Hackamore Breen, with his Colt .44, did all that a man could against a carbine at that distance. But he was wise enough to spring back behind a tree. Jesse Bodine, walking warily, bore down on him, stalking him as a man stalks his game in any jungle.

He got a glimpse of Breen's elbow and shot at it; this time his bullet merely tore through shirt fabric, not even burning the flesh. Even so, it was a rare, good shot.

Breen emptied his gun at him, then jerked farther back, altogether out of sight, to break the gun and refill the cylinder. And Jesse Bodine, knowing what the man must be about, came stalking his game, closer and closer.

They fired together, and Breen's bullet cut the air whistlingly at Jesse's ear, and Jesse's bullet chanced to catch Breen's gun on the very tip, flipping it out of his hand, numbing his gun arm tinglingly. And Jesse, seeing and understanding, bore down on him with a whoop.

His attack was like that of an Indian leaping upon a paleface whose scalp he particularly hungered for.

"Throw down your gun, Mr. Breen," he said in a sort of singing, jeering way, "or I'll shoot your guts out, and you know it. Throw down your gun and let me use my knuckles to carve my initials on your face!"

Breen, with the muzzle of Jesse Bodine's carbine threatening his midriff, with a quick memory in mind of the sharpshooting he had just seen, threw down his gun and jerked his hands skyward. Then Jesse Bodine laughed at him, and whether or not Hackamore Breen had ever heard a man laugh like that, it was certain that little April never had.

"I'm not going to kill you today, Mr. Breen," said Jesse Bodine, very polite. He couldn't help that, "Mr. Breen," because it was part of a habit; part of a gambler's habit that he had in part caught from Claude Purcell, in part had been born with; and, though done with gambling for good and all so far as cards went, he'd ever gamble with words and with his life. As now he gambled. He threw down his own gun.

"I'm not going to kill you today after all, Mr. Breen. I've a friend, Ransome Haveril, who has the right before me. But I'm going to send you back to someone who, when she looks at you, will say, 'Why, you've been visiting with Duke Bodine!'"

A sort of blue murder came stormily into Hackamore Breen's eyes, and a cruel gladness blossomed on his lips; man to man, like this, he was very sure that he would beat the slender erstwhile gambler into a bleeding pulp. Breen's hands were big and hard and competent. And moreover, he had an ace in the hole.

But just then Jesse Bodine was not so much an individual with a private grievance as a cold steel tool in the hands of men's destiny. The battle fury which ran through him was like an electric current along a copper wire, a dispassionate sort of thing that could blast and destroy as a streak of lightning blasts and destroys. He tore into Hackamore Breen like a lean, clean arrow into a buffalo.

And there on the ground about them, like broken toys, were Breen's four men, watching them with goggling eyes. Perhaps they weren't quite sure whether they were dead or alive, awake or asleep, with such rapidity had disaster smitten them. Any man of them could have shot Jesse Bodine then as he and Breen tied into each other; not a man of the four even thought of moving, held partly by the shackle of pain from his wound, partly by the chain of sheer, bemused wonder. And for a time April was, like them, spellbound.

As Jesse Bodine hurled himself at the man whom he longed with an infinite longing to beat down into the earth, that blue fire in Hackamore Breen's eyes grew hotter with a new, exultant flash. For Breen's ace in the hole was a big-bladed sheath knife dangling from his belt. He whipped it out and brought it sweeping down with every intent and hope of splitting his enemy wide open.

And very close did he come then to achieving his heart's desire, but perhaps he was a trifle overeager, overconfident. The broad, gleaming blade, razor-sharp, would surely have made an end of Jesse Bodine but that Bodine saw it in the last nick of time, and was as swift and sure as chain lightning in avoiding it by a shuddersome, narrow margin, and blocking the murderous downward sweep by catching Breen's descending wrist in a clutch that gripped and locked like steel. The two men began a fierce struggle then for the mastery of the weapon. . . . April's heart stood still and she stopped breathing as, in fascinated, frozen horror, she watched them strain with the ultimate ounce of strength residing in two rather glorious bodies. Their lips were retracted in the savage and rigid balancing of their efforts, their hard-set teeth were bared so that they, too, were like fighting weapons, and the sweat ran down their faces. For an instant they resembled still statues of gladiators more than living men.

Jesse Bodine began to laugh softly. She could hear his laughter and wonder at it.

"It's no good, Mr. Breen," he said. "I'm squeezing the blood out of your hand. I'm putting your nerves to sleep, I'm paralyzing your right arm. In a minute I'm going to damn near kill you!"

The two men's faces had turned a hot, purplish red with fury wedded to desperate exertion, and their veins stood out as though they would burst. Now, however, all the color drained out of Hackamore Breen's cheeks, which slowly turned a dead white as the vise clamped tighter and still tighter on his wrist, twisting it unmercifully, stabbing him through with pain. Then the knife fell from his paralyzed fingers, and for an instant the two men stood motionless, free of each other, glaring into each other's baleful eyes.

And then, always the swifter of the two, Jesse Bodine bored into Hackamore Breen the second time and began keeping his promise, battering him, battering his congested face with both fists smashing like iron hammers, so that Hackamore Breen reeled backward; and still Jesse Bodine drove his smashing, piston blows into his face, into his body, mostly into his face, crushing his lips against his teeth, breaking his nose, making him into an exhibit for Lady Kate as he had said that he would. Breen did all that a man could, sling blow for blow, but from the drop of the knife he was beaten, and what was more he knew it and Jesse Bodine knew it. In the end, quick in coming, Jesse's clubbed fist came up like a stone in a sling—and Hackamore Breen went down, flat on his back, and lay as still as a dead man.

"Got you, damn you," panted Jesse Bodine.

Then, out of a blur of sound, he heard a shrill, agonized scream from April, and for the first time saw her. And in time he saw, too, what it was that brought that warning scream to him.

"Jesse! Jesse! Look out!"

One of the men on the ground, one of Hackamore Breen's men whom he had shot through the leg, had heaved himself halfway up, propped with one hand on the ground, and with his other hand had dragged to him Hackamore Breen's fallen Colt revolver. That was what April saw when she screamed, what Jesse Bodine now saw just in time. This man on the ground was not six feet away from him; he could scarcely fail to kill, give him another thin slice of a second. But that was what he was not to have.

Jesse Bodine did the one thing possible, and in doing it took every chance of running all the way into death's arms. He leaped at the man with the Colt, instead of springing aside, and, leaping, he kicked out at the uncertain hand holding the weapon. The toe of his boot crashed into the other man's wrist; the gun flew wide, exploding in the air; the man crouched back whimpering and staring stupidly at his hand which seemed to dangle from a broken wrist.

Swiftly as the thing was done and over with, already April had come running. She snatched up one of the fallen rifles; she stood there shaking, menacing them all with it, her eyes blazing with such anger it seemed impossible her sweet eyes could ever harbor. And then she railed at them, crying wildly:

"I'll kill you! I'll kill every one of you! You horrid things, you damned beasts! Don't so much as move a finger, any one of you, or I'll blow your damned brains out!"

Not a man of them moved. They scarcely breathed. Jesse Bodine stared at her incredulously. Then, "Good girl, April," he said in a quiet voice, and, still looked at her queerly and with newborn understanding of her. "I'm still alive, and it's because of you, little April."

Then he turned from her and took up his carbine.

"Boys," he said to the Breen men, "the party is over. You get to hell out of here, off my land, anywhere you like and any way you can. And take Mr. Breen with you; go dump him back on his own land. And don't any of you ever show up here again as long as you live. Get going."

The men got away to their horses as best they could, and dragged Breen along with them and heaved him into a saddle and rode away. Only then the rifle slid out of April's grasp and she buried her face in her hands and began to cry stormily.

Jesse Bodine held her in his arms; he didn't say a word, just held her close and let her cry. But swiftly she got herself in hand; there were hitherto unsuspected wells of strength, deep down, in April Crabtree. Gently she freed herself, giving his arm a light little pat, smiling up at him even before she wiped the tears away.

"I was so frightened, Jesse," she said quite simply. Then she wiped her eyes and added: "It was a glorious thing, the way you fought them all. Do you mind if I feel mighty proud of you?"

"If it hadn't been for you—"

"Sh! But let's go away from here now, shall we?"

They went in silence to their horses and turned back toward the Lazy Creek ranch house, but just before they came within sight of it April stopped her horse and said tremulously:

"Jesse, you go on and leave me here. I guess I'd better be all by myself for a little while. Oh, I'm crazy, but I can't help seeing it all happening over again; I can't talk about it to the others yet."

"But, April—"

"Please, Jesse."

He nodded. "I'll be looking for you. If you don't show up pretty soon I'll come back for you."

"I'll be all right. I'll follow along in a few minutes."

She watched him out of sight through the trees, then slid from her horse and lay down, her face hidden in her crossed arms. And there she lay when a few minutes later Ransome Haveril, riding this way, found her.

"April!" he cried anxiously, in a flash standing over her. "You've been hurt!"

She sat up then and summoned up that brave little smile of hers which now was like a pale glow of light on her pallid face.

"No," she told him. "Just lying here and thinking!"

He shook his head. "You can't fool old man Ransome. Something has happened. What is the matter, April?"

"I'm just being a silly girl; they say girls are always silly after everything is all over. Yes, something has happened, but it came out all right."

And then she told him.

Ransome sat down beside her, staring angrily off into the distance.

"Jesse ought to have killed him," he muttered. "Why didn't he?" He turned his brooding eyes back to her. "Do you know that Breen thinks he is going to marry my—Did you ever hear of a Lady Kate, April?"

"Yes. Everyone has, I suppose. But what about her, Ransome?"

"Breen thinks he's going to marry her. That's why I wish Jesse had killed him. That's why I'm going to kill him myself."

"But, Ransome!" She stared at him in wonder. "Lady Kate? I thought that—You're not in love with her, are you? I thought that you and one of the Moraga girls—"

"Can't a man love two girls at the same time?" he asked curiously.

She shook her head vigorously. "Of course not. You know better than that."

Keeping his eyes, baffling now, steady on hers, he demanded:

"Not even if one of the girls is his own sister?"

"Lady Kate—your sister!" she gasped.

"And what's more you knew her once. Remember? Kate Haveril?"

She looked stunned. "Kit Haveril! Kate Haveril, Lady Kate! But, Ransome—"

"She's over there now, at Breen's. Fixing to marry him. And long ago, before Jesse and I started west, to California, Jesse and Kate were sweethearts. Now see what has happened to them!"

"Ransome!—No, no! Let me think!"

Jesse and Kit! The two people whom she, a tiny girl, then a girl of sixteen, had loved so desperately! She thought back and back, and remembered so many things!

She looked up, no longer the white-faced, trembling girl, but with a flash in her eyes now and color in her cheeks. She hesitated, then asked swiftly:

"Has Kate changed terribly, Ransome? I won't believe it!"

"How do I know? I've hardly seen her. Changed? Yes, of course; you wouldn't know her for the same girl. But she's not—Damn it, she's not the sort they say she is!"

"Of course she isn't! We all change, don't we, Ransome? But she is too lovely, down deep, to be really what people say Lady Kate is. You and I know that. But tell me, does she still love Jesse?"

"How do I know? How can she, and be about to marry Hackamore Breen?"

"People are funny, you know," she said wisely, and then went on with her questioning. "Does Jesse still love her?"

"How do I know?" he muttered for the third time. "How does anybody know anything about anybody else? Jesse love Kate? Hell, yes! Of course he does, though maybe he doesn't know it. He has never once looked at another girl."

"That's Jesse," nodded little April. "You're right. Of course he loves her. And she loves him." She jumped up and brushed dead leaves from her clothes. "Let's go now, Ransome."

Then, as he, too, got to his feet, she surprised him by laughing softly.

"If you had only seen what Jesse did to that Breen man just now, you'd know that he loves her! With all his heart and all his body, with everything that's in him! Oh, I'm glad now that they fought! Just the way they did! I just wish Kate had been there to see!"

As it happened, though Lady Kate had not seen actually with her own eyes what had just taken place on the debated watershed, she was seeing it vividly and pretty accurately right now with the eye of her mind. For when Hackamore Breen, slumping in the saddle, came home to El Monte, his men looking sick in their saddles, Kate Haveril

266

was out under the big oak below the house and was first to see them. Breen would have given pretty nearly anything he possessed to have been able to keep out of her sight for a few hours. There was black, dried blood on his face, his bruised lips were swollen, his nose was a shapeless swelling, one eye was purple, his clothes were torn.

Solicitously Kate ran to meet him.

"Why, Willard! You—" She gasped out the few words, then grew rigid and silent. Her first thought was: "What has happened to him? Who would do this to him?" And in a flash she answered her own question! "Jesse Bodine has done this to you!"

That infuriated him. It was worse than rubbing salt into a raw wound. How should she be so sure that that damned Bodine had done this to him, that Bodine *could* do this to him?

Hackamore Breen's last grip on himself went then with the acid of shame added to the pain and humiliation he had already endured. He said things which at the moment he himself did not realize he was saying, used words to say them with which he never should have used. Not only did he curse Jesse Bodine uphill and down-dale, shouting out incoherently what he was going to do to that gambler and crook, but he went so far as to drag Lady Kate into the arena of his fury. He named her the sort of thing which he had heard her named in the mining camps, he accused her far more rightfully than he knew of having an eye on Duke Bodine.

Lady Kate turned her back on him and went to the house and to her one friend on earth just then, so far as she knew, Big Belle.

Big Belle had heard every thundering word, and she had seen, too.

"Serves you right and I'm glad of it," she said sourly. "I've told you what for a man he is, and you shut your fool eyes. Now you ought to know! And you ought to know what for a man Jesse Bodine is too, by this time! Huh! You loving him and him loving you, and you trying to make yourself make eyes at Hack Breen!"

"We're leaving here right away," said Kate. "Come with me to pack our things."

"Where do you think we're going?"

"Anywhere but here! Back to San Francisco, I suppose. Come; hurry."

"Hold on a minute, child," said Big Belle, and her voice softened to a sympathy which was ever ready in her. "You really mean this? It's not just a flare-up?"

"You know that I mean it!"

Big Belle nodded. She did know because she had a shrewd eye in her head, and she knew people, Lady Kate better than most. And she had noted these last few days that Lady Kate looked now and then strangely at Hackamore Breen, and

Belle something more than merely guessed that the girl, seeing so much of him at his own place, was getting to know him better than she had ever known him until now, and was getting enough of him, and was realizing that fact before it was too late. Unless, Big Belle was thinking, it was too late already.

"If you really want to get into the clear and out from under all this," she said gravely, "better use your head instead of just your hands and feet. A feller sometimes travels faster and goes further, using his noodle instead of just paws and hoofs."

"What on earth do you mean?"

"I'm ripe and ready to go the minute we can make a getaway," said Big Belle. "As ripe and ready as you are. But I sort of know what Hack Breen's like, and just about what he'll be thinking! He'll have his notion where we're going, whether he's right or wrong. Think he'll let you scamper over to Jesse Bodine right now? I called you a fool a couple of times, but you ain't! Keep your shirt on, kid, or Hack Breen'll see to it that you *never* get away!"

"I see what you mean," said Kate miserably. "Oh, Belle!"

"Shush! And stiffen your backbone and play mollycoddle. When you and me go, the hell with any packing! We'll sneak out by the dark of the moon, grab a couple of horses and high-tail without nobody knowing."

This time it was for Kate to whisper an urgent, "Sh!"

For she heard Hackamore Breen's heavy tread at the front door.

CHAPTER XVII

APRIL MAGIC

A few sunny days passed by during which, had a stranger passed this way, he must have exclaimed, "How serene, how filled with peace and plenty and all good things is this pastoral life in California!"

At the Lazy Creek Ranch everyone was busy, everyone seemed happy; there was much to do and much was being done. Bud Weaver and his henchman-uncle, Lonesome Pete of the mournful visage and enormous, drooping mustaches, were overflowing with plans for the renascence, then the general betterment toward perfection of a ranch which they both swore was the finest up-and-down spread this side Texas, or th' other side, either. And both, as cheerful about the matter as any two crickets, having heard of Jesse Bodine's encounter with Hackamore Breen and his merry men, were overeager for a return engagement.

"Ever since once I played poker with that coyote that time, over to Yellow Jacket," said Bud Weaver, "I been hoping! Glory to come, what a day it'll be when he gives me a show to shoot his eyes out!"

Scarcely less interested and optimistic was old man Crabtree, April's father. And Ransome Haveril and Don Felipe Moraga and Captain Leigh, all three of them more of the time at Lazy Creek than anywhere else, were richly in accord with all this, with all that was going forward on the ranch and with high hopes for a showdown with Hackamore Breen.

Meantime busy hands were pleasantly occupied everywhere, within and without, at the Lazy Creek ranch buildings. Two carpenters—at least two men who called themselves carpenters, and had hammer and saw, and who accepted a ten dollar a day wage with the tacit understanding that they were not to overwork—were making or mending floors, patching roofs, rebuilding and enlarging here and there. Bud Weaver and Lonesome Pete, with a half dozen of Jesse's Indian *vaqueros*, had driven in the first nucleus of their new herd, bought down in the Sacramento Valley, and had added a dozen saddle horses.

Supervised by April Crabtree, there were always three or four Indian women cleaning house. A six-horse team strained in from San Francisco bringing household furnishings and supplies by box and barrel. April was planning a rebirth of the ancient flower garden and orchard; she had commandeered a couple of young Indian bucks to dig a ditch from the creek farther up in the hills to bring a rivulet close to the house.

The carpenters made a long plank table for the dining room. There were evenings when anywhere from a dozen to a score sat at table together, and happy evenings they were. Bud Weaver could play the mouth organ; Lonesome Pete had a surprisingly fine tenor voice; April sang songs like "When the Roses Bloom Again," and "Her Bright Smile Haunts Me Still." Don Felipe played the guitar and sang Spanish love songs. Sometimes Captain Leigh made April dance with him to Bud's music, and then Don Felipe sulked and glowered and maybe got up and said that he had to go back to La Fiesta—and then little April ran off to her room, and no one knew whether or not she wept.

These were queer days for Jesse Bodine. For the most part he was silent, off somewhere by himself as much as he could manage. For him it was a time of a glad fulfillment and of an empty sorrow. For one thing, he saw an old, old dream emerging from insubstantial shadowland and becoming a glorious reality. He was building himself a place like a kingdom; it spread across miles and miles and yet other miles, someday, he vowed, it would spread still farther and farther. He had under his rooftree many human souls; in a way they belonged to him. He had the fine sense he had so lacked during his hectic gambling life of accomplishing something good and real and abiding. He was going to have large herds; wild hay he had in plenty, but he was going also to have vast fields of man-high waving grain.

But he did not have what he wanted most of all.

He rode at times alone to the crest of a low-lying ridge from which one could almost look across the miles to the Hackamore Breen ranch house. Once or twice he saw smoke from its chimneys. And at these times, afraid for Lady Kate and hungering for her, he asked himself why he had not killed Hackamore Breen and made an end of an unendurable situation. He couldn't quite answer his own question, so mixed were his motives. Maybe he hadn't killed Breen because the man belonged to Kate Haveril; it was unthinkable that he should destroy anything that Kate wanted. Maybe he hadn't killed Breen because, had he done so, he must have shut the door for all time between himself and Kate. What he had done was the right thing after all—Beat Hackamore Breen half to death, then send him back to her! She would understand that—just as if he had made her any other gift. A gift, say, of a thin, fine gold chain—or a diamond.

April began to find it difficult to get anything done, with so much requiring her attention. And that was because, if it wasn't Ransome Haveril seeking her out, it was Don Felipe, and if not Don Felipe, then Captain Leigh; and, if none of these, then even Bud Weaver or actually Lonesome Pete pulling his drooping mustaches mournfully at her, and with much to say. She had never had so much attention in all her life; it flustered her.

"Mercy!" gasped little April many's the time, as with both hands she thrust the fallen curls back and away from her rosily flushed face.

"Listen to me, April, I'm going clean crazy," said Ransome Haveril, and she sat down and folded her hands in her lap and listened. "Those Moragas! They're the cream of the earth you know, and all that but—they know I'm in love with Juanita and that she's in love with me and that we want to get married—so what do they do? It's just like they built a high fence between us; there's always her mother or some old woman with eyes like a rattlesnake and a black shawl over her head, watching us, spying and listening. If I could only get her alone!"

"The Spanish people are funny that way, I know." Little April nodded. Then she puckered her brow. "I'll help you somehow, Ransome, when I can. Don Felipe has asked me to visit them soon, and I want to. But just now we're so busy here!"

This was Ransome's constant complaint, and many the time he drew April apart to have her solace him if only by sympathetically listening to him boiling over. Down by the creek where she had gone to superintend the Indian women busied with the household washing, and where Ransome had gone seeking her, Don Felipe

Moraga followed. April's sweet blue eyes rounded as she saw him approach, as they always did. What a note the young Spanish don always struck, stepping along in the smallest, tightest, shiniest black boots in all Alta California, with his enormous sombrero with its silvered band, with the dagger thrust through his scarlet sash, and his ivory-handled pistols and his thin white cigarette! And the look in his great, black, smoldering eyes! He made little April shiver; always he did that, and something sang and sobbed in her heart.

Don Felipe stood with his hands on his hips and looked at them. Almost he sneered; not quite that, nor did he quite scowl, for she was a lady and Ransome was his friend, and he himself was a gentleman. But the *almost* was thinner than one of his cigarette papers split in half. Well, after all, friend though Señor Ransome Haveril was, was he not supposed to be deep in love with Don Felipe's little sister? *Aja*! Then explain his always making love to this little señorita who was like a little white dove with pink feet, making love with her and breaking her heart for love of him! *Caramba*! As the saying goes, Don Felipe was a jealous young man.

Today April looked her very prettiest. It was not that she had done anything very particular to paint the lily. But she had been thinking, "Don Felipe will come today!"

Before now little April had surprised others.

Today she was going to surprise herself. She saw Don Felipe coming; she said quickly to Ransome:

"Ransome, please do something for me? Hurry up to the house as fast as you can, and tell those Indian boys working on the springhouse not to do anything more with it until I get there. Tell them to—tell them that they can rest in the shade until I come. Hurry, won't you, before they spoil the springhouse?"

So Ransome, planning to return immediately to talk about Juanita some more, hurried away.

Don Felipe came on down to the creek. He looked very young and very dignified.

April drenched him with a smile and gave him her hand. He kissed it and all of a sudden thawed.

She said: "Howdy, Don Philip. I am just going up along the path a little way to the pool under the waterfall; I want to see if there are any flowers for the house. Will you escort me?"

He put his hand on his heart.

The water came splashing down into a crystal pool over a great white rock. There was a mossy, shady, secret place on the bank to which the path led. For an instant April and Don Felipe stood on the brink, peering over where April seemed to think some water flowers might be. She lost her balance, screamed as she fell, and went down under the glassy surface.

He couldn't swim a lick, but nevertheless he went in headlong after her. The two of them might well have drowned, but after all it was but a narrow pool and they scrambled ashore. His face was dead white.

The result was, dripping as they were, he took her into his arms. She clung to him, and he strained her tight. He poured his love into her ears, and wise little April, with her head down on his breast, smiled. She lifted her face and he kissed her.

"I love you with all my heart and soul, with my brain and my body, with everything that is in me!" cried Don Felipe.

"That's the way I love you," sighed little April.

There are some people who seem born to get their fingers among human heartstrings. Too many, perhaps, blunder and make discords and even cause the strings to snap. Some few, like April Crabtree, who all of a sudden became an interfering little body, have a touch as light and strong and sure as sunlight.

Ransome monopolized her for a brief while. Then came Don Felipe, a greater monopolist. Still, in his turn, there was Captain Bobbie Leigh. And by the time he cornered Miss Crabtree—or thought that he did, because their secret conference was of the same order as her falling into the pool—she knew a lot from Ransome and Don Felipe about him and Don Felipe's glowing sister, the laughter-loving little Rosa whom, once,

Hackamore Breen had wanted—until the horse episode. They were all young, and California was young, and youth is mating time, and there is nothing very much you can do about it. And some young ladies like April, very much in love, can't help wanting to see everybody else in love and happy. Matches are willingly made by such heavenly hands as little April's.

"Captain Leigh," she promised, all eagerness, "I have been asked by Don Philip's mother and father, he told me yesterday, to visit them. I am going to do it! And I am going to tell Miss Rosy everything you want me to!"

And April all the while was daydreaming and night-dreaming, too, of Jesse Bodine and Kate Haveril. The "Kit" she had loved so long ago! And her fingers fairly tingled. . . .

That noontime Dan Comstock, the sheriff from Yellow Jacket, rode down to Lazy Creek, seeking Jesse Bodine. He and Jesse squatted on their heels out by the barn, and talked.

"Remember the day you brought the stage into Yellow Jacket, Bodine?" asked the straight-from-the-shoulder Comstock, with those hard, icy-blue eyes of his trained like guns on Jesse's face.

"I remember."

"The bandits killed Long Peters that day, remember? You didn't know him alive, but you brought him in dead. Well, happens he was a friend of mine."

Jesse Bodine looked his interest, a notch above mere curiosity. Long Peters was a long time dead now, no matter whose friend.

"Maybe I told you that time," the sheriff went on, "that I couldn't figure out whether the job had been pulled off by Joaquin Murietta or by the Bedloe gang. You might not remember that. But, me, I don't forget easy. And something you said sticks in my mind. It was like this: You said you didn't get a chance to see the bandit captain clear, him being masked, but you heard his voice when he yelled out his orders. And you said it was a voice you'd know again if you ever heard it. You might remember that?"

Jesse Bodine scratched the ground with a bit of twig he had picked up, dropped from the wide branches of the oak spreading above them. And he gathered his brows thoughtfully. Then he nodded.

"That still goes, Sheriff. I've thought sometimes I might hear that voice again, somewhere, in one place or another, but I never have. Yes. If I heard it now I'd know it."

The sheriff for a while watched Jesse's twig-scratches in silence. At last he observed.

"I ain't a great hand for monkeying around with other folks' business, Bodine, but, like most, I got a sort of natural curiosity. I've heard tell that you and your neighbor Hackamore Breen don't jibe, as the feller says."

"Well?" Jesse asked him, noncommittal, since he didn't get the drift.

"I might ask you to do me a favor," said Comstock.

"Ask ahead. It's yours, unless there's some good reason to the contrary."

"Thanks." Comstock stood up. "It won't be long; maybe tonight. I'm not riding far before I'll be back."

"I'd like to have you put up with us as long as you can," invited Jesse, and he too got to his feet. He tossed his twig away and hooked his thumbs in his belt and said mildly, "You're not hinting that Breen was one of the men that stuck up Long Peters' stage, are you?"

"No, not exactly."

"I didn't suppose so. Anyhow it wasn't his voice I heard."

"No. No such luck. Hack Breen's too crafty a bird for anything like that to happen to him. Well, I'll ride along and maybe I'll see you later—and maybe we'll have something to tell each other. For one thing, if there's trouble between you and Breen, I'm not on Breen's side. So long, Bodine."

"Ride lucky," said Jesse.

He had plenty to think about during the afternoon and plenty to do. The sun was midway down in the west when one of his Indian boys sought him out and handed him a folded bit of paper. Up went his brows. The boy grinned and explained:

"Señorita Avrille!"

A note from April?—The Indians called her Señorita Avrille—That was funny. She was right up yonder at the house, wasn't she?

There were just a few penciled lines:

> Dear Jesse, please do what I ask right away, won't you? It's terribly important. Come to the watershed place. And wait there, if you have to, a little while. I'll explain.
>
> April

It certainly was funny! He frowned over the thing and naturally could make neither head nor tail of it. Well, it was clear that April had ridden ahead and that she had sent for him to follow. And she said "right away." Not for a second did he have the slightest thought of keeping her waiting. He got his carbine, shoved it in its leather on the saddle and rode.

It was a serene, pleasant afternoon and the pines made a shadowy solitude all their own on the slopes where the only sound was the soft whispering of their never still branches, and splotches of sunlight were pure gold. It struck him that it was a rarely beautiful day, and overhead were the California skies as he had dreamed them and had first seen them, a glorious blue with a few stilled white clouds like enormous puffs of cotton, and the clean fresh resinous tang of pine was in the air. He noted all this somewhere in the depths of his mind, and breathed deep of it and in a way gloried in it, for it was all his, the fertile earth and the hills and the running water and forests and the sky above—but all the while he was wondering about April. And when he reached the spot where he had contended with Hackamore Breen and his men, and there was no April there, he began to feel uneasy. From the beginning he had been perplexed; now he began to experience a first shadowy apprehension.

He read April's note again to make sure; she had said: "Wait, if you have to a little while. I'll explain." He eased himself sideways in the saddle and waited.

He knew April's handwriting; she had helped at making lists of things needed to replenish a larder or to be used in house-beautifying; he had no thought of any sort of trickery. His act in bringing along his carbine was simply a matter of custom nowadays. But when he presently heard the quick beat of a horse's hoofs he noted with a first flick of suspicion that they were oncoming from the direction of the Breen ranch. Another moment and he saw the rider coming straight toward him through the pines and made out that it was a girl.

He did not know that it was Kate Haveril until, riding to meet her, they came around a clump of buckeyes and met with only a few feet between them.

If he was startled, no less was Kate Haveril. They looked at each other wonderingly.

"Kate!" he exclaimed, and his gladness, surprised in him, rang in his voice.

She looked at him level-eyed from under the broad brim of her hat, and whatever she felt she hid from him. For a moment she was quite still, and it was a moment in which he, like a man athirst come upon a desert spring, drank deep of her sheer loveliness, and his eyes hid nothing. He was not just now the gambler, Duke Bodine, pokerfaced. He was very much like young Jesse Bodine of faraway Pleasant Valley.

Kate said in that lovely voice of hers, "I came here to meet April Crabtree."

"Why, so did I!" said Jesse Bodine.

"She wrote me a note that an Indian boy brought over—"

"She wrote me a note!"

They looked at each other gravely. Then a quick smile touched his lips and he said very softly, "You are just like a wild rose, Kitty."

And a warmed rose tint swept up instantly into her cheeks. "Kitty! You are like a wild rose!" *Kitty!* Not since those long-and-long ago days. And she was like a wild rose now, not in the least the Lady Kate of the scarlet gown and ostrich plumes. She was dressed plainly like a country girl with a long skirt, since she rode a sidesaddle, and she wore a boyish shirt open at the throat. And Jesse Bodine saw in the sunlight the golden flash of a fine gold chain about her white throat!

He came down out of the saddle and went to her and put up his hands, bidding her with his eyes to come down. Suddenly he thought how little she looked, how sweet and demure up there on top of the tall horse, how like tender wild flowers her eyes were. He didn't say anything; he just stood there looking up at her, holding out his arms.

Kate said in a small voice: "April played a trick on us. Is that it, Jesse? You didn't do this, did you?"

"No. Our God-blessed little April did it! Shall we let her have her way in this today, Kate Haveril?"

Her expression did not change; her eyes were unaltered in their grave steadiness and were very, very serious. But slowly she let her reins slip out of her hands to rest on her horse's mane, and then she reached her hands out to him. And when she came down it was to melt for an instant into his embrace. But, "No, Jesse," she said firmly. "Let me go. I will talk with you—"

He put one hand to her throat and lifted out the little gold chain. From it dangled the small bauble of a locket that had come once upon a time from the Pleasant Valley general store. Now, for companion piece, there was a diamond ring strung with it on the chain, and he knew it for the ring Duke Bodine had given the adventuress, Lady Kate, that night in the lusty young city by the Golden Gate!

He laughed quietly, deep down in his throat, and drew her into his arms again and kissed her, and both were thinking the same thing, how they had longed until they burned with the longing for a kiss when they were boy and girl sweet-hearts, and how only now did they kiss for the first time.

And Kate threw her arms about his neck, tight and tighter, and began to cry, and as far as the records go there never was any Lady Kate after that.

They sat together on a big fallen pine that last winter's storms had brought down to provide them a seat for today, and clasped hands and looked at each other, Kate trying to read in his clear eyes all that had happened to him since he had gone away and broken her heart, he trying to read likewise something of the maturing Kate since she with her scornful laughter had killed something within him. Whatever it was that was killed was alive again now, and her broken heart was no longer broken. An almost unendurable joy rose up within both of them.

"I love you with all my heart," said the girl very

simply. "Even when I hated you most, I loved you! Oh, Jesse! Have we found each other again?"

"It's some sort of magic," he whispered.

"April magic," she said. "Was there ever on earth anything so dear as April Crabtree?"

They had so much to say to each other, picking up the ancient, lost pattern, running back over the years, and April had to be told about by each of them. Kit Haveril, the runaway boy, and April at sixteen! Jesse Bodine, the young man, and April only at the beginning of her 'teens.

"And now she is beautifully in love with a fine fellow, one of the young Moragas of La Fiesta," said Jesse, "and we're going to give them such a wedding as never was or will be on land or sea—except ours, of course!"

But after all they were not here now to talk of April. They fell again to talking of each other, trying to get a million things said in a dozen words, and at times they had to stop to stare soberly at each other in new wonder, or to laugh for no particular reason—or for him to draw her close again and kiss her.

CHAPTER XVIII

THE SHOWDOWN

As the first lamps and candles were being lighted at the Lazy Creek Ranch that night, Sheriff Dan Comstock came again looking for Jesse Bodine.

"I've been doing me some Nick Carter stuff," said the sheriff, when he had Jesse alone in a little room which April was converting into an "office" for Mr. Jesse Bodine, owner and manager of the Lazy Creek Ranch.

"Who'm I? Dick Merriwell?" grinned Jesse Bodine, highly good-humored.

"Listen, kid. I'm going to ask you a favor, and that means you're helping me. After that—Dammit, I'll shed my blood on your side the fence."

"Fair enough," laughed Jesse. "Let's go, Sheriff."

"We'll take us a little ride then, Bodine."

They passed through the big living room which, with logs blazing in the deep old black fireplace and music of mouth organ and Captain Leigh's singing, and the tapping of light feet as Don Felipe instructed little April in *La Cachucha*, was a very gay place. Jesse perforce stopped to draw Kate aside and have a word with her.

For Kate had come straight home with him,

making good her freedom, not even returning for a word with Big Belle. And that was because that word had already been spoken. When she had received April's note she had shown it to Belle, and that buxom lady had said eagerly:

"Here's your chance, child! You meet your little friend, then keep right on going! You'll hardly be more than out of sight when I'll make my getaway too. We'll meet half a dozen miles out on the wagon road, San Francisco-bound!" And Kate and Jesse had gone on to the meeting with Big Belle and had brought her here along with them. So now Patriarch Jesse Bodine's household was more than ever patriarchal. He had laughed over it with them and had vowed to grow a beard, a good long white one. And Kate had laughed, too, very gay, and had promised him that at this rate of carrying the world on his shoulders he'd not have to worry about any shortage of white hairs!

Now he drew her outside for a stolen moment, a brief half-explanation, since he lacked information for a full one, and a clinging kiss. "Come back as soon as you can, Jesse!" and "Don't you know that I will, Kitty darling?"

Toeing into his stirrup, he asked Comstock, "Which way?"

"Down to Shingle, to Shingle John's. You've been there, I heard."

Yes, he remembered the time—when he had gone to a meeting with a man named Frank

Brewster, and had been too late, Hackamore Breen arriving before him, when Hackamore had killed Brewster, and Jesse Bodine had shot Hackamore. And Shingle John, an unlovable character anyhow, had been disgruntled because among them they had made an untidy mess of his place.

Jesse Bodine waited for the sheriff to say something further, but Comstock rode on in silence, and Jesse asked no more questions. As long as a man knew where he was going, he could wait until he got there to find out what was at the end of the trail.

After little more than an hour's ride they arrived at Shingle, tiny, dim-lit settlement in a lazily flowing bend of Lazy Creek, and dismounted in the dark a hundred yards away from Shingle John's. When the sheriff removed his spurs and hung them on his saddle horn, Jesse Bodine did likewise; it was a tacit understanding between them that they walked in silence. Comstock led the way, keeping in the dark, around to the rear of Shingle John's. That was where, Jesse recalled, the card room was, the room where he had come upon Hackamore Breen killing Brewster.

When they stopped under a small, high window, it was quite dark, the window shaded or blanketed; yet the card room was tenanted and sounds came freely enough to them—a chair moving, the chink of coins, a glass against a bottle, then a man's voice.

Then, out of comparatively long silences, several voices. Men at poker, silent for the most part. A man laughed. It was a winning voice. Also it chanced to be the voice of Hackamore Breen, who always had to jeer when he won.

The poker game went on and, outside, Comstock and Jesse Bodine stood quite still, eavesdropping. Again a voice burst out explosively, an extraordinarily unpleasant voice, rough and discordant, neither high-pitched nor low but of a metallic quality that rasped on the nerves after the fashion of a slate pencil squeaking on a slate. A voice difficult for one man to describe to another, yet one which, once heard, would be hard to forget.

Jesse Bodine's grip shut down hard on Comstock's arm.

"That's the man!" he said. "That's the voice! I'll swear to it!"

"Thanks, Bodine," said Comstock, and drew a deep breath of satisfaction. "I was already well-nigh sure of it. That's Jake Bedloe. All right; let's go."

"Where this time?"

"Back to your place. I'm accepting your invitation to eat and sleep at Lazy Creek. Riding along, I'll tell you a thing or two." And as they rode, "If we don't travel too fast," Comstock said, "maybe we can talk this out before we get to your place." He removed his Stetson and rumpled his hair and clapped his hat on again. "I guess we better begin with Hackamore Breen."

"I'd rather end with him, but have it your way."

"*Bueno, compañero.* Hack Breen is out to burn you down and you know it and the whole damn country knows it by now, and knows the reasons why. You shot him once at Shingle John's; you beat him to the draw in getting the Lazy Creek Ranch away from him: you shot him again over a poker game at General Bright-Hampden's place on Nob Hill; they say you beat hell out of him with your fists the other day; on top of all that, there are folks that say you stole his girl—"

"We don't have to talk about girls tonight, do we?" said Jesse Bodine.

"No. But anyhow there are reasons, like I've mentioned, why Hackamore Breen wouldn't cry if you dropped dead. Likewise, he wants the watershed, and you're holding him off that, too. All right. He's going to get your hide if he can. Right?"

"Go ahead."

Their horses had slowed down to a swinging walk. Sheriff Dan Comstock took off his hat again, this time hanging it on the horn of his saddle; then he rolled a cigarette, taking his time.

"All right. Now for Jake Bedloe. By the way, you heard Breen with him just now? They are old side-kicks. The day you brought the stage in, like I said, I figured the stick-up job was Joaquin Murietta's or Bedloe's. Just guesswork, by the earmarks of the way the thing was done. So I just hung fire and kept hoping. But there was one thing I did pick up that helped, and it was a gun that somebody had left out there by the Cotton-wood Bridge. There was blood on the gun; I guess you or your friend Ransome or somebody else in the stage must have shot one of the damn robbers in the hand. Anyhow, there the gun was and what is more, I knew that gun the minute I got my eye on it. An old-timer, long-barreled, with the sweetest looking horn handle you ever saw, with a sort of half-moon where your thumb goes. Sure I knew it; it used to be mine. I lost it in a poker game more'n three year ago.

"Well, it didn't take me anywhere fast, but it sure took me far! I started back with the man I lost it to and traced the damned thing from man to man that owned it since, and three years' time eleven men had carried it! None of 'em had kept it long; well, that wasn't surprising." He chuckled with obvious enjoyment. "Hell, Bodine, the gun looked fine, but it just wasn't worth a single damn; maybe if it had been I wouldn't have let it go so easy over a card table. And among them eleven men, two of 'em was dead; shot dead! That kind of a gun it was. And following the trail of that gun through eleven owners, two of 'em dead, was a tarnation of a job. Anyhow, I got it done a month ago. And it was Dick Bedloe, Jake's brother and one of the gang, that had owned it most recent. And only a couple of weeks ago I saw Dick over to Dry Town. He had a scar on the back of his right hand you could see from across the room."

When he paused a moment, Jesse Bodine observed thoughtfully: "It looks like you've come pretty close to nailing that Cottonwood Bridge job on the Bedloes. What with the gun and my remembering Jake Bedloe's voice."

"It's just about twice as much evidence as I need," said Comstock with satisfaction. "All right. Now here's where you're going to be interested. One thing, like we've said, Hackamore Breen is out to pull you down and dig you under and pile rocks on top of your grave. Another thing, Hack Breen and Jake Bedloe are friends. Another thing, Jake Bedloe is staying at El Monte now, and his two brothers are due to show up there most any minute. That's something, ain't it?"

"It's a hatful," muttered Jesse Bodine, and thought of Kate Haveril and little April and Mrs. Crabtree and her daughter with her two babies, all at Lazy Creek.

"And here's the funny thing, only maybe I don't exactly mean *funny*. Over in Nevada City the other day where I was helping out at Happy Renfrew's birthday party, there was a fight in a saloon and a man got killed. He was a half Injun that I kinda liked, seeing he did me a pretty big deed of kindness three-four years ago. Being as he was dying anyhow, I kind of tried to make things easy for him. He stuck it out two days before he cashed in his chips. At the end he was sort of half crazy, fever, you know; he did a lot of talking. He'd been with the Bedloe gang; I knew that. He jabbered about them; most of all he jabbered about their swag. He still craved for his share, I guess. He had it in his head that they'd been hoarding up the loot from a lot of highway robberies, meaning to split the pot when it got as rich as they wanted it. And he knew where they'd hid it. Guess where?"

"How in hell should I know?" asked Jesse Bodine.

"They picked themselves out, says my half-breed Injun, a likely spot, an old deserted house way to hell and gone, a place nobody'd lived in for a long time and where nobody'd most likely live for years to come. A place called—Got it, kid?"

Jesse Bodine stared at him.

"My place!" he said.

"Lazy Creek! Why not? Somewheres in your house, I'm betting you my shirt against your thumbnail, all that swag is hid—and Mr. Jake Bedloe wants it—and you can look out heap pronto for a midnight visit from the Bedloes and Hackamore Breen and all their little friends and companions!"

"Good God, man! They'll kill like a bunch of Indians on the warpath! And look at the folks I've got there!"

"Thought you might get interested," said the sheriff, and put his hat on.

There remained little to say, so they put their horses to the gallop. A few further words were jolted out. Comstock surmised that Bedloe would have six or eight or maybe ten men with him; there might be that many of Hackamore Breen's men, if they did decide to attack, and to do so with joined forces. But what was the use doing any further guessing? They knew roundly now what the game was.

Kate Haveril was wearing a diamond ring on her thumb. And about her neck was a fine gold chain, and its dangling locket hung *outside* her dress! And she was proud alike of chain and locket and ring. And you should have seen those glad lovely eyes of hers!

"Love me, Jesse?" she whispered.

"If I don't love you, Kate Haveril, there are no stars in the sky, and no God backing the stars up, and the grass was never green! Come here, where you belong!" She stepped swiftly into his arms.

While Dan Comstock joined the others, Jesse Bodine told Kate first of all of the purpose of his visit to Shingle, of Jake Bedloe being there with Hackamore Breen, then of the sheriff's theory.

"It's quite likely he's right all along the line," he concluded. "Breen and Bedloe are hand in glove; Bedloe's up here for a purpose; the bandit gold is no doubt cached somewhere in this house. It isn't hard to guess what's in the wind, is it?"

Her hand tightened on his arm. She said, serious but unafraid:

"They'll raid us! Of course. For Willard to try to make you pay with interest all you've done to him, for the Bedloes to recover their treasure."

"So you see, dear girl, you mustn't be here. Right away, tonight, while Breen and Bedloe are playing poker at Shingle John's, I'll get the big wagon ready. You and April and Mrs. Crabtree and Ann and her kids are going over to La Fiesta. The boys can do as they please, go or stay. But you womenfolk—"

"I wonder why it is," said Kate, and sounded merely curious and meditative, "that men seem to think, when it's a question of the danger of getting killed, that a woman should feel any different about it than a man does? How do you figure it out, Mr. Bodine? And even when it comes to shooting, why is it that a man always figures a woman can't line up sights and pull a trigger? I've often wondered about that! Tell me, won't you, you who know—"

He caught her back into his arms and kissed her words away. And then he laughed softly, proud of her as always.

"Just the same, to please me, you'll go?"

"No," said Kate. "I'm darned if I will. I'll do anything on earth, I think, to please you, Jesse Bodine, except one thing. I won't ever leave you again. I've had enough of that for one lifetime."

They went back to the others in the living room and there Comstock, at a nod from Jesse, told them all he knew of the Bedloes and of the present condition of affairs. The sheriff's face was grave; when glances shifted to Jesse Bodine they could make nothing of a pair of inscrutable dark eyes, but all sensed in him as in the sheriff a conviction of danger to the household.

Despite that, here is what happened:

Lonesome Pete, the sorrowful one, of all people, let out a whoop of glee that resounded through the big old house, and before he had said a word his thought had been caught and had spread a sort of wildfire among them. The Bedloes' swag, hidden right here, somewhere in the house! *Wheee!* A Treasure Hunt!

From Kate Haveril, her glad eyes laughing, to little April, all excitement, to old man Crabtree, to Bud Weaver and Captain Leigh and a couple of household Indians, through them all went a sort of merry-mad excitement. What on earth could be more fun than coming at the Bedloe gold before the Bedloes did?

That started Jesse Bodine laughing, and when

Jesse Bodine laughed others simply had to laugh with him. They were like a holiday crowd, say a Christmas gathering, ready to burst open the doors and go trooping in where the tree was.

For one thing, the womenfolk refused, as Kate had refused, to budge. That was settled, unless their menfolk ganged up on them, tied them and hauled them away. Well, then, why not spend a pleasant evening treasure hunting?

They lighted a score of candles and the few lamps on the place; they went singly or in couples—Don Felipe and April were never more than a yard apart, and most of the time forgot what they were looking for in the knowledge of what, more precious than robbers' gold, they had already found. From the start it was just a game. Just the same they went forward on the understanding that the only rule to apply was that of "Finders keepers," and really did use their wits and their eyes as well as lively tongues, quick hands and scampering feet.

To be sure they found nothing that night—that is, no bandit loot—but they did have a good time. And they halted safely this side of tearing the house down. And, in a way, they thumbed their noses at any Bedloe-Breen menace.

And in the end the house grew quiet and the candles were blown out. . . .

But out in the barn, with a couple of lanterns, were Jesse Bodine and the sheriff. And one by one the other men, having received a quiet word during the hubbub, came to join them.

"Dealing with bad men is one thing, dealing with womenfolk is another, as maybe you boys might know," said Dan Comstock, and took off his hat and hung it on a harness peg, and mopped his brow. "Now, I've talked aside with Bodine here, and we've got another idea. It's like this:

"You see, I sort of wanted to let things drift until the Bedloes showed up here to grab back what they cached here, so me, I could grab it off of them. Well, hell, it's nothing but gold anyhow, so what the hell? If we wait that long, we wait until they're ready, until the rest of Bedloe's friends show. Here's the other way of it: I go out right now, tonight, back to Shingle John's, and I say, 'Jake Bedloe, you're under arrest for robbery, murder, holding up the stage and killing Long Peters!' And to make my play sort of even, some of you boys come along. That way there won't be any raid a-tall on the Lazy Creek. And, likewise, that way, most likely we'll tie the can to Hackamore Breen's tail; if he don't happen to get shot, I can arrest him for chipping in with Bedloe in defiance of the law. If we ride fast we'll most likely find them still at poker at Shingle John's. Bodine agrees."

"Gentlemen!" exclaimed Captain Bobbie Leigh. "May I ask what we are waiting for?"

"There's not a chance in a hundred," said Jesse

Bodine, "but we can't afford to overlook that chance that we might miss the men we're looking for and that they might show up here while we're somewhere else. One of us has to stay here and keep an eye open. First we decide who's to stay; then we go stir up the Indian *vaqueros* and see that they've all got rifles, and scatter them in the dark outside the house. If they see any flock of riders coming they're to blaze them out of their saddles as they come along. It's only an hour and a half to Shingle; the same to get back if there's nobody there. And it's still early. Like I say, there's scant danger of an attack here while we're away, but anything can happen."

Captain Bobbie Leigh was answered.

The men looked at one another, asking with their eyes the same question, "Who's going to stay?" Almost to a man they were prepared to say: "Not me! I'm coming along!"

"Mr. Crabtree," said Jesse Bodine, "you're elected to hold the fort here until we get back. You're the man for it. For one thing, you're pretty much of a stranger here and don't know any of the men we're looking for; another thing, you'll want to be near your family. Am I right?"

Crabtree sighed and scratched his head and pulled at his mustache, and sighed again.

"I'd sort of like to traipse along of you boys," he said, downright envious and open and frank about it, "but I guess Bodine's right. I'll stick and

I'll take care o' things. Only if you boys do get a chance to sock that outfit, give 'em an extra shot for me, won't you? Now I'll step along an' round up the Injun' camp. So long, boys."

So they went for their horses and rode on their way toward Shingle in a soft clear night of many stars. They strung out along the trail, seven of them, Sheriff Dan Comstock and Bud Weaver and Lonesome Pete chancing to ride at the fore, Jesse Bodine and his old friend, Ransome Haveril, next, Captain Bobbie Leigh and Don Felipe Moraga crowding them hard in their eagerness. And Jesse Bodine and Ransome fell to talking.

"It's sort of like old times, Jess, riding together," said Ransome.

Jesse Bodine nodded. He harked back to the time when he and Ransome, out to get firewood among the hills rimming Pleasant Valley, had cast their lots together for the great adventure. And he thought, too, "Here of late my mind keeps going back to Pleasant Valley . . ."

They rode swiftly with always the top thought in their minds, all of them, that they were leaving Lazy Creek and their womenfolk there, not too well defended in case of a miscarriage in their plans. They wanted to get to Shingle with all possible dispatch, to make sure.

And when they saw the reflected glint of stars, broken waveringly in the creek bending about

Shingle, they were down from their saddles like one man, and were hurrying, silent and swift, to Shingle John's. There was a light in the main room where the bar was; they moved noiselessly to the rear, stood a moment under the dark window—and heard voices.

"They're still at it," said Comstock, relieved.

"They're not playing cards, though," said Jesse Bodine. "Listen."

From within came a confused storm of voices. Breen's voice was to be distinguished, and it strove to dominate. That metallic voice of Jake Bedloe's was unmistakable.

"Lookee," muttered Bud Weaver. "I remember one time down in Texas—"

"This is one hell of a time to start tellin' stories," mourned Lonesome Pete.

"Anyhow," snapped Bud Weaver, "a man without a horse is only half a man! How do we know what's going to happen now? So a couple of us fellows steps back and hides our horses good and plenty, where nobody but us can find 'em. And a couple of us goes and lets their horses loose, counting 'em first to see how many men we're stacking into, and scatters their riding stock clean to hell. Then we step up and say, 'Howdy, gents!' That's what remembering old Texas days does to me, you damn old sidewinder," he informed his uncle Pete.

"It's a mighty nice idea, Bud," said the sheriff.

"Listening to them men talking in there tells me one thing: The two other Bedloes have come, and likely there's more with them. Let's take care of the horses first, like you say."

So Bud and Lonesome Pete, and Captain Leigh and Ransome Haveril hastened away to dispose of the two sets of saddle horses, returning hurriedly, when Bud Weaver reported:

"There was eleven of their horses, all with their saddles on 'em, tied out by John's barn. Whether they all belonged to the Breen-Bedloe crowd, we don't know; anyhow we set 'em high-tailing, and anyhow likewise Breen and Bedloe is afoot. Now!"

"I been tellin' you," grumbled Lonesome Pete, "you're always getting too damn previous. Who wants to hurry anything?"

Comstock, who had been all the while listening intently to the voices in the card room, made his succinct report:

"Breen and Jake Bedloe are in there. Likewise the two other Bedloe boys; that's four of 'em. Then there's others I can't swear to—Jim Oliver, for one, I'd say, and Injun Tuckalee for another, and three-four others, and all helling to go places. Like Bud says, boys, let's go get what we come for. Anyhow there ain't many more of them than there are of us."

He led the way, Jesse Bodine falling in step with him, around to the front of the squat, toadlike plank building. They shoved the swing doors open and entered the main room where the bar was.

The place was lighted by a couple of coal-oil lamps with darkened, tinny reflectors. It was very quiet. Besides the bartender, Shingle John, there were only four men in the place. Two of them, tired looking miners, sat disconsolate at a dim corner table; a half-breed drooped over the near end of the bar, looking without interest into the bottom of an empty glass; a young cowboy, evidently awaiting someone, sat playing solitaire.

At the quiet tread of feet, Shingle John looked up; he was behind his bar on a high stool, glancing dully through the torn sheets of an old copy of the *Atlanta Constitution*. But when he made out who his callers were, in what a compact body they arrived, how many of them there were and yet how a single expression seemed to be stamped on all faces, he came erect and his eyes were like pin points of light.

"What the hell do you want?" he demanded uneasily.

First of all Sheriff Comstock, though not thinking altogether of himself, saved his life right then, and at the cost of but a bit of clear thinking added to a ten dollar gold piece. It chanced that he knew the half-breed draped over the end of the bar, and signaled him with the quirk of an eyebrow.

"Poco-poco," he said, forking over the gold

piece, "get on your horse and ride hell for leather to Yellow Jacket, and tell Doc Dabney I said to come on over right away!"

"Somebody seek?" murmured Poco-poco.

"Not yet, but soon!" said the sheriff. "Get going, kid."

Poco-poco, only slightly more mystified than usual, hurried away. Comstock glanced about him at the readiness on the faces of the men backing him up, said briefly, "Seven to eleven—lucky numbers, and seven's the luckiest!"

And then he lifted his voice to carry a mile and sang out:

"You, Jake Bedloe! Come out and come shooting, or come with your hands up! It's Dan Comstock talking! Do like I say and make it quick; else I burn this damn house down and shoot as you pile out!"

A roar came from Shingle John!

"No, you don't, Dan Comstock, damn you! I don't have my place all messed up again, and I don't have it burned down—"

"Shut up!" admonished Comstock, and called loudly again: "Hear me, Bedloe? Come get it or come walking soft. You, Hackamore Breen, stay out of this or chip in, just as makes you happiest. Step along, Bedloe!"

There was a heavy, somehow electric silence. Behind the closed door of the card room there was, no doubt, a hurried, whispered conference.

307

But Jake Bedloe did not happen to be the patient kind of man, nor was he afraid of the devil on horseback; certainly he had no fear of Dan Comstock.

The door opened and Jake Bedloe stepped into the front room. He was an enormous man, some six or seven inches above six feet, broad and powerful, a lusty young black-bearded giant. He came out with his hands lifted no higher than his floating ribs, and he carried a heavy, ready gun in each hand. And as he stepped through the door, Hackamore Breen stepped lightly behind him, and then there were the two other Bedloes, much like Jake in looks, and Injun Tuckalee and Jim Oliver, and the rest of the eleven of them. And their eyes were steady and hard and murderous. Men like those men know when the showdown has come.

"Well, Dan?" said Jake Bedloe in that harshly discordant voice of his. "What's it all about?"

"Me, I'm the law," said Comstock. "You're under arrest for highway robbery and murder and all that sort of thing, mostly for killing Long Peters at Cottonwood Bridge. Want to come quiet?"

"Maybe we better talk it over, Dan," said Jake Bedloe.

Glances licked through the dim light like spurts of flame. Jesse Bodine's eyes and Hackamore Breen's met. Comstock said:

"We'll talk at the jail in Yellow Jacket, Jake.

And it's my bet you'll hang inside twenty-four hours unless you wink out right now. Make up your mind!"

"Dammit!" yelled Shingle John, and from behind the bar started flourishing a stubby, sawed-off shotgun. "You shut up, you boys, and clean out, or—"

The man was half drunk, and also he was deep-bitten with indignation that his place should be chosen for a free-for-all such as this promised to be, and he was jerking about the place in a paroxysm of sheer nerves. Whether or not he meant to shoot just then, whether he hit the target he had in mind, if any, was never to be definitely known. A shaky finger on one of the two triggers precipitated a general bedlam; the explosion of his buckshot-loaded shotgun was like that of a cannon, and his discharge, tearing over Comstock's head by a safe margin of four or five feet, blew the swinging lamp into atoms.

Comstock, whether or not under a misapprehension, threw his gun down and shot Shingle John through the upper chest. . . .

Shingle John dropped out of sight behind his bar, and there was the loud clatter of his falling shotgun. The uninterested bystanders vanished like puffs of steam over a hot stove. Red gun flashes ripped through the semidark. Two or three men of Bedloe's following whipped back into the card room to leap out through the window and get away anyhow they could. Lonesome Pete grabbed Bud Weaver's arm. "They're runnin' out on us!" yelled Lonesome Pete. "Let's go get 'em!" and he and Bud Weaver ran out and to the back of the house.

In half a dozen seconds the front room was acrid with smoke, and the place was almost swallowed by an utter dark; a chance shot, or one winged with intent, exploded the second lamp. Kerosene leaked out and fire caught along the wall and licked hungrily at the dry boards, making a small, lovely plume of flame from a resinous knothole; it gave the only light.

There came a burst of shots from outside. Lonesome Pete and Bud Weaver were arguing it out in the smoke with the trio who had fled either to make their escape or to run around to the front of the house and thus attack the attackers from the rear.

The flare of pitch fire shot up a tall, wavering plume of thick smoke as black as ink. There was no light save the fitful light, red and evil and without avail, of guns spitting. Through the sound of firing burst the crash of breaking glass; a man had hurled himself toward safety through a window.

Something struck Jesse Bodine in the side of the head, staggering him. His first thought, "I'm done for." But it wasn't a bullet; just something hurled at him, whether a bottle or a stone or an emptied gun, he did not know. The last thing he had seen reasonably clearly was Hackamore Breen, and Breen was shooting at him, with a gun in each hand. Now, steadying himself, he saw a dark form slide by him, headed for the swing doors. He couldn't be sure that that way went Hackamore Breen, he just guessed and hastened in pursuit. Another dark figure crashed into him; that was Ransome Haveril, he knew from Ransome's strident cursing, Ransome's angry shout: "Get out of my way, dammit! That's Breen and he's mine!" Jesse Bodine and Ransome crashed through the swing doors together.

Jesse Bodine, still dizzied and half blinded from the blow he had just received, half fell down the steps into the dark of the road and lost sight then of both Ransome and Hackamore Breen. But he steadied himself as he saw several other forms come lunging through the swing doors, one of which was now hanging crazily on a single, twisted hinge; he held his fire; he couldn't make out who they were.

Then he heard a raucous voice never to be mistaken, and a very big man was almost on top of him and was firing with both hands as he charged, and Jesse Bodine fired back point-blank, and the big man's thick body was absorbed in the dark; where it went, Jesse Bodine did not know until a few minutes later when he found it at his feet.

Bud Weaver and Lonesome Pete came reeling

back, insubstantial shadows in the night. Each had an arm about the other, and they staggered, but were shouting defiance of everything on earth this side of Texas or the other side. Both had been shot, both were alive—and they had taken care of the men who had tried to duck out through the card room window.

A storm of shouts and shots within doors was like a sudden crash of thunder. After it, there shut down a heavy silence. It was so still there at Shingle John's that a whisper carried far and true. It was scarcely more than a whisper from someone in the dark that all heard:

"Finished?"

There was no answer. But presently the opaqueness of silence was troubled by a thin sound, that of a man somewhere moaning. Jesse Bodine went up into the saloon again; Bud Weaver and Lonesome Pete came uncertainly in his wake. He heard Ransome Haveril's voice from the outer dark, calling:

"All right, Jess?"

"All right, Ran. You?"

"Sure. Fine. I got him, Jess."

"That's good. Come ahead."

They brought a lamp from the card room and looked things over.

Shingle John was dying. He kept muttering curses at them, at all of them, damn their eyes, they were making a mess of his place . . .

CHAPTER XIX

SIX WHITE HORSES

. . . Hackamore Breen was dead, shot through the side of the head. Jake Bedloe lived to be hauled off to Yellow Jacket and very promptly hanged. Injun Tuckalee was dead with four bullets through him. Bud Weaver had a bullet through his arm and one searing his middle body, and Lonesome Pete as long as he lived would carry a sagging, stiff shoulder and a scar along his high, bald forehead. Captain Bobbie Leigh came close to dying, shot twice, and would have died that very night except for the prompt arrival of that very rough-and-ready yet equally expert surgeon, Doc Dabney, with his kit of tools and his bawdy songs. (And subsequently Captain Bobbie Leigh was grateful for the bullets through him as well as for Doc Dabney's prompt arrival, for, hauled back to Lazy Creek, there came to attend him and the others, all the pretty girls from La Fiesta, and of course among them was the elusive laughing Rosa! With little April in attendance, furthering matters!) And Sheriff Dan Comstock had not dodged all the flying lead; that night he lost a thumb, but was glad it was off the left hand, and didn't seem to mind that for a month he went lame in his left leg. For he had his rope on Jake Bedloe, who had killed Long Peters at Cottonwood Bridge, and one of the other Bedloes was dead and the other vanished into the night for all time.

"I'm riding back to Lazy Creek for a wagon," said Jesse Bodine.

But he had ridden only a half mile when he met a wagon hurrying from Lazy Creek to Shingle, John Crabtree whipping up the horses; and in the wagon were three mattresses and clean cloths for bandages and two girls, and the girls were Kate Haveril and April Crabtree.

Bud Weaver had a bit of money left, and so had Lonesome Pete, and they had a couple of friends, cattlemen, down in Texas who had a little money, and Jesse Bodine loaned them ten thousand dollars. And so Bud Weaver and his friends bought in El Monte, and the name of Hackamore Breen, and the Breen feuding over so much spilling water, was forgotten. But, in due course, with forgetting one thing, it may be that something else is remembered. . . .

It was Jesse Bodine who did the remembering, to begin with.

He and Kate had ridden in an early, pearly dawn to the crest of Black Pine Ridge. From there you could see, Jesse vowed, half around the world in either direction! He further stubbornly maintained that if you'd look steadily east and then would whirl around as fast as light to look straight west, you'd see *all* the way round this great big beautiful world of ours.

"Ours! All ours, Kate!"

She reached out and squeezed his hand; they gave themselves to each other with their eyes. They leaned together from their saddles. . . .

And it was then that Jesse remembered.

He said very quietly, speaking the words drawlingly, taking his time with them to get everything quite clear:

"Kate, listen. We're happy, Kate." He drew a deep breath; so did Kate, and she nodded. Happy, yes! They were happy! That was one point thoroughly made and accepted.

"Our being happy," said Jesse Bodine, "started a long time ago and a long ways from here. Back in Pleasant Valley, Kate. And, even if I haven't said anything about it much, I keep on remembering how the little path wriggled along Buckeye Creek, and how the fields looked from the hills—and how your house was right over yonder, and our house was right out that way . . . and our folks, Kate—"

"Oh, Jesse! I know!" There came a sob into her throat, and her eyes glistened and her fingers wrapped themselves tighter than ever about his.

"Yes." He nodded slowly. "You see, Kate, it's going to be fun. Ransome and the little Moraga girl are going to get married; so are Bob Leigh and the other little Moraga girl, and April and Don Felipe. And so are Kitty Haveril and Jesse Bodine!"

He laughed softly and Kate, for whatever reason, blushed like the fresh tips of a wild rosebud just opening.

"So," said Patriarch Jesse Bodine of Lazy Creek Ranch, "here's the idea: We give a party, Mr. and Mrs. Jesse Bodine. We outfit us with four big wagons, four horses to the wagon, with canvas tops in case it rains. One for the Bodines, one for Mr. and Mrs. Ransome Haveril, one for Mr. and Mrs. Bob Leigh and one for Señor Felipe Moraga and his little Señora, April! And we start off on a honeymoon, strung half across the country so that one wagon doesn't crowd the other, *and we go all the way back to Pleasant Valley!* And there we have a big dance and barbecue, and we pick up the rest of the Haverils and Bodines, and we all come back to Lazy Creek to live happy ever after! Shucks, Kate, it's just around the corner! I bet we can make it inside a year!"

And how Kate Haveril got from her horse onto his horse and into his arms, and why she should have been sobbing, nobody knows. . . .

In another early, pearly dawn the caravan started.

There were the four big wagons, each with four horses ready to go, each with a driver, so that the Bodines and Haverils and Leighs and young

316

Moragas could take life easy and have the teams travel on if they wished. There was a fifth big wagon, creaking heavily with provisions. There were a dozen saddle horses brought along, since one does not want all the time to ride over the undulating ways, mountains and hills, valleys and plains, on a wagon seat. There were a dozen of Jesse Bodine's Indians riding before and behind, hewers of wood, drawers of water, killers of game.

The Crabtrees and Bud Weaver and Lonesome Pete and some of the Moragas and still others waved them on their way. With them was the gravely smiling padre who had been a house guest these three busy days.

Jesse Bodine and Kate Haveril were no longer Jesse Bodine and Kate Haveril, but one now in all things. It was a new mystery, still unfathomable, always to be a mystery. One, now, not two; yet Jesse Bodine said to the girl lifting her melting eyes to his:

"Kate! Quick! While they're starting, let's run on ahead. Just you and me, Kate, around the bend. On foot!"

She didn't know what he meant, but hand-in-hand with him she ran willingly, laughing; crying a little but laughing more.

"Remember, Kate! When I was such a fool in Pleasant Valley? When I left you? And you said —You said what?"

317

"That—that—What did I say, Jesse?"

"Something about a carriage!"

She couldn't remember right away, with all the excitement. Then she did remember, and laughed at the memory.

"Oh, Jesse, I was just a silly little—"

"But what was it, Kate?" They were still running, growing breathless, too. "What was it you said?"

"That you meant to come back—in a glittering carriage—with six white horses and—"

"Look!" cried Jesse Bodine. "Your wedding present, my dear!"

They came around a sudden bend through the pines and Kate gasped, and stopped in her tracks. *"Jesse!"*

It was Jesse Bodine's surprise for his bride. There, fresh from San Francisco, was a glittering new coach drawn by six white horses!

They ran together, hand in hand, as they used to run along the banks of Buckeye Creek. He lifted her up to the carriage seat and climbed up beside her. He cracked the whip, and the six white horses were off at a gallop.

And so in the lovely dawn, growing pink now, they were laughing, these two; but in their eyes was something far transcending mere laughter.

Then other whips cracked, and they were on their way, Duke Bodine and his Lady Kate leading their caravan back to Pleasant Valley.

Center Point Large Print
600 Brooks Road / PO Box 1
Thorndike, ME 04986-0001 USA

(207) 568-3717

US & Canada:
1 800 929-9108
www.centerpointlargeprint.com